The Legend of Jubal Courtney

Courtney

BOOK 1: CHASING THE NEXT SUNRISE

I0641411

Creative Texts Publishers products are available at special discounts for bulk purchase for sale promotions, premiums, fund-raising, and educational needs. For details, write Creative Texts Publishers, PO Box 50, Barto, PA 19504, or visit www.creativetexts.com

The Legend of Jubal Courtney: Book 1: Chasing the Next Sunrise
by Jared McVay

Published by Creative Texts Publishers
PO Box 50
Barto, PA 19504
www.creativetexts.com

ISBN: 978-1-64738-047-2

The Legend of Jubal Courtney

BOOK 1: CHASING THE NEXT SUNRISE

by

JARED MCVAY

CREATIVE TEXTS PUBLISHERS
Barto, Pennsylvania

Thank you to all my readers. To you I dedicate this book.

Thank you to my publisher, Dan Edwards, for having faith in me

And a huge shoutout thank you to Jerri Burr,

whose help is more than you know.

TABLE OF CONTENTS

PROLOGUE

From the journal of Jubal Courtney

1802 -1906

The date is December 28th, 1859 - three days after my fifty seventh birthday.

I do not take pen in hand because I am some powerful magistrate who has done great things and want them recorded for all time – nor am I a rascal pirate who has ravished the seas, taking from others as an easy way to make my living by stealing what is not rightfully mine. I take pen in hand as a man who has faced life and endured. By all rights, I am not a young man. As a matter of fact, many might consider me, old, but I am still able to chase the next sunrise and when it comes right down to it, I don't want to die, but I'm not afraid to, and I will fight as long as I'm able.

Survival of the fittest is a way of life that has been with us as long as man has been in existence. He has had to stand up against wild animals, overbearing rulers, men who want what he has, along with mother nature's cruelty – and somehow, he survived.

There are men who survive any and all the hardships life throws in their path. Then, there are those who crumble when life gets hard. As I look back at what I've seen, it seems the majority are content to be ruled by men not worthy of the position, while others are born into slavery and want to be free, but are too afraid to try. Life seems to be a paradox.

For me, life has always been an ever-changing battle. Out of the frying pan and into the fire, as some would say. I was forced from being a free man who wanted nothing more than to do my work, have a small adventure from time to time and live a happy life. But forces beyond my control took over and I was forced into several lives far from anything I have ever dreamed of. Like the time I went from a peace-loving man to being a slave. It was a hard pill to swallow but I watched and waited, taking their abuse until I could find a way to be a free man, again. But escaping was not enough. They hunted me down and I was once more, thrown back into slavery. Even so, I was not beaten. Freedom was the force that drove me on - and in the end, after many years and thousands of miles of long, rough roads – I found solace - a long, long way from my home in Ireland.

I'm hoping by writing this journal, someday, someone will read it and be helped in their fight against the forces of life, fate, or whatever it may be called. Only with great tenacity, can man prevail…

ONE

My journal begins far down the road from when I was born, but I will do my best to recount the events of my life leading up to the situation I find myself in. Will I have a future to write about? Only God, or fate, or the powers that be, knows that. As soon as the snow melts, they will come for me. Of that, I have no doubt. Hopefully I will be ready for them.

We are born… then sometime later, we all die. Death is imminent, but it's not something we like to think about or discuss. But sitting here, all alone in this log cabin, with four feet of snow outside and my possible demise only weeks away, it's something I have to give thought to. I don't want to die, and I'm hoping I don't, but if the inevitable happens, so be it. But for now, as I await my future, I will take the time to chronicle my life's events. I do this because my woman, Calling Bird, asked me to do it, several years ago, before she was taken from me by the ones who seek my death when the snow melts.

As I think back, I find it compelling that we move from a mortal existence to whatever lies beyond - some not caring, while others dwell on it their whole lives. Where or what happens after we pass on has always been a mystery to me, but I don't dwell on it. What we do in between being born and moving on, is to me, the important part. It's what some people call, destiny, fate, or the will of the Gods. The way I see it, maybe life is decided by the decisions we make - good or bad. There is no actual guide books that I know of, but you can be sure of one thing, every one of us has an opinion. Yes, I know many of you reading this will say the answers are in the Bible, which could very well be true. But then again, which Bible? How many different religions and Bibles are out there? I don't rightly know. But I do know, each one has its own slant on things. In Ireland where I was born, Catholics were the majority, which ma and pa were, but the ruling class were Protestant, and never a day went by that they weren't fighting about something.

1

CHASING THE NEXT SUNRISE

I'm not saying I'm not a God-fearing man, but you have to admit, a good number of wars have started and been fought in the name of religion. Kind of makes a man wonder.

So much for that. I have to take a break and make some ink to continue writing with. It's not hard to make, just time consuming. I use ash from the fireplace, mixed with some water and a drop of vinegar. And when it's mixed all together, it does a fair job. My writing tools are made from wild turkey feathers. I shave the ends down to a point. Of course, I need something to write on. Two years before Calling Bird was taken from me, she insisted I buy some paper when I went down to Denver to sell my furs. Never thought I would ever use it, yet, here I am.

While I was making my ink, I ate some hardtack and a chunk of elk meat that was hanging over the fire, along with a cup of tea. Like my tea, I do. One of the few things I treat myself. There is also a bag of coffee beans, which I also have come to like.

Now, where was I?

Putting religion aside, I was never able to understand why my life turned out the way it has, although, from time to time, I have given it serious thought – and I always come to the same conclusion… The way my life has had so many twists and turns I have no clue what guides it or what will happen next or what the powers to be have in store for me, or how I'll deal with it when it comes. In the end, the way I see it, we don't have any choice but take what life throws at us and move on. To me, life is like a fast-flowing river - once you stick your finger in the water, it's gone and you can never touch that same water again. We can look back – even dwell on the past, but we can never go back for a do-over.

It's dark outside and I need to get some rest if I'm going to be clearheaded enough to remember all there is to say.

-

There is at least four feet of snow on the ground and it's still falling, with flakes as big as silver dollars. I'm sitting here with memories washing over my brain like a flock of wild turkeys running from a wolf. I built this cabin for Calling Bird, a beautiful, young, Shoshone woman I helped escape from the Utes, seven years ago.

They say I stole her, and maybe I did, but whatever it was, we've been fighting over her ever since, even though they took her from me a long, long, two years ago, I continue to grieve over her death.

Men come up here to hide away from what's going on down below, but usually don't seem to live too long. Either the Indians or wild animals get them. There are lots of bears and wolves up here, along with cougars. Mostly, the men aren't prepared for this kind of life, for it can be cruel. Not being able to adapt, they die of starvation or freeze to death. Me? Somehow, I've always been able to adapt to whatever situation I happen to be in. Knowing what the winters are like up here, I have two sides of elk meat hanging in the corner, a large sack of beans and enough coffee to last until the big thaw comes in the spring. I cut and stacked enough wood to last out the winter, so I don't reckon I'll freeze. But, in case I do, I guess that wouldn't be the worst way to go; maybe better than being killed by the Utes.

As I look back on my life, I have to chuckle. My life has been a long, twisted road with more turns than a mountain trail. Along the way, I've rubbed shoulders with men of honor and men who should have been put down the day they were born. I've seen good and bad times and been on death's door more times than I like to think about. And as far as I know, a good many of those men are dead – but that's just a guess since I haven't been down to civilization in a coon's age. Maybe when good weather comes, and I don't lose my hair to the Utes, I might venture down, just to have a looksee at what has changed. Which I'm guessing will have me scampering back up to high country quicker than a rabbit hunting a hole.

Some folks like all that crowdedness and the noise, along with the fast-paced living, but not me. I love the quiet of the mountains where a man is free from other folks trying to run your life or trying to stay alive as a slave, working with no pay til you're nothing but skin and bones. After all the things that's happened to me, I've had enough of civilization to last me three lifetimes. At least that's the way I think about it right now.

I'll take living up here where my biggest worry is wrestling with some mean ole bear or coming face to face with a bunch of Indians who want my hair as a trophy.

CHASING THE NEXT SUNRISE

Although, I have to admit, being a mountain man can have its downside. From time to time a man likes to wake up next to a woman on a cold morning and snuggle a little closer – to get warm. For me, Calling Bird filled that void. To the best of my knowledge, she'd never been down to a town and had no desire to go. But she did like to sit and listen to stories about my past. She would shake her head in wonderment and tell me how glad she was that we didn't live down there. I surely do miss her a lot. She always made me feel like I could do anything I set my mind to.

Like I said, she used to tell me I should write down the things that have happened to me so folks would know what all I've been through. Of course, I just laughed, saying, "Who in their right mind would want to know about my life, or even care, for that matter?"

Now, as I sit here in my loneliness, her words come back to me and since I don't have anything else to do, I sharpened some turkey quills, made a good sized pot of ink, set out two candles I made out of left over cooking fat with some pieces of cotton string for wicks. I did all that, just so I can write down what I can remember about my life and all the hills I climbed and valleys I walked through.

Don't exactly know what I'll do with it when I'm finished, but I'll worry about that, later.

TWO

Even way back, when I was just a young'un, I do believe I was looked at favorably by the Gods – otherwise, I should have been dead at least half a dozen times.

I was born in Macroom, Ireland back in 1802 and growing up in Ireland during the early eighteen hundreds was not easy – not with all the poverty people had to endure because of the war dealt to us by that English bastard, Cromwell, and then, a few years after that, came the Protestant, Catholic wars, with big land owners pushing to control everything.

The way the story goes and I'm sure it's true, Cromwell and his soldiers invaded us and devastated Ireland. He took some fifty thousand prisoners and sold them as indentured laborers to British colonies in North America, and beyond. When the war between the Catholics and the Protestants came around, several years after that, the rich land owner Protestants set the rules and controlled the purse strings. They even went so far as to say a man whose religion was Catholic upon his death, could not leave his property to his oldest living son, which in my case was me. It was to be sold off to the highest bidder, which was always a Protestant.

As I look back, I'm guessing pa did a passel of thinking to come up with a plan to get around that law, which in the end, after all his effort, didn't work out all that good. But at the time it was the best he or anybody else could come up with. Within a few weeks after I was born, pa drew up papers making me a partner in his business and half owner in all the property he had, so that when he passed, it would be mine without him leaving it to me.

Macroom, Ireland is located in the valley of the River Sullane - a tributary off the River Lee, about twenty-five miles west of Cork. We lived at the edge of town, at the foot of the Boggeragh Mountains. Pa owned and ran the local livery stable and blacksmith shop. Ma was from up north a few miles, and was well book learned. She'd secretly been trained as a schoolteacher, but she wasn't allowed to teach because she

5

was a Catholic. The Protestants wouldn't allow it. But we got around that, too. There was a small room on the back of pa's blacksmith shop where me and a few others learned to read, write and do our sums at an early age. It was all hush, hush, of course, with all of the Catholic families promising not to say anything about ma teaching us. If word had gotten out it would have been the end of the school, and probably the blacksmith shop, too. And maybe even ma and pa. At the least, they would get a public whipping.

Except for the big landowners, most of the folks who lived in Macroom were poor and survived mostly because of the barter system, since they had little or no money. They traded with the crops they grew, or services they could render, like pa did with his smithing and horse boarding. We were neither rich nor poor, but we had a roof over our heads and food in our bellies. Pa kept a couple of cows out back of the house, so we had milk to drink and ma had milk and cream for baking. And we got vegetables from the small garden ma kept along the side of the house. Couple that with the smithing pa did for most all the horses in the county, which included making harness and other such things they needed, we lived better than most. Even the Protestant land owners liked and used pa for more than just his blacksmithing. He was handy at fixing or making things.

Pa liked to recite what he called, words to keep us on the straight and narrow; like the time I came down with the croup, he told ma, "What butter and whiskey can't cure, there's no cure for."

Ma just smiled, patted him on the cheek, and said, "Yes, love, you're right."

Earlier in his life, during the time before he met ma, pa worked as a shipbuilder. During those years he saved his money, and although he was allowed to purchase only one acre of land, he made the best of it by buying an acre of forest land at the edge of town. He used the lumber from the trees he cut down to build the house, the blacksmith shop, the barn and corral, leaving some trees to fill out the back part of the property like a small forest. I always liked to go with pa when he went into our small forest to hunt for game. That's where I learned to, not only shoot, but hit what I shot at. Lead and powder was scarce and he taught me not to waste it, which came in handy in later years. There wasn't much game in the small forest because they would hear us coming and be gone by the time we got there. But pa, being the kind of man he was, he set traps and we almost always found something waiting for us. Smiling as he skinned whatever it was, he trapped, pa would say, "A cabin with plenty of food is better than a castle filled with hunger." Pa was like that with his sayings, and seemed to have one for almost every situation.

-

Night comes early here in the mountains in the wintertime, like it is doing now – so I'll put down my pen for a minute or so and add some wood to the fire in the fireplace. Next, I took a sliver of burning wood and lit two of the bear-fat and string candles I'd made. What I like about fat burning candles is that when they melt, they just keep feeding themselves, so they last longer than wax candles. All I have to do is find me a bear that is willing to be made into food, a warm coat, and candles from his fat, which ain't none too easy.

With a piece of elk meat that had been roasting over the fire, along with some beans and coffee, I filled my belly and lit up my pipe, thinking I would write some more before my eyes get too tired.

-

Now where was I? Oh yeah, when coming up on a bear I recommend you have your guns loaded and your powder dry because bears typically don't just stand there and point to where they want to be shot. No, sir... If he or she feels like you're invading their territory, they're going to be hell-bent on making sure you wish you'd never even heard of them and even sadder that you're looking at them, eye to eye.

I remember one time when a bear snuck up on me without me noticing and caught me unawares. I was afoot, leading my horse to give it a break on the steep incline we were climbing, along with leading a mule I was using to pack what few belongings I had.

It seemed like that ole bear came out of nowhere without any warning. One minute the trail was empty, and the next, there he stood - a big ole black bear, standing on his back legs and growling like he was madder than a wet hen.

If I haven't mentioned it yet, I'm a good-sized man. I stand an even six feet tall and that ole bear was looking me right in the eyes. He was nigh on to as tall as me and I swear he weighed on the high side of four hundred pounds. I was still fairly young and a good thing, too, because my rifle was in the saddle holster, so all I had was my pistol and my knife.

With lightning fast speed, I pulled my pistol and got off a quick shot because he was almost on me. Now, like I said earlier, pa taught me to hit what I shot at, but he hadn't said anything about having a horse and a mule trying to rip the lead rope out of your hand so they can run away, nor the adrenaline rushing through an already frightened brain as you try and shoot at an angry bear. Between trying to control my panicked animals and getting off a quick shot, well, I hate to admit it but all my shot did was wound that ole bear in the shoulder and make him even madder than he already was.

Being fair to meddling size, young, and strong as an ox helps a lot when it comes to wrestling a bear. And lucky for me, I carried a Bowie knife and kept it razor sharp.

I didn't have any choice but to turn my animals loose and let 'em run so I could meet that ole bear, head on.

We must 'a fought for close to half an hour before I was able to get my knife into his lungs and heart, and by then, I was worn down to a frazzle and bleeding from at least a dozen claw marks.

Of course, that was a long time ago and now I've learned a thing or two about watching for bears and always keeping my rifle handy, along with listening for unusual sounds, like a bear walking on dry, crackling, leaves.

THREE

Sorry about getting sidetracked, but sometimes I need to explain things.

According to a paper ma had, I came into this world around one in the morning on the 25th of December, in the year, 1802. Guess I was what you might call, a Christmas present, although I'm not sure ma thought so. They say I was long and skinny, with a full head of fiery red hair. And when the woman acting as midwife, smacked me on my backside to make me cry, well, pa said I just up and got stubborn and clinched my jaws together and refused to utter a sound – which lasted for the first two years of my life.

I guess it takes me awhile to get over a grudge – or maybe I just didn't have anything to say.

On my second birthday, ma let me sit next to the Christmas tree while I opened my one and only present. The reason we only got one present each, was because of ma's rule. She didn't want us to look like we had more than we did, so's not to set the neighbors tongues to wagging. Anyway, although I can't recollect exactly what I got that year, they say I looked up at them and said, "Thank you," which they told me, later, almost gave both of them a heart attack.

Even with that outburst, I still didn't have a lot to say, and still don't. I'm more of a thinker than a talker - although, sometimes when I'm stumped about something, it's easier to figure things out if I talk about it out loud. Of course, seeing a man with long red hair walking around in the forest, talking to himself makes the Indians think I'm crazy and that's good because they're afraid to harm someone they think is touched in the head... Brings bad luck in their way of thinking. Most of them have never seen a man with red hair before and they're not sure what to think about that. So, whenever I see any of 'em, I jump up and down and wave my arms for them to come to me, while I sing some bawdy song. They turn and run like a pack of wolves was after 'em. But then there are a few braves who don't care about spooks and such when it comes to wanting revenge and they are the ones coming for my scalp, come spring.

It's funny how superstitions cause folks to act as they do. Me? I'm not the superstitious type. I try to look at things with both eyes wide open, and study whatever it is 'til I figure it out, even if I have to talk to myself to do it. Then again, there are things that a man just can't figure out, like trying to explain something to a hard headed mule when he clearly doesn't care one little bit about what you're saying – or, how to understand the way a woman thinks.

I'm sure pa had a saying about that one; I just don't recall what it was.

All my young life, I always believed pa was the tallest and strongest man in the world. Of course, back in those days, I was pretty small compared to him. Even so, pa stood head and shoulders above all of the other men in town. I'm guessing he stood several inches over six feet tall and weighed at least two hundred pounds.

I once saw him punch ah charging bull right between the eyes with his fist and drop him to his knees. Being a blacksmith makes a man, strong, and with his size, it just made him look more formidable. Of course, I tried not to rile him much – even though that didn't work out too well during my younger years, but it was ma I feared the most. When her eyes got all fiery looking, I headed for anyplace out of her sight.

Like I said earlier, ma was a small woman, who, when standing full up, barely reached pa's shoulder. But make no mistake about it, even with being small, she still ruled the roost at our house.

Pa being the silent type and ma the strong willed one, and always wanting to do things her way, things usually went the way she said. But to be honest, she was protective of me and pa.

Ole Doctor Brenan, who was the richest man in town, and a Protestant as I recall, owned a farm up north of town and asked pa to make a new set of harness for his horses – then claimed they didn't fit right and refused to pay pa, which made ma mad. She went up to see for herself and when she saw his horses with the new harness, that fit them perfectly, well, she came back to town and cut herself a switch, then went into the doctor's office and commenced to whip on him, right in front of all his patients. He run and ducked and tried to get out of the way, but she stayed right on him til he gave her the money he owed pa. And before she left, she dared him to try and do something to us for standing up for ourselves - and he never did. I think he was scared of ma, too.

I must have been in the neighborhood of six or so when ma took me into town with her one day. It had rained just before we left, and like most young boys, I liked to jump in the puddles to make a splash. I saw this puddle and I run in front of ma so I could jump in it and make a splash, which I did. It just so happened that a man came walking past at the same time I landed with both feet in the middle of that puddle, and splashed muddy water on his pant legs.

Made him mad, it did, and he reached out to slap me, but ma was right there and grabbed the man's arm, then kicked him in the shin and when he yelled and bent down, she kicked more water on him, saying, "You touch my boy again and I'll shove your face down in that puddle and hold it there!" I swear, her eyes were spitting fire and daggers, both at the same time.

That man must have seen it too because he turned and ran on down the road.

I think pa was more comfortable at the blacksmith shop than he was at home, which didn't mean he didn't like coming home, because he did. Being on the same property, our house was just a short walk to the blacksmith shop and when pa heard ma ring the supper bell, he would close up and come a running. Ma run the house and pa run the horse boarding and blacksmith shop which is why he felt more at home there, where he was the boss and could create things with his hands.

And me? I guess I've always been the adventurous type which seemed to always bring trouble my way because of one thing or another.

As I think back, I was somewhere around three when trouble started following me around. Ma had baked a berry pie of some kind and sat it on the window sill to cool.

I was still too short to reach it, but that pie sure did smell good and it got my mouth to watering. I remember standing on my tiptoes and reaching up to grab the pie. I had to strain and even then, I could barely touch the edge of the pan, which, when I curled my fingers over the edge and pulled down – well I reckon you can guess what happened next. The pie tipped over and landed on top of my head. Lord ah mercy I thought my hair had caught on fire and I was going to fry my brain; the pie was still that hot.

I ran for the water bucket on the other side of the kitchen to put the fire out, and in doing so, I left a trail of pie scattered all over ma's clean kitchen floor.

Thinking back, that was the first of many times I wore out a switch or felt the sting of ma's hand on my rearend. I don't think ma had ever heard anything about spare the rod, spoil the child, so, as you can bet, I was never a spoiled child.

Don't get me wrong, ma and pa were good to me. They praised me when I did good and punished me when I did bad, which I believe to this day is a good way to raise a child, although, I never got the chance with the way my life turned out.

My next encounter with a switch came when I was four. Our water came from a well out on the side of the house not far from the back door to the kitchen, and one afternoon I got to wondering if there might be any fish in the water down there, and apparently, I leaned over a mite too far, and the next thing I knew, I was learning to swim.

I was lucky ma needed some water about then and heard me yelling.

She grabbed the water bucket and tossed it in, and when it landed next to me, I heard her call down to me, "Grab ahold of the rope and hang on!"

It's probably a good thing I was still small, because, like I said, ma was not a big woman and she might not have been able to pull me up. I looked at that rope and wondered if I should just stay down in that well because I knew what was coming when I got out. And I was right, too. She grabbed me by the ear and dragged me into the kitchen, then grabbed me by the shoulders and shook me back and forth so hard my teeth rattled, saying, "What is wrong with you, boy? You could 'a drown!" Then she bent me over her lap and whooped me on the butt with her hand until her arm got tired. And when she stood me upright, she pulled me up close to her and squeezed me so tight I thought she was going to crush my lungs. Right then is when I learned I didn't know much on how women think. One minute she was whooping on me, and the next, hugging me tight.

Years later I realized all those whippings ma gave me was because I did things that caused her to be scared that I might hurt myself really bad, or worse – but during those younger years, I didn't have sense enough to understand that, and just kept on doing dumb things.

As I look back, those years weren't all about me getting in trouble – there were a lot of good times, too.

When I turned nine, pa gave me a fishing pole he'd made himself, over in his blacksmith shop. It was made from a metal rod and where he got the reel and line, I'm not sure, but it became my most prized possession. And of an evening, when the weather was nice, he would take me down to the Sullane River, which like I said, is a tributary off the River Lee and taught me to fly-fish. Before that I'd just used a piece of line and a hook with a worm on it, with a piece of cork for a bobber.

At first, I didn't catch much, because the sun put a glean on the water and I couldn't see very well because I didn't wear a hat to shade my eyes. Pa gave me one of his old hats and insisted I keep trying. And sure enough, it wasn't long until I could cast almost as good as pa, and began to catch some good-sized brown trout, which I took home to ma. Of course, back then we mostly spoke Gallic and a brown trout was called a, Breac Donn.

By the time I was ten, I figured I was one of the best fishermen in all of Ireland, or at least our part of the country. Pa had told me to never go fishing without him, but of course that went in one ear and out the other. I loved to go fishing. I remember one time when he and ma were busy one evening. Some folks gathered down by the river so they could talk about things without Protestant ears hearing and going to spread the tale.

Anyway, when me and the other young folks were told to go find something to do, I looked around and figured the weather was just right to catch some fish. So, when I said something to the other boys about it, several of them, girls included, said they wanted to go with me to see if I could live up to my bragging.

On the way down to the river I heard one of the boys say, "I'm bettin' he'll be lucky to catch anything bigger than bait. To my way of thinkin', he's all blow and no go."

Well, I stopped right there and turned around and stared down at him. Just then I remembered something pa once said and I told him, "Mister Shemesh, just so you'll know, it's often, a man's mouth has broken his nose."

He looked down at his feet and mumbled something under his breath, and when I asked, "What was that you said?"

Tommy O'Leary stepped up next to Billy Shemesh and said, "He said he's sorry and he really didn't mean what he said."

I stretched out my hand with the fishing pole in it and asked, "Maybe you'd like to show me how to do it right?"

When he just stood there with his jaws clinched tight, I turned and headed toward the river. I'm not sure which shut him up, pa's saying, or the fact that I was the bigger of the two of us and had a bit of a reputation for having a quick temper.

I guess, as I think back, I did want to show off the skills pa had taught me and without stopping, I waded out into the river, up to my knees, and showed them what I'd learned about casting.

My fly landed right where I wanted it to and I began to reel it back in, giving a slight jerk now and then.

I was looking over my shoulder, explaining to everyone on the bank what I was doing when the big trout hit my fly and almost jerked the pole out of my hands. Oh, he was a big one, all right! I jerked back on the line and the fight was on! When he leaped into the air, everybody on the riverbank let out a gasp, including Billy Shemesh.

Trying not to show it, I was scared I might not be big enough to land him. He was so powerful he was dragging me out into deeper water, but I was determined to bring him in and I kept fighting to the loud encouragement from the boys and girls on the bank.

Then the inevitable happened, I stepped off into deep water. Down and down, I went until I was in well over my head. Still, I wasn't willing to give up. I bent my knees and pushed hard, driving myself back toward the surface, and when my head cleared the water, I gulped in as much air as I could before I was dragged back down to the bottom of the river, again. I don't know how many times that happened before one of the girls ran for help.

When pa and the others got there, I was nowhere to be seen. I was still under the water because my foot got stuck between two rocks and I was having trouble getting it loose. I held onto my pole with one hand as that big ole trout kept fighting me, while I tried to loosen my foot with the other hand.

The next thing I knew, pa was grabbing ahold of me and pulling me to the surface, with me still trying to land that fish. And with his help, we hauled in a big ole brown trout that weighed twenty-one and a half pounds – the biggest trout anyone in our town had ever caught.

Even though I was the talk of the town, and Billy Shemesh was eating his words, I don't remember anyone ever mentioning the paddling I got for going off to the river without pa, and scaring him and ma half to death.

During those years I learned a good number of things that helped me in the years to come – like, how to fish and track game - how to clean and dress what I caught, for eating; or how to tan a hide, and how to think for myself. This was all good except for the fact that in my younger days I didn't always do the thinking for myself part very well.

I was thirteen when pa took in a thoroughbred horse to board. He was a beauty – a dark chestnut that stood sixteen hands. Pa had gone to take some harness to one of his customers and I was left to look after the place for an hour or so while he was gone.

I climbed up on the wooden fence of the corral and studied the big horse as he pranced around, his tail was raised in an arc, his head held high and his mane was flying back from his neck. He was magnificent! And that's when my common sense went flying out of my head.

I got down and ran to the house and returned shortly with an apple. I climbed back up on the fence and held the apple out to him.

He came to me slowly, his neck stretched out, his nose sniffing. When he got close enough to reach out and take the apple, he did so, real gentle like.

As he drew it into his mouth, I leaped from the fence and onto his back.

For about twenty seconds I had the ride of my life. I had a handful of mane and was glad I did because he reared up on his hind legs, whinnying at the top of his lungs, and when he came down, his back legs went out and he began to buck, twisting and turning to get me off his back.

Of course, I thought I was a good rider, but I'd never experienced anything like this and when I lost my grip on his mane, I went flying into the air.

If you've never been bucked off a horse that stood sixteen hands and was another three feet in the air, well let me tell you, it's a long way to the ground! I landed on my head, neck and shoulders and felt pain in all those places.

I rolled over to get back up on my feet and when I did, I looked up and my eyes went wide. He had reared up and I saw his front hooves coming down at me.

I was barely able to roll over and get out of the way as his hooves slammed against the ground where I had just been.

I came to my feet and ran for the fence and just as I reached the top, I felt his teeth clamp down on my backside. I went headfirst over the fence and landed flat on my back.

When I was able to get my breath back and open my eyes, the first thing I saw was pa. He was standing there, glaring down at me. "Have you not learned anything from the things I've tried to teach you, boy?" he asked, his eyes filled with sadness.

I didn't get a whooping, that time, but I did get a long talking to and after he calmed down, pa asked, "You want to learn to ride, do you?"

At this point I have to tell you about Irishmen and racing. It's in their blood – they're born with the drive and there was a big race track just north of town on the other side of the road, across from the local doctor's farm. Pa took me up there and because of who he was, he was able to get me a job exercising the racehorses. I think he was hoping I could get this yearn to ride horses, out of my system. At least that was the plan.

Instead of getting tired of riding, by the time I was fourteen, I was jockeying for one of the owners. The horse's name was Radala, which translates in English to, Fast Runner, and that he was. He stood seventeen hands and ran like a pack of wolves was chasing him. The wind in your face, the power between your legs and the challenge of beating the other horses is a feeling beyond description. Radala and I won six races together before my brief jockey career ended because of two reasons. First, Radala hurt his right front leg and was retired and put out to pasture to sometimes help bring a new colt into the world.

And second, I got a sudden growth spurt and it wasn't long before I was too big to be a jockey – but still not too big to exercise them. But after racing around a mile track on the back of a horse that weighed more than a thousand pounds, and crossing the finish line in first place, exercising them wasn't enough and lost its appeal.

I still worked for pa at the blacksmith shop and helped ma when she needed it, but I was constantly looking for a new adventure.

FOUR

It was pa's friend Amos MacGillycuddy that taught me to sail.

From time to time on a Sunday, Pa and me would hitch up the buggy and take a trip over to the River Lee and meet up with Mister MacGillycuddy. He had a twenty-six-foot sailboat and loved to sail up and down the river. His wife had passed on and they had no children, so I guess sailing took his mind off his loneliness.

Well, let me tell you, I took to sailing like a young lad takes to seeing a pretty lass that makes his heart go pitter-patter. And after only a few lessons, I was sailing the boat by myself while Mister MacGillycuddy and pa were emptying some bottles of ale and seeing who could tell the biggest tale. I'm not sure but I'm guessing that it was pa who won.

Being in command of a sailboat is right up there with being a jockey, feeling the wind in your face and the sails full as you glide up or down the river. It's you and Mother Nature – and you're in control. It's a feeling that's hard to explain… although, the feeling that your willpower is stronger than Mother Nature's can get a fella in trouble as I would one day find out.

The following year, on a Sunday, Mister MacGillycuddy was out sailing by himself and his boat was hit by a huge floating log that tore a hole in the side, and sunk it.

Pa told me Mister MacGillycuddy had never learned to swim and he went down with his boat. His body washed up on the shore a few miles downriver from where the boat was found sitting on the bottom of the River Lee. And for some reason, they left it there.

I'll never forget what Mister MacGillycuddy told me one Sunday. It sticks in my mind still today. He said for me to always mind my p's and q's because the river was cursed and would eat me up if given a chance. Then he recited a saying, and since he never learned to speak English, his words went something like this, "Mise ab Sulan, fuar, fada, fireann - Anois an t-am, ca bhfuil an dunie," which, when translated, meant, "I am the River Lee, long, mean and masculine. Now is the time. Where is the person I am to drown?"

I don't know if he was just making that up to impress me, or scare me, or what, but I missed Mister MacGillycuddy, his boat, and our Sunday sailing.

It was about then pa seemed to start ailing some, so I spent a lot of time caring for the horses and learning more about being a blacksmith.

By the time I was fifteen, I was nearly as tall as pa, but not yet up to his weight, but I knew my way around the blacksmith shop pretty good. In fact, he allowed me to do a lot of the work so I would be ready to take over when it was time for him to sit in his rocker and tell tall tales about his younger days.

I was seventeen when I walked into the barn and found him lying on the floor next to a stall he'd been cleaning out. The doctor said his heart just gave out from all the hard work he'd done during his lifetime. And the day we put him in the ground, I swore never to work so hard that I would die as young as pa did. He was only forty-two.

In fact, now that I was the sole owner of everything, I gave thought to selling the place and go traveling, but then what would become of ma? So, I stayed, and found out how hard it was running the place by myself. I was nearly as good as pa had been so there was never a lack for work, but the hours were long and tedious.

I had been working the horse boarding and blacksmith business for close to a year when the police came with a piece of paper telling me I wasn't the legal owner. I told him he was wrong and took the paper from the desk showing I was a legal partner since the day I was born. But he just laughed ant told me the paper wasn't worth the ink it was written with.

Pa's idea of making me a partner instead of trying to leave the place to me sounded like a good idea, but them Protestants didn't see it that way. The doctor wanted the place and he had the law and the judge on his side, and there wasn't a thing I could do to stop him. As I look back, I figure it was his way of getting back at ma for the switching she'd given him and the embarrassment in front of his patients.

Oh, they pretended to be all law abiding and all and told me instead of just kicking us off the place immediately, the doctor would buy it from me – not for what it was worth, but for pennies on the dollar, and give us two whole weeks to get out of the house so the man he'd hired to take my place could move in with his wife. And as you can guess, the new blacksmith and his wife, were Protestants.

Of course, ma cried a lot, but in the end, she decided to go live with her younger sister and brother-in-law up north, in Killarney. He was head master for the Ross Castle Properties. Truth be told, he was the superintendent over their farms and race horses. But it was a good job and better than many men had in those days. They had an extra bedroom and ma could help around the house.

My brother-in-law offered me the job of blacksmith on the farm, but I said, "Thank you, but no. I'll be moving on."

FIVE

With my inheritance stolen by the doctor and ma living up in Killarney, I was eighteen and free as a bird and just about as penniless. Except for a few farthings to get by on until I could find work, all I had was my fishing pole and the few clothes I owned. I gave ma the rest of what money was paid to us. Along with the money she had put by for a rainy day, she could go to her sister's place with her head held high, knowing she could pay her own way and not be a burden. Not that she would have, but having some money in her purse made her feel better.

With nothing more than my fishing pole and the few pieces of clothing I owned, that were thrown into a flower sack, I hitched a ride with a man going to Cork to pick up some dry goods he'd ordered for his store. He was short, bald and grumpy. "Ah man can hardly keep his head above water these days, what with the price of everything. It's ah shame the way some folks get rich off the backs of us poor, honest folks tryin' ta earn a livin'." The man was a Protestant and owned a dry goods store. I seriously doubt he'd ever lacked for anything in his entire life.

During the entire trip, all the man did was complain about how the Catholics had it all.

I just nodded my head and kept my mouth shut about the way the Protestants had stolen what was rightfully mine, because I'm sure he would have tossed me off his wagon, leaving me to walk the whole twenty-six miles to Cork. As pa used to say, "God is good, but never dance a jig in a small boat."

I was let off down on the wharf where he was to pick up his goods. He didn't say anything, he just stopped the wagon in front of the warehouse and got off and went about his business. There was a salty breeze coming off the water and it tickled the inside of my nose. I had never smelled the ocean before, nor had I ever seen so much water. I was paralyzed for a few moments, watching as sea gulls flew about.

After getting down from the wagon, I knelt down and dipped my fingers in the water, then put them against my tongue. I had read that ocean water was salty, and now I knew it was true. They were right, sea water was unfit to drink. What a shame, since there was so much of it.

I looked at the sky and from where the sun was, high overhead, I knew it was close to noon. Plus, I could feel the rumble in my stomach.

Just down the wharf a short distance I saw a sign swinging in the breeze that read, Murphy's Pub & Grub.

I had never been in a pub before but figured now was as good a time as any to see what they were like. Pa used to have a liking for them.

The place was crowded, but I found a stool at the bar and climbed on it and looked around. Except for the women waiting on the tables, the place was filled with men of all size and description. Grey smoke from their pipes and cigars floated heavily against the ceiling, and the whole place smelled like smoke and fish, along with what I guessed to be a mixture of whiskey and ale. The men were all talking loudly and the women who waited on the tables laughed at their bawdy jokes.

The sound of a woman's voice caused me to turn my head. "What'll it be, sweetness?"

I sat there, my eyes wide and my mouth hanging open. No woman had ever spoken to me that way and I didn't know how to react. She was younger than ma and a bit taller – but still a fetching woman with a big smile and a lot of cleavage showing.

She laughed and said, "Close your mouth, darlin' or you'll be eatin' flies for lunch."

I closed my mouth and tried to clear my throat but nothing came out.

She laughed, again, and said, "New in town, are ya?"

I could only nod my head.

"And you'd be obliged ta know what would I recommend," wouldn't ya?.

Again, I nodded my head. This was crazy because I had never been shy around girls before. But this was no girl. This was a full on woman, and she was making me feel very uncomfortable with her forward attitude.

"You ever eaten fresh seafood?" she asked.

"No... no ma'am," I stammered.

"There's no ma'am, to it, sweetie. The name's Sarah. Sarah O'Hara. But you can call me whatever you like, as long as you call me." She said with a wink of her eye and a chuckle on her lips.

Well, I could feel the skin on my face tighten and I knew my cheeks were as red as the beets ma grew in her garden, or the hair on my head, for that matter. Somehow, I was able to stammer, "Yes, ma... Sarah."

She looked at my fishing pole leaning against the bar, then down at the sack with my clothes in it and asked. "So, you really have just arrived in our fair city, haven't ya?"

Again, I nodded my head, but was able to say, "Yes, just a few minutes ago."

"So, to introduce you to our fair establishment, it's the best in the house you'll be ah needin', then we can discuss where you'll be stayin'," she said as she turned and went into the kitchen, shouting something about a large bowl of clam chowder.

And in less time than you could say, Jack Sprat, she was back, sliding a bowl of clam chowder in front of me, along with a plate with a small loaf of soda bread and butter next to it, followed by a tankard of ale. I looked at it and then back to her.

She smiled and said, "Eat! We'll talk later." And with that, she whirled and went to see a man who just came in and sat down a few stools down from me.

I had never eaten clam chowder – only fish from the river near where I grew up, and I had to admit, it was good. And I enjoyed dunking the soda bread in the thick soup. I wasn't sure what kind of fish a clam was, but I was thinking about having a second bowl. I took a drink of the ale and studied it a bit. It wasn't as stout as what pa used to drink, but it was tasty.

Waiting for her to return, I sat there, thinking about what she'd said about a place to stay and wondered if she had rooms to rent and how much they'd be? I needed to be some watchful over what little money I had.

When she returned, she leaned her elbows on the counter, giving me an eye-full, and asked, "So, handsome, where do you plan on spending the night?"

"I don't know – what with me just getting here and all, and still without a job, yet. Do you know of a place that isn't too expensive? Like I said, I don't have a job, yet, and the coins in my pocket are a bit light."

She gave me a smile that sent chills down my spine and said, "I think I might be able to find you a place for the night, if you don't mind sharing my bed."

Well, at that, I didn't know what to say. I had never been with a woman before and for sure, I was a bit nervous and her forwardness scared me something awful.

I needin have been worried about what I was going to say or do because the man who had just come in and sat down a few stools away, got up and walked over and stopped next to me.

"Did I hear you say you were new in town and looking for employment?" he asked.

"You did, and I am," I told him, hoping he would rescue me from this awkward situation.

He nodded his head and asked me, "You wouldn't happen to know how to sail a boat, would you?"

My eyes grew wide and I smiled and said, "Yes, sir. I do. I love to sail. As a matter of fact, I used to…"

The man patted me on the shoulder and said, "That's good. Yes, that's very good, indeed. You're hired."

And with that he put money on the counter to pay for my meal and fairly dragged me outside.

"She's just down this way he said," as we walked down the to where a beautiful sailboat sat, bobbing on the water.

"By the way, my name's Byron Campbell. And you? What do they call you, lad?"

"Jubal Courtney. I'm just in from Macroom. I…"

"Fine, fine," he said. "And you said you can sail a sloop?"

"Aye, I can. I sailed…"

"Good, good," he said leading me aboard the boat.

"She's thirty-four feet long with an eleven-foot beam, I need you to leave right away because I promised the new owner I would deliver the boat within the week."

"Within the week?" I asked, wondering what I was getting myself into.

"Oh, it won't take morn' two or three days, what with good winds and all," he said, ushering me down below. "As you can see, there is plenty of food and water and a map of your sailing route."

I looked down at the map lying on the table and it just as well could have been written in hieroglyphics as far as I was concerned. I'd never learned map reading and I started to protest – maybe even back out of the deal. "I'm not prepared to leave right away. I…"

"But you have to! I will pay you in advance."

He reached in his pocket and laid ten pounds sterling on the map, then looked at me and nodded his head.

I stared down at the money and my nerves went to tingling. I even forgot about the possibility of spending the night with Sarah from the pub. That much money would set me up good. I looked at him and asked, "Where did you say I was to deliver the boat?"

Mister Campbell looked at me and smiled. "Falmouth. And if you leave now, you should get there in no more than three days."

Now, I admit, I didn't know all of the seaports along the coast of Ireland and for sure, I'd never heard of this one, so I looked down at the map and asked, "Would you mind showing me on the map?"

His finger traveled from Cork, out across the ocean to the tip of England and a short way up the backside of the land jutting out from the mainland. "Right here. Falmouth, England."

I took a deep breath and asked, "Did you say, England?"

Mister Campbell got a concerned look on his face and said, "You did say you are an experienced sailor, didn't you?"

I looked down at the map and it didn't seem all that far. Then I looked at the money, again and smiled. How hard could it be? "I'll be leaving within the hour."

He helped me get the boat away from the dock and out into the bay. It was rigged just like Mister MacGillycuddy's boat, only bigger. There was a breeze coming off the land and I put up the jib sail and tied it off on the port side, then moved the main over to the starboard side in a wing on wing position, and the boat began to move forward toward the open water of the ocean.

CHASING THE NEXT SUNRISE

SIX

I felt proud of myself and turned my head and saw Mister Campbell standing on the wharf. He was smiling and waving. I waved back, then turned back and guided the boat out into open water.

I had never sailed on the ocean before. In fact, until that day, I had never seen the ocean, and I got a knot in my stomach. It looked much bigger out here than it did on the map.

I took a deep breath and told myself, "You can do this. According to Mister Campbell, it's only two hundred and fifteen miles. Isn't that what he said? How hard can that be? By my reckoning, if I stayed on course, I should be able to see land in another day or so, and then the rest should be easy."

As I stood with the tiller gripped in my right hand, I noticed the sails begin to flutter.

Now that I was out, away from land, the wind had shifted and was now coming from the southwest. After tying off the tiller, I readjusted the mainsail to the starboard side and adjusted both the main sail and the head sail. With the wind coming like it was, it wanted to take me northeast instead of southeast like the map showed I should go.

I ran down below and studied the map as best I could. From the look of it, the tip I was to go around was east of Cork and a little bit south.

Back at the tiller, I stood looking out over the vast ocean. There was nothing to see but water and sky, and my mind began to jump around like it did when someone was in the outhouse and I had to wait. What if I stayed on this course and the current took me south of where I wanted to go? What was it pa used to say? "The best of luck is what you make for yourself."

I studied the sky, then the ocean as the boat went up over one wave, then down into the trough, and back up over the next one. It would be like this for at least two days with me not knowing if I was sailing true or not. Sailing on the ocean was a lot different than up and down a river where I could see both banks, and I wasn't sure I hadn't bitten off more than I could chew.

CHASING THE NEXT SUNRISE

I concentrated and could see the map in my mind. If I sailed too far off to the northeast, I would wind up in Wales. But if I sailed just slightly to the northeast, I would run into the west coast of England, then I could safely sail south to the end of the peninsula, go around it and up the short distance to Falmouth. That seemed the safest thing for me to do, so I veered the boat slightly to the northeast and tried to relax.

As I stood, holding the tiller to stay on course, a big whale came to the surface, blew water into the air and then dove back down. I stared at it, shaking my head. I had never seen a whale before and suddenly my knees began to shake. What if a whale came up under me on its way to the surface? It would tip my boat over and I would become shark food. Did that really happen? I had no idea. But in my mind, it could. "Clear your head, Jubal and think only positive thoughts," I told myself. I looked off to starboard and could see the whale in the far distance. "He's gone and you have nothing more to worry about," I said to the wind, and shortly, was able to breathe easier.

By now I was getting hungry so I tied off the tiller, again, and went down below to see what food Mister Campbell had put aboard. What I found was some salt pork with maggots crawling around in it and the biscuits were so hard they were like rocks. There was a small, oil stove to cook on, but only one pan. The only decent thing I found was the small keg of good water and a few bottles of ale. I decided I wouldn't be eating any salt pork, but what I could do, was use it for bait! I had my fishing pole and I could fish. I knew nothing about saltwater fishing, but hoped it wouldn't be any different than fishing in a river.

After checking the sails and adjusting them just a little, I put some salt pork on my hook and let it drift off the stern of the sailboat. The baited hook couldn't have been more than thirty feet aft of the boat when a fish attacked the bait and my pole bent almost in half and was almost jerked out of my hands. Very quickly I slacked off the line and let the fish run, but when it came back toward the boat, I wound up the line as fast as I could, bringing it closer to the boat each time, until finally I got it up close. And when I saw the big sea bass, I couldn't believe my luck. I also knew I couldn't haul it in with the line I had. The fish was too big and the line would break, for sure.

I looked around for something to hook it with, but found nothing. In desperation and because I was really hungry, I tied a piece of rope around my waist and the other end to the boat, then I jumped into the ocean. I was a strong swimmer and I had no trouble grabbing the fish by the gill and heaving it aboard the boat.

That evening I dined on sea bass, fried biscuits and a bottle of ale. It's amazing what a little food in your stomach will do for your attitude. I stood at the tiller, gazing out across the water and watched as my first day at sea came to a close.

Shortly after the sun disappeared beyond the western horizon, dark clouds covered the moon and all around me. Except for a few stars here and there, it was so dark I couldn't even see the bow of my boat. My world had suddenly turned black. The only sound was the wind blowing against the sails, and the waves slapping against the side of the boat.

Suddenly, a nasty tasting bile begin to build in my throat and my heart began to beat faster. I suddenly realized I was out in the middle of the ocean with no one to turn to if something went wrong. I tried to calm my nerves by telling myself, everything was going to be all right. The sails were set and the tiller was gripped tightly in my hand – and, and I was sailing in the direction I wanted to go.

As I stood there, staring into nothing but a black void, I heard one of pa's sayings as it popped into my brain. "A good laugh and a decent night's sleep are the best cures for almost everything."

I leaned my head back and gave out with a hearty laugh, that was carried by the wind, out across the ocean, and just like that, my fears disappeared. After tying off the tiller, I went down below and lay down on the bunk.

With the sound of the waves washing across the hull of the boat and the gentle rise and fall as it plowed through the ocean, I was soon lulled into a deep sleep. My first day at sea had been a long and somewhat exciting one.

I don't know what time it was but it was still dark when seawater cascaded down the open hatch and drenched me from head to toe. I leaped to my feet and was thrown back down onto the bunk as the boat rolled from side to side. My first thought was the boat was going to capsize with me in it. I knew I needed to get topside as quickly as I could and find out what had gone wrong.

It took all my strength to get myself upright and make my way out onto the deck. I closed the hatch before any more water went down below and possibly sink the boat. The boom for the mainsail was trying its best to rip itself from the rigging and both lines on the tiller had broken and it was swinging back and forth with the rolling of the boat.

I wasn't sure what a monsoon was, but I was convinced I was in one. Water was falling from the sky like I was standing under a waterfall, and the wind was so strong it was all I could do to keep from being blown or washed overboard and I could feel panic trying to take control of me, but I gritted my teeth and screamed, "I will not let you defeat me!"

I grabbed the tiller to try and stabilize the boat, but I got no response. It just moved back and forth. I turned and looked over the stern but all I could see was black, foamy water as it crashed over the back end of the boat. I couldn't see the rudder but I knew it had to be swaying back and forth at the whim of the raging water. The pin attaching the tiller and the rudder must have slipped out, separating the two, leaving me at the mercy of the storm and the heavy seas. With no way to steer, the only thing I could do was drop all sails and hang on for dear life, and pray the boat didn't capsize and the storm would soon pass as I waited for daylight.

If I died out here, the only one who would know would be Mister Campbell, and when I didn't show up in Falmouth, he would probably think I had absconded with his boat. And if he did know about the storm and realized I could have been lost at sea, he would know nothing about my mother or how to let her know I would never be coming back.

Three hours later, as the sun came over the eastern horizon, the only thing remaining of the storm was the backside of the black clouds as they moved on to the northeast. The sky was clear blue with only a few puffer clouds drifting lazily along and the temperature was already becoming balmy.

The sun was on my right, which meant the boat was pointed north. I had absolutely no idea where the storm had taken me or what my position was. Since the storm had hit during the night and by the time I got topside, the boat was spinning around and around uncontrollably. Since I was without a rudder, the storm could have taken me north or south of my log line. I had no fancy instrumentation or any way of figuring out my location. I could feel my blood pressure rising and I needed to calm my nerves and use some of that common sense pa used to speak of.

I opened the hatch and went slowly down the steps leading to the salon and stopped short of going all the way. My best guess was, there was close to ten inches of water covering the floor of the salon. Enough to make a mess, but not enough to sink the boat.

At that moment, I was glad I had had enough sense to close the hatch or the water coming over the side, along with what was falling from the sky, would surely been enough to send me to Davy Jones' Locker.

Wooden boats all leak, and that's why they have bilge pumps, but this was more than just leakage. I waded into the water and grabbed the wooden handle and began to pump.

It took almost three hours to empty the water from the salon area and when I'd finished, I opened the six port holes to let air in so the inside would dry.

Fortunately, the water hadn't gotten high enough to do any damage to what little food and drinking water I had. So, after rummaging through the larder, I found a jar of blueberry jam, and some tea, which rose my spirits some. I cut the biscuits in half and fried them to soften them up, and then smothered them with jam. When everything was prepared, I went topside and sat next to the tiller and stared across the water as I ate my breakfast and drank some tea.

At this point, my biggest concern was repairing the tiller-rudder problem. Without a rudder I was doomed to go wherever Mother Nature wanted to send me. The boat had reversed itself and was following the southwest flowing current, taking me out to sea, away from land, or maybe back to Ireland, I wasn't sure.

After putting something in my belly, I felt a little better and once again, went down below to see what I could find. An hour later, exhausted and frustrated, I went back up on deck. I had found nothing I could use as a pin to hold the rudder and tiller, together.

CHASING THE NEXT SUNRISE

The waves were quite large and slow rolling, which gave me the idea to check the connection up close; and after once again, tying a piece of rope around my waist and the other end to the boat, I leaped over the stern and swam up close to have a look-see at the tiller arm and rudder. The saltwater burned my eyes, but it was clear enough for me to see that I had been right. The pin holding the two together had somehow come out and was now at the bottom of the ocean – which of course was unretrievable.

After climbing back on board, I walked forward and stood looking out over the ocean, trying to figure out what I was going to do? I assumed that eventually I would find land, but how far away was it? And did I have enough water to last that long? I could always catch fish to eat. At least, I hoped so. But I would need water.

I turned around to go back to the cockpit when I discovered two things that shocked me. A bucket was tied off to a small chest - both sitting in front of the mast. Somehow, I hadn't noticed either of them. The bucket was filled with fresh rainwater from the storm! What was in the chest, I had no idea.

After taking the bucket of water below and filling my jugs, I came back up topside to see what was in the chest. When I hunkered down, I could see there was a padlock in the hasp.

It took me the better part of an hour before I found the key hanging next to the stove in the galley.

With trembling hands, I opened the chest and felt a large smile fill my face. It was filled with tools, extra things to help with repairs, including a box with four metal pins for the tiller!

It took close to half an hour to get the pin in place. Hammering under water is not the easiest thing to do, as I found out. But it was worth the effort.

When I climbed back aboard and tested the feel of the tiller, I shouted, "Wahoo!" I was once more in control of the boat!

By now the sun had passed its midpoint and was drifting toward the west and I had a decision to make. How far off course had the storm taken me and what direction should I point the boat? The only thing I knew for sure, was that my destination was off to the northeast – somewhere.

With that in mind, I pointed the bow toward the northeast and trimmed the sails to get the best speed I could.

With a bottle of ale in one hand and the tiller in the other, I sailed toward my unknown destination with hope in my heart, which is the only thing I could do.

That night, I slept in the cockpit, just in case Mother Nature decided to throw another storm in my way. The night sky was filled with a full moon, bright stars and a steady wind pushing me ever onward.

Somewhere during the night, I drifted off to sleep and awoke to the sound of thump, thump, thump. I jumped up and looked around, wondering what had broken this time. But instead of something having broken, the foredeck was covered with flying fish. Mother Nature was furnishing my breakfast… Maybe as an apology for the storm.

After my belly was full of fish, biscuits, jam - and tea, I felt somewhat renewed and when I went to the bow, somewhere in the far distance, I thought I could see land! I wished I had a telescope to get a better look, but knew I didn't. I would have to wait a bit longer.

I adjusted the sails to get the best speed I could, then tied off the tiller and went up on the bow, again. I stood, holding on to the down stay, and stared out across the water.

After what I perceived to be at least an hour, I could see it was land and I ran down below and retrieved the map.

As I got closer, I compared what I was seeing to the map and the hair on the back of my neck stood on end and my heartbeat quickened. The land looked very much like the picture on the map!

How this happened, I wasn't sure, but I thanked the Gods for bestowing their kindness on a young man who had let greed overtake his common sense.

The sun was directly overhead as I sailed into Falmouth and tied up at the pier.

A man was sitting in a chair in front of one of the buildings, and when I stepped onto the dock, he stood up and waved.

He hurried down to where I was standing and we shook hands. "Glad to see you made it. When that storm passed through, I got a little worried. Did it give you much trouble?"

I grinned and said, "No trouble at all. She's a sturdy boat and sails well."

"Well, here's a little something to show my appreciation for getting her here on time," he told me.

My eyes went wide as I looked down at the five pounds sterling he laid in my hand. All I could say, was, "Thank you."

SEVEN

There I was, in England, free as a bird, with a pocket full of money. Right away, I got myself a room and a hot bath and shave, then some new clothes befitting a young gentleman. I wanted to look good when I went looking for employment. What type of work I was going to look for, I hadn't the foggiest idea, but whatever I chose, I wanted to look good. I had the beginning of a resume. I could groom and exercise horses, I was a fair hand at blacksmithing, and I was now considered a blue water sailor. But first, before I tied myself down to a job, I decided to give Falmouth a once over.

It was a lively seaport with friendly people, which surprised me. I'd been told the English leaned toward the snobbish sort. I also ran into other Irishmen, along with men from France, Germany, Spain and even Italy.

There was a fair maiden who helped me into manhood. She was pale skinned, with blonde hair and blue eyes. I'd never seen anyone with blonde hair before and I told her so, right off when she brought my supper on my first night in Falmouth. One thing led to another and the next thing I knew, she was in my room at the hotel, helping me off with my clothes.

By the following morning, I was in love, but she soon put that idea out of my head when she told me she was married to a sailor who was due home any day now.

For the rest of the day, I was a broken man, wandering the streets, thinking of myself as a fool. Women were fickle and never again would I be taken in by a big smile or the swaying of a woman's hips.

Two days later I learned the reason Mister Campbell wanted me to leave in such a hurry. The keel of the sailboat was filled with stolen gold that he wanted out of the country, which explained his urgency and the large amount of money he paid me to get me to leave.

The man who took delivery of the boat had it hauled out and put in the shipyard, and in the middle of the night, was dismantling the keel to get the gold, when the authorities showed up. He began shooting at them, but when he ran out of ammunition they rushed in and arrested him. I was still asleep when they came banging on my door.

How they knew about me or where I was staying, I don't know for sure – but I was glad there was not a lass in my bed to further complicate things.

I was startled to learn the news and after a lot of questions the police decided I was not a part of the theft and left me standing there wondering what I might have done, had I known about the gold?

For the next few days, with money in my pocket, I wandered around Falmouth, with no real destination in mind other than looking for work, of which I found none that suited me. Mucking out horse stalls was not what I had in mind.

My third day in Falmouth, I broke my vow to never let another woman get close to me. Riegan Daly was petite, with hair as black as coal, and eyes that matched and the voice of an angel. She tended bar at the Crab & Suds – a place I stopped in for lunch. Without realizing it, she made sure we hit it off and I came back when her shift was finished.

She was two years older than me – cute as a new born pup, and a whole lot smarter about man/woman relationships than I was, even though I'd had a brief encounter with a married woman. But after two days, or should I say, nights, with her, I knew I had to move on. She was taking a bite out of my finances and I still didn't have a job.

I was standing on the dock, looking at the boats tied up to the pier and the bigger ones anchored out in the bay, when a man of around forty or so, stopped next to me and asked, "Are you a sailing man?"

I turned and looked at him. He was tall, with a roughish look about him, with streaks of gray in his hair and deep blue eyes and a smile that made the sun blush. He was an Irishman for sure, and dressed in a captain's uniform.

"You might say so," I told him. "I just sailed a thirty-four-foot sloop over from Cork, Ireland, single handed, I did."

"Did you now? And what are you up to now, lad?" he asked, appraising me from head to foot.

"Not that it's a big secret, but since you asked, I'll tell you. It's work I'm looking for and if you know where I might find some, I'll be happy to listen," I told him.

"I like your spirit, I do. And yes, I might know of some work if you're interested," he said slapping me on the shoulder.

"I'm listening," I told him. I was being a little more cautious this time. "What might the work be and how much does it pay?"

"You'll be working for me. I'm the captain of that ship out there in the harbor, the two masted schooner. I'm making a cargo run up the coast all the way to London, with stops in Bournemouth, Southampton, Brighton, then up the Thames to London. I'm looking for one more deck hand and you look able enough, and if you passed through that storm a few days back, you won't be wasting my time by hanging your head over the rail for most of the trip like the man I had to let go."

I looked him over good, and decided he was on the up and up. "You didn't say what the pay is," I said, glancing out at the ship. I had never been on a schooner before, or a ship that big, but figured I knew enough to get by.

"The pay is ten shillings per week and it's a two-week trip. When we get to London you will have your choice to stay or leave the ship. We have a good cook aboard and he keeps a good larder. What say you? Will you be coming with me?"

I wasn't sure how deep into England I wanted to go, them being my mortal enemy and all, even if they had all been decent to me so far. If it was anything like what I'd read about, London would be something to see. "Can you give me a few minutes to get my things from the hotel?" I asked, turning toward the hotel.

"Be quick about it, lad. I'm hoping to sail with the next tide."

Since the ship was already loaded, most of my time between Falmouth and Plymouth was spent learning about the rigging, which wasn't all that much different than the two boats I'd been on, except that the sheets were square rigged and only the two sails up front were tri-sails. Walking her deck was a far cry from the smaller boats I'd been on and the captain hadn't lied when he said the cook was a good one. I hadn't eaten so good since ma went north to live with her sister.

The first night we had mutton stew that would melt in your mouth and a sweetbread that was as tasty as any I had ever eaten. And for dessert, we had bread pudding, with tea.

CHASING THE NEXT SUNRISE

I was the youngest of six crewmen and we all slept in hanging berths in the forward part of the ship, leaving the rest of the ship for cargo – minus the captain's quarters and the galley, that is.

What really caught my interest was the cargo loading and unloading boom, which I found out, was to be my new job. The man who ran the loading and unloading took one look at me and assigned me to the haul line. I was one of four men who pulled on the rope to lift or lower the cargo off and on the ship or shore.

In each town we put into, we unloaded a few crates and loaded that many back aboard. And in each town, the men went ashore to frequent the pubs – but not me. I was not going to waste any more of my money until I knew more about what my future looked like. Not long before pa died, he gave me some advice that struck home, now. "No matter how tall your father or grandfather were, boy, you've got to do your own growin'."

I never realized what he meant by that until now. A young man, such as myself, had no one else to look after him – not my pa or grandfather. And it didn't matter what they'd done, I had to make my own way.

I still had fourteen pounds sterling I kept tucked away inside the belt I wore, and no one was the wiser, and that's the way I wanted to keep it. I'd been listening to some of the men talk and the word was, a man with at least ten pounds, could wind up with a business of his own in London. I wasn't sure what business that might be, but I had that much and more and I was eager to get to London to find out what my future might hold, even though I'd heard my mother say, "London is nothing more than a huge den of sin and inequity." I guessed I would need to see for myself.

By the time we got to Brighton, the last port before London, I had not only become a top hand at cargo handling, but had made an improvement to the rig by trading out the single sheeve dolly for a three sheeve dolly, which made pulling up a heavy load, much easier, and with less wear and tear on the rigging.

I wasn't sure how the ship was going to go up the river until one of the men explained that the ship had only a five-foot draft. He said it was long and narrow, giving the ship, not only its stability, but allowed it to go into water no deeper than seven feet.

As we drew close, I stood on the bow with my mouth hanging open and my eyes as big as supper plates. London was more than I dreamed it might be and when we were anchored and the cargo unloaded, I told the captain I would be staying in London. He wasn't happy to see me go, but understood. "If London gets to be too much for you, lad, keep an eye on the docks and if you see the Radala tied up, give me a shout. There will always be a place for you on my ship."

I thanked him and after collecting my money, I went ashore with the rest of the crew, only I wouldn't be coming back.

EIGHT

After two days of wandering the streets of London, I understood what ma meant, and was tempted to get back on the ship and go someplace else – anyplace else. From the deck of the ship, the city had looked to be a fine adventure. From the stories I'd heard, London was this grand city of kings and queens – of fancy carriages – castles and all the things wealth can bring and new beginnings for a man with gumption and a few bob in his pocket.

But what I saw was a black cloud hovering over the city. And when I walked the streets, the smoke gagged me and the soot clung to my clothes. When I had to cross the street, my feet sank ankle deep in mud and horse dung. The muddy streets were covered with it and the stink was enough to gag a maggot. And the Thames? A river I was told was a grand river, was filled with sewage and garbage. Yes, I almost turned around and went back to the ship.

But, alas, I didn't and now that I look back at it, my decision to stay was a good one. If I had gone back to the ship, I would have been aboard when they were attacked by pirates and six of the crew were hung from the yard arm. Only a skeleton crew made it to a port in Jamacia, where the ship was sold and the money split among the ones left. What happened to them, or the captain, no one knows. They just disappeared and were never heard from, again.

Had I been among the crew, would I have been one of the ones hung, or one of the men left stranded in Jamaica?

What I did was, hire on to ride with a man on his wagon, who was hauling a new anvil to a blacksmith on the far outskirts of town. I had helped load it and was to help unload it.

"Has London always been this filthy?" I asked of him as the wagon slowly made its way away from the muck and mire of the city.

He stared straight ahead for some time before he took a pipe and a bag of tobacco out of his coat pocket and filled the bowl, then stuck the stem of the pipe between his teeth. After putting the tobacco away, he took out a piece of flint and a striker. He held it over the tobacco and scratched the flint with the striker making sparks that finally ignited the tobacco. He puffed until he had it going, then put the flint and striker back in his pocket.

"I'm thirty five years old," he said as he puffed on the pipe and slapped the reins gently on the rump of the horse, who paid little attention, but continued on at his slow, steady pace.

The man looked much older, because of the dark pigment of his skin and the structure of his bones, but I held my tongue.

"As long as I can remember, London has always been a breeding ground for sickness because it has no sewer system. And until they do, it's gonna be just like you see it today. Why people flock to London is beyond me, but they do and each bloody year. the growing population just makes things worse."

We rode along in silence for some time before I asked, "Where is this blacksmith shop we're taking the anvil to?"

He dumped the dead ashes from his pipe and said, "Less than a mile further down this here road. Smithy's name is Baumgartner, Silas Baumgartner. A good man, he is, but gettin' a bit long in the tooth, if you get my drift?"

I did. I'd heard that saying before. "I do," I told him. "But surely, he has sons to help him, doesn't he?"

"Had two sons and a daughter, he did. But a few years back, they got the fever. His wife and all three children died. And I'm bound ta tell ya, he ain't been the same, since."

When we arrived, a tall, rawboned man came walking out to us, his feet shuffling in the dirt. His clothes were dirty and looked like he'd been wearing them for some time. He had big hands that were dark tanned and calloused. From what I'd been told, the man couldn't be older than his mid-forties, but he looked to be in his seventies. His eyes had the look of a man who had taken a look at what life had to offer, and had given up. Immediately, I felt sorry for him and hopped down and took the anvil in my arms and asked him, "Where do you want me to put this?"

He pointed and said, "There, on the corner of that table."

I looked at the table and wondered if it was strong enough to carry the weight of the anvil, let alone, do the pounding to shape things put on it.

I placed the anvil on the table where I was told and quickly stepped back as the table leg buckled under the weight and the table crumbled, tossing the anvil onto the floor.

Silas just stood there, staring at the broken table and the anvil laying on its side. He gave a sigh, then pulled a dirty rag from his pocket and blew his nose.

I picked up the anvil and set it to the side, then hauled the broken table over and set it near the fire he used to heat things up, then walked outside.

I was about to go back when I spied a pile of oak posts. I leaned my head around the corner of the opening to the barn and asked, "Does that pile of wooden posts have a purpose?"

Silas thought for a few seconds, then said, "Not that I know of. Why? You wantin to buy them?

I grinned and said, "No, sir. I have a better plan than them just laying around out there and turning to worm food." Without another word, I hauled them inside and in short order, I built a new table that would hold the weight of a horse. And when I was finished, I mounted the anvil on the far end of the table where it would be most useful.

And that's how I went to work for Silas Baumgartner. At first, I didn't make any money, just board and room. But after I repaired things and gave the place a new coat of paint, which I paid for, folks took notice and began to stop by. And when they saw the work I could do because of pa's teaching, we had work running out our ears. And Silas? Well, he perked up and became a living, breathing human being, again.

After the first year, Silas made me a full partner, which made me a happy young man. Business was good and my savings was growing leaps and bounds. Now, don't get me wrong, it wasn't all work and no play. There were several ladies who lived nearby whose company I enjoyed. And there was a tributary off the Thames that had clean water and the fish seemed to have a special attraction to my bait and hooks.

One of the ladies I saw from time to time, was a schoolteacher and she got me to reading of an evening. Ma always encouraged me to read and had books laying around but not like these. The books she encouraged me to read were, The Politics of Aristotle, a novel - Tale of the Tub, a play called, The Way of The World, and others she thought would broaden my knowledge. She was very nice, along with being attractive. Her only flaw was, she wanted to get married and have a large family. "At least six children," she told me.

I was far from considering anything like that, and when I told her so, she asked for her books back, and that was the end of our relationship.

I heard some time later she married a man who owned and operated a print shop, and even later that she had written a book that her husband printed. Never did find out what the title was or what it was about. I always thought I would have liked to have read it, just to see if I had been mentioned.

NINE

Silas came to an end none of us want to be a part of. I lived in the top part of the barn, above the blacksmith shop and Silas stayed in some rooms at the back, on the ground floor. Silas had gone to see a sick friend and was still not back when I decided to call it a day. I went up to my room and after reading a little, my eyelids became quite heavy. I hadn't been in bed long enough to be fully asleep when I heard his cry for help.

I leaped from the bed, pulled on my pants and ran down the stairs and out into the street in front of the blacksmith shop. He was lying in the middle of the street. He had been bludgeoned to death and the blood from his headwound was soaking into the dirt.

I knew he was gone before I checked, but I did, anyway. The street was empty and I felt the anger rise inside me. I desperately wanted to find whoever did this and show them what a slow, torturous death would feel like. Silas was my friend and I wanted revenge!

With tears running down my face, I searched two blocks before finding a Bobby, and told him about Silas.

Of course, at first, I was suspect. The partner who wanted the place all to himself, which of course was ridiculous. The man or men who killed Silas were never found and I was eventually cleared and the final analysis was – killed by an unknown assailant.

For the next seventeen years, I threw myself into my work until one day I told myself, "Enough. I'm thirty-five years old and I have to get on with my life."

After work that evening, I cleaned up and went to a nearby pub to have supper and a mug or two of ale. I had twenty-nine pounds on my person and more hidden beneath the floor in the blacksmith shop, under the anvil that stood guard over the hole. Come morning, I planned to look for a buyer so I could go adventuring.

After supper, I went up to the bar for a chat up with the barmaid, Lucy. I had two more pints of ale and promised to be around when she got off at midnight.

To kill some time, I walked down along the river to get some fresh air and watch the boats sailing back and forth. Maybe I'd buy a small boat and go sailing, myself.

I hadn't been standing there, long when I heard a woman scream, "That's him! That's the man what killed and robbed my husband!"

I turned just in time to see a woman and a Bobby approaching me.

I looked around to see who she was talking about and in horror, I realized she was talking about me.

"Madam, you are mistak…"

That's all I was allowed to say before the policeman hit me alongside my head with a fist that felt like a sledgehammer.

By now I was even bigger than pa had been, but the policeman was also a big man and the punch to my head staggered me back a couple of steps before I landed on the ground, flat on my rearend.

Lights were going off and on inside my head and the taste of blood in my mouth. I must have bitten my tongue or the inside of my cheek, when he hit me. Everything was spinning. Something was wrong, terribly wrong.

I'd had a good day. Three of my customers had paid their bills and for the first time in a long time, I was feeling good about myself. I'd treated myself by going to the pub for dinner and a few pints of ale. And I was supposed to meet someone, but I couldn't remember, who?

I was still in the throes of trying to remember when the Bobby jerked me to my feet and asked the woman, "You sure this is him?"

The grey-haired woman took no more than a few seconds before she said, "That's him. I'm positive of it."

I suddenly found myself accused of robbery and murder. This couldn't be happening to me. I was innocent and I tried to tell the Bobby just that, but he paid me no attention.

Two more Bobby's arrived as the woman ranted and raved about her husband being bludgeoned to death by a man who was big and broad shouldered and had fists the size of hams – which described yours truly, from head to foot.

Knowing I was innocent, I didn't resist when I was told I was under arrest. It was all a big mistake and I knew when I got the chance to explain it, I would be released, and life would go back to being dull and normal, again.

At the station my large sum of money was taken from me. I tried to explain it was money received from three of my customers who had paid their bills, but they turned a deaf ear and threw me into a cell. Over and over, I told them I wanted to speak to a barrister, but it was like they were hard of hearing.

For the next three months I sat in isolation, never speaking with a barrister. They fed me nothing but mush and cups of stale water.

When the morning finally came and they opened the cell door and told me I was going in front of a judge, I walked out of the cell, forty pounds lighter than when I went in, and looking like some creature from the swamps.

Along with several others – mainly, thieves, drunks and one man who had embezzled company funds, we were taken into a court room and sat down on a wooden bench on one side of the room, to the right of where the judge would be sitting. The room was quite large and filled with spectators.

"What day is this?" I asked the Bobby who sat me down.

"Why, it's January 26, in the year 1838. Why do you ask?" he said with a surprised tone.

I said nothing but counted in my head and realized I had been locked up for over three months. What had happened to my business? What about the horses I had been boarding? Those and several other questions raced through my brain, along with the fact that I had missed my thirty-sixth birthday.

The judge was a portly man of upper age, and looked to be in a bad mood. His name was Ezekiel Brownstone Darthwater, and had been assigned to decide our fate. His eyes were strawberry colored and his cheeks had red streaks in them, like those of a man who liked his liquor. His robe was stained and his wig was sitting a bit off center, which made him look lopsided. He staggered when he walked and had to be helped up to his seat. He had a scowl on his face and it was obvious he was in his cups and would rather be someplace else – like maybe taking a nap.

As each prisoner came in front of him, the judge disposed of each man, quickly and with what I believed to be harsh sentences. I was the last called to stand in front of him.

When my name was called, I had a lump in my throat and I was suddenly as nervous as a young lass on her wedding night. Each of the convicts before me had been sentenced to a penal colony I had never heard of – a place called, New South Wales. I knew the country of Wales was not all that far away, but why send us there? And why would the people of Wales want a bunch of criminals coming into their country?

"Jubal Courtney, you are charged with murder and robbery. How do you plead, guilty or not guilty?" the judge barked as he glared down at me.

I didn't need a mirror to know that after three months in a cell with no chance to clean himself up, or shave, I looked no better than a street urchin.

Squaring my shoulders and standing up straight, I said, "Not guilty, Your Honor."

The judge looked at me and made a harrumph sound, then looked out over the crowded courtroom and asked, "Is the woman here who accuses this man?"

Matilda Hilderbran stood up from where she was sitting at the back of the room and said, "I'm here, yer Honorable." She was dressed in less than fashionable clothing and her hair looked like a bird's nest. The judge was less than impressed by her looks, but, she was, after all, the victim, and the only witness.

The judge watched as the elderly woman walked slowly down toward him. He scratched his cheek, wondering who would want to rob someone who obviously had very little to offer in the way of money, or anything else, for that matter. When she was standing in front of him, the judge asked, "Can you tell the court if you see the man who attacked your husband and beat him to death before robbing him? Is he anywhere in this room?"

Matilda turned and stared at me for what seemed to be a long time. Her eyes told me that she was filled with hatred. She raised her arm and pointed at me and said, "That's him. That's the man what killed my poor

Henry and then robbed him of every farthing we had. He's a bloody murderer, he is, and he deserves ta hang!"

She turned and looked back at the judge, saying, "Yer Honorable, he's ah mean 'un, he is. I was afraid he was going ta kill me too. I was afraid for me life, I was."

The judge looked down at Matilda and said, "Thank you. You may go back to your seat."

I tried to protest, asking if I could ask the woman a few questions, but the judge shook his head and said, "Sit down! If you wanted a say so, you should have gotten yourself a barrister."

"I tried. I asked for one – several times, but no one paid me the least bit of attention," I said. I could have been talking to a deaf and dumb mute for all it got me. And as far as the people in the courtroom were concerned, they were there to see men sentenced to the gallows, or worse.

The judge looked out across the crowded room and asked, "Is the arresting officer here, today?"

"I am, Your Honor," a husky, middle-aged Bobby said, as he stood up, straightened his jacket and approached the bench.

"You are the officer who arrested the defendant?"

"I am," he said.

"And at that time did the witness, Mistress Hilderbran identify the defendant to you as the man who murdered her husband and stole his wallet?"

"Yes, she did, Your Honor," the Bobby said, nodding his head.

"And at that time did you search the defendant to see if he had the man's wallet on him?"

"I did, Your Honor," the Bobby stated.

"And did the defendant have the man's wallet in his possession?" the judge asked as though he was getting bored with the sing song questions and answers.

"Well now, about that, Your Honor. I found a large sum of money on him, but not the wallet Mistress Hilderbran said her husband was carrying. But it is my belief he threw the wallet away, which would make sense to me, and what I would do if I was the thief," the Bobby said with confidence.

That last part was actually, nothing more than speculation, and the officer's opinion, but the judge let it slide. His stomach was growling and he was getting a headache. He wanted to go home and take a nap.

"How much money did the defendant have on him at the time of his arrest?" the judge asked, trying to seem interested, before making his ruling.

"He had twenty seven pounds and some odd change on his person, Your Honor," the Bobby said.

"And did Mistress Hilderbran mention to you how much was stolen?" the judge asked.

"She did, Your Honor. She said her husband was carrying their life savings – nine pounds, sterling, Your Honor. I'm guessin' the rest must 'a come from other robberies that we don't know about, yet."

"I protest!" I yelled, which yielded me a cuff on the back of my head by one of the Bobby's, who said, "Keep your mouth shut. If the judge wants to hear something from you, he'll ask a question."

The judge excused the Bobby without giving me the opportunity to examine him, and then turned to me. "Master Courtney, you said the money you had on you came from three of your customers – payment for work you did for them. Is that still your contention?"

"That is correct, Your Honor," I said, looking him in the eyes. "And I would…"

"And are those men here today to testify in your behalf?" the judge asked, cutting me off.

I looked around the room, knowing they wouldn't be there, then turned to the judge and said, "Your Honor, I have been held in jail for the past three months and have not been allowed to speak to anyone, nor have I been given the opportunity to try and find those customers, or even seek the help of a barrister. But to answer your question, the men for whom I did the work were men passing through town and I have to assume, they are no longer in the vicinity."

"Then, the answer would be, no," the judge said.

"May I speak freely, Your Honor?" I asked in desperation, realizing things weren't looking good for me.

"Be brief, Master Courtney," the judge told me. "It's been a long day and if you don't have something significant to say, I feel I have enough information to render my decision."

I knew the judge had already made up his mind against me, but I also knew I had to try one last time. I was never one of those people who were blessed with elegant speech, but as my father told me many times, "Being smart is ninety percent common sense."

"Your Honor," I said, trying to form the words in my head. "I am a simple man – a blacksmith by trade - taught by my father, who was also a blacksmith. I'm not a rich man but I make a fair living because I'm good at what I do. I've never cheated anyone in my life, nor have I ever robbed anyone or committed murder. Your Honor, I am innocent of these charges and if I may say one more thing… First, when this was supposed to have happened, I was at least a block or more away, walking along the docks. It was getting dark, and in that kind of light, it would be hard for anyone to see an attacker well enough to describe him as well as the lady did. Sure, the man may have been close to my size, but believe me, Your Honor, it wasn't me – just someone who looks a lot like me. And one last thing, I don't know who did this to her and her husband, for which she has my condolences. And from what I've seen of her, she and her husband were probably honest, hardworking people – and with that in mind, I would gladly give her nine pounds to see her back on her feet." I said this, hoping the judge would see that I was not a criminal, but an honest man who was willing to help.

The judge looked down at me and leaned his chin against his folded hands.

After what seemed to be a long while, the judge spoke. "Master Courtney, that was quite a speech; something a smart minded criminal might come up with. I salute you. You're an Irishman, aren't you?" he said with a sneer, like being Irish was in itself a criminal charge.

I could see the look on his face and knew I was a condemned man. "I am from Ireland, your honor, but I don't…"

He raised his hand to shut me up, then said, "You Irish come over here and think you can drink and raise bloody hell, and we're supposed to just look the other way. Well, not in my courtroom."

Before I could reply, he continued. "That you would offer to return the victim's money convinces me you are guilty. You have gall, Master Courtney, I'll give you that. Based on your little speech, I take it you expect me to let you walk out of here a free man to rob and maybe kill, again?"

My heart sunk and I knew the next words from the judge would be to send me to the gallows, and I have to say, I was surprised by what he said.

"Jubal Courtney, it is the court's judgement that you are guilty as charged of both robbery and murder - and yes, the lady will get her nine pounds back; which will come from your funds. The rest of the money will go toward your passage to the penal colony in New South Wales. As far as your business goes, it has already been put up at auction, and has been sold. That money went to pay the court fees."

I couldn't believe what I was hearing. I felt numb. I was innocent, but no one seemed to care. How could they have sold my business before coming in front of the judge? Something didn't make sense. I was brought back to reality by hearing my name spoken. I looked up and the judge was staring down at me with a frown on his face. The room was so quiet you could hear a fly breathing.

"Jubal Courtney, for the charges of robbery and murder in the first degree, I sentence you to be imprisoned in the penal colony in New South Wales for the rest of your life. And may God have mercy on your black, Irish soul."

The judge looked at the Bobby standing nearby and said, "Take the prisoner away and put him with the others. Court is adjourned."

In a cloud of disbelief, I was taken along with the others and thrown into a large room that had only two small windows, high above the floor. Both were too high to reach, and too small to climb through. My brain was too numb to even think about escaping. I had just been sentenced to life in prison for something I hadn't had a hand in. I tried to think of what pa would say about a situation like this, but came up, empty. I guess he was never confronted with anything like this.

I found an empty space in the far corner of the room and sat down with my knees drawn up to my chest and my arms wrapped around my legs. I could hear the others speaking to each other, but I had no idea what any of them were saying – I was that lost in fear. At the age of thirty-six, my life was over. I was branded, 'Criminal,' on my left shoulder, and I would be spending the rest of my life in prison.

TEN

The following morning, along with sixty other prisoners, I was taken to one of the ships anchored in the harbor - The Ocean Star. We were lined up in three rows on the main deck as the captain paraded back in forth in front of us.

With Wales being a country attached to England, I wondered why we would be taken aboard a ship, when we could just as well be carted in wagons, and in my way of thinking, taking a lot less time. But the more I thought about it, the better I liked the idea of going by ship. Maybe, at some point, if I could see land, I could jump overboard and swim to freedom. I could also be eaten by sharks, or maybe not.

The captain was a tall, skinny man with muttonchop sideburns that showed a lot of gray. His eyes were a blazing green, and his Adam's-apple bobbed up and down when he spoke. "You have been put in my charge because each of you is a criminal, which means you do not deserve to live with decent people. You are the scourge of the earth and I have been contracted to take you to your new home in New South Wales, where you are to spend the rest of your miserable lives at hard labor. We will be at sea for well over a hundred days, and a good many of you will not survive the trip because I have no tolerance for disobedience."

A hundred days at sea? Just to get up to Wales? That couldn't be. From the map I'd looked at, Wales was closer than Ireland, which was no more than a three-day trip.

The captain looked around for someone to use as an example and when his eyes locked on me, he grinned. I was the biggest and strongest looking of us all.

"You," the captain said, pointing at me. "Step forward."

When I did as I was ordered, four crewmen grabbed me and tied me to the mast, then ripped open the back of my shirt.

While the prisoners looked on in horror, I was given ten lashes with a whip.

Gritting my teeth, I endured the humiliation and pain without uttering a sound, but when a bucket of saltwater was thrown against my back to wash away the blood, I passed out from the pain.

When I opened my eyes, I was lying on my stomach on a cold, damp, floor. Getting into a sitting position took every bit of strength I had, and when I was sitting upright, I looked around and realized I was being held in a cage in the bottom of the ship. Hanging near the passageway leading topside, were two, oil burning lanterns. Because of the black smoke they emitted, they gave very little light to see by.

I could hear the waves crashing against the outside of the ship and felt the rise and fall as it plowed its way through the water. We were at sea.

"Here, have a drink o' water," a voice to my left said.

When I turned my head, I saw a scruffy looking man holding out a dipper of water in my direction. "Go on, take it," the man said.

The man's name was Alex Morehouse. He had been convicted of stealing food for his family after being dismissed as a crewmember of this very ship. "Couldn't find another ship ta take me on, and I couldn't stand ta see my family go hungry," Alex told me.

The following day when we were taken topside to scrub the deck of the ship, Alex eased up next to me and in whispered tones as we worked, told me the ship would sail south down along the coast of Africa and go around what was called the horn, past a city by the name of Cape Horn - a trip of over eight thousand miles. And after a stopover at Cape Horn, we would sail down into what was called, the roaring forties because of the heavy winds, which would take us east at a dangerous speed.

Alex went on to tell me the second leg of the trip to our destination at Sydney, Australia, would cover more than six thousand miles and would be the most dangerous part of the trip. "You'll need ta keep a sharp eye, least ya get washed overboard."

I was overwhelmed by what he was saying. "What about New South Wales? I thought that's where we were to be taken? Isn't that just a short run up the west coast of England?"

Before he could answer me, I was kicked in the ribs and told to keep my mouth shut. "No talking, unless you're want 'in ta feel the whip, again," the bosuns mate said.

I closed my mouth, bent my head and went back to scrubbing the deck.

We didn't get another chance to speak until the evening meal, which wasn't fit for an animal, let alone a human. But, since it was eat or starve to death, we ate. We were sitting on the deck with our backs leaned up against the railing.

Alex leaned over close and whispered, "New South Wales ain't nowhere close to the country of Wales, mate. It's what they call the place in Australia."

Australia? How could that be? I knew of its existence because of the geography ma had taught me, but for the life of me, I couldn't picture it in my head.

"How long will the trip take and how do you know so much about this place?" I asked, not remembering what Alex had previously told me.

"Like I told ya, I was a crew member on this very ship. I was the navigator and when I disagreed about the route to take on this very upcoming voyage, the captain sent me packing. I wanted to stay north of the roaring forties because I believe it is safer, but the captain didn't see it that way. He wants ta be shed of us as fast as he can, and if some of us die along the way, it's no skin off 'in his nose. He's already been paid."

Yes. I remembered the judge saying I would be paying my own way to hell.

During the evening meal of cabbage soup with small worms swimming about in it, Alex repeated his tale to the rest of the prisoners. "Just keep yer mouth shut and do as yer told and just maybe, you'll survive the trip, although I ain't sure jumpin' overboard wouldn't be ah better option."

Of course, he'd never been there, himself, so he could only speculate what a life of hard labor in a foreign land would be like. And in my mind, if they were sending us there, it must be a place no sane person would choose to live.

The trip to Cape Horn was the same thing day in and day out. We were brought up, given buckets and brushes, and told to clean the decks. Some of us were chosen to throw fishing lines over the side and catch fish to be eaten by the officers and the crew. One poor chap, a fellow they called, Ames, was so hungry he bit into one of the fish he hauled aboard and began eating it right there on the deck.

For the few morsels of fish he consumed, he received twenty lashes and saltwater thrown on the open cuts on his back. I'm sure the angels in heaven heard his screams. That night we were, again, fed a gruel that had worms in it. When no one was watching, I tossed mine over the side.

Ames was not in the work line the following morning and rumor had it that he came on deck during the middle of the night and fell over the side of the ship and had drown.

I'm sure not a one of us believed that because at night, we were under lock and key and we all knew Ames didn't have a key.

After forty-four days, the ship put in at Cape Horn to replenish its food and water supply, along with taking on a passenger who for no reason I could understand, wanted to go to Australia.

As we found out, later, he was a Dutchman named, Willem Smit. Willem had a degree in mining and had heard Australia was teeming with resources such as gold, silver and coal, just waiting to be pulled from the ground. Apparently, he wanted his fair share of the riches. As the story went, it was there for the taking if only a man had the intestinal fortitude and substantial finances.

His money came from the fact that he robbed a wealthy man in Germany, then fled the country before the police got wind of him. He was hiding out in Cape Town, waiting for a ship going to Australia when The Ocean Star came in.

He not only booked passage, but bought twenty of the indentured men from the captain who would later report them being swept overboard during a storm in the roaring forties. It was extra money in his pocket and what the authorities in Sydney didn't know...

The first week of sailing southeast from Cape Town was a little bit rough, but nothing to worry about. We went about our daily routine as we so far, had. But when we hit the roaring forties, life aboard the ship changed. The wind howled twenty-four hours a day. The sea was choppy with huge whitecapped waves. Cold waves of seawater came crashing down on the deck, washing away anything not tied down, including prisoners and crew members. By the end of the first week, we had indeed, lost six men from being washed overboard. In water such as the roaring forties, if a man was washed overboard, he was lost because he was instantly swallowed up by the raging water.

The rough water also created seasickness among a good many of the prisoners. It was only through Alex, who was friends with the cook, that saved them. He was able to smuggle saltine crackers to his fellow prisoners, which helped calm their stomachs. I was one of the lucky ones who never seemed to be affected by the heavy seas and pitching, rolling, ship.

Willem Smit never seemed to be affected, either, and spent a lot of time studying the prisoners. I saw him looking at me and making notes in the small booklet he carried. It wasn't until the ship anchored in Sydney that he made his final decision. For what he had planned, he would need healthy men – men who could survive hardships.

The captain lined us up on the deck and allowed Willem to walk up and down the line, pointing out the ones he wanted. Alex and I were among the twenty men selected, and were held back to be offloaded after the rest of the prisoners had been taken ashore.

ELEVEN

The night was filled with dark clouds that hid the moon when the twenty of us were put into long boats and rowed, under the cover of darkness, to shore, far from the main landing, at a place called, Rose Bay.

Four covered wagons were waiting and we were put into two of them. And for the next two weeks, we traveled deep into the interior, finally stopping at a small mountain range. Here, we were unloaded and immediately we began clearing the land for building a house for Willem and then two other buildings - one to hold the prisoners and the other one for the guards. A large tent was erected where tools were stored, Willem took a corner for his bed, trunk and small desk. The guards had cots along one side. We slept on the ground, outside the tent, which didn't go too well since there was an abundance of scorpions and other biting insects, like, lizards and snakes. During the first month, we lost three men and another six were too sick to work. The only upside to all of this was the cook, bless his ugly heart. He fed us well, if you can say, eating snake, lizard and this huge animal they called, a kangaroo, was eating well. At least there was plenty of it.

After six weeks of grueling hard work and fighting off the heat and bugs, the buildings were completed, and we were given two days to rest before the mining began.

I don't know about the rest of the country, but that part of Australia is hot and humid during the day and cold at night. The wind blew day in and day out, covering everything with a thick layer of dust, which also went into your mouth and up your nose.

On the day the mining began, picks and shovels were given to some of the men, and told where to begin digging.

While some of the men dug a tunnel into the side of the mountain, some of us were given saws and axes. We were taken higher up on the mountainside to chop down trees to use to support the interior of the tunnel, which was seven feet high and ten feet wide. It was hard, backbreaking work, but at least, like I said, we ate well and only worked twelve-hour days. He needed us to stay healthy.

Some three hundred feet inside the mountain they struck a humongous vein of coal.

Willem seemed to be overjoyed with this and threw a party where he allowed us to gorge ourselves on kangaroo steaks and all the ale we could drink.

Because of my size and ability with an axe, I had been assigned to the tree cutting team and had not had to endure digging the tunnel, which I later found out was taking its toll on the men. Picking at the earth inside the mountain created a great deal of dust and the deeper they went, the less the air circulated. Breathing the coal dust went down into their lungs, causing them to cough up blood at night - Alex among them.

Six months after the mining had begun, nine men died from breathing the dust and the rest were in bad shape.

I could see Willem was concerned, but not for the men, per say. He was worried about all the men he was losing and the rest, working at only a fraction of their normal speed.

To my dismay, I was put on the digging crew. I knew the consequences of breathing the coal dust and wanted none of it. As pa always said, "Plain ole common sense outweighs education every time." And with that, I put a thick piece of cloth over my nose and mouth to help keep from breathing in the dust. On the hour, I took the mask off and shook it out as best I could, then put it back on.

When the other men saw what I was doing, they began doing the same thing and at night there was less coughing and spitting blood.

From the first day I was sent to the mine, I began thinking about escaping. I had no idea where I was or where I would go, but anything was better than a slow death from breathing coal dust.

Three weeks later, my chance came when Willem left to go to Sydney to try and buy more indentured men to replace the ones that had died.

Once Willem was gone, the guards relaxed, thinking we were too afraid of what would happen to us if we tried to escape. Besides, with this place being so far from civilization, where could we run to?

CHASING THE NEXT SUNRISE

I had looked in all four directions and all I could see was miles and miles of miles and miles. There was only one dirt track leading away from the mine, which since it was the direction Willem took, it must lead to Sydney.

I gave thought, if given the chance to escape, I would not go in that direction. It would be the first direction the guards would search and secondly, what if I ran into Willem on his way back. The land was flat as a board and no vegetation worth speaking of, so there would be no place to hide.

The only real chance I would have would be to go farther into the interior where I might have a chance to hide and possibly find game to eat. Water might be another worry. We had to dig a well that was sixty feet deep, to find decent water, but I couldn't stop and dig a well whenever I got thirsty. I would have to take a chance that I would find water from time to time. It was a big land out there and I might die, but it would still be better than working in the mine and die from my lungs getting clogged up with coal dust.

On the evening of the second day after Willem left, black clouds rolled in. Lightning filled the sky, crackling as it struck the earth, followed by the rumbling sound of thunder. A mixture of rain and small pieces of hail plummeted the ground. Everyone, including the guards, were hunkered down inside their respective buildings. Rain didn't come often but when it did, it came hard, like it the heavens were angry.

Outside, under a bush, I had hidden three gourds, filled with water, yesterday, hoping for my chance to come. This storm was giving me my chance and I was going to take it.

When I could hear snoring all around me, I eased my big frame out of the back window of the slave building and headed for the water filled gourds, then ran into the night, not knowing where I was going, except, into the unknown west. I just wanted to get away. I would deal with the consequences, later. By now, I was used to facing new challenges - of which this looked to be a big one.

Between the dark sky and the pounding rain, the night swallowed me up in just a few minutes. Hopefully, no one knew I was gone and wouldn't until morning, giving me a decent head start.

Traveling was not easy, but I was still strong and able. I tried to set a pace that, come daylight, would put some distance between me and the mine. It would take them time to realize I was missing, and more time to find my trail, if indeed they ever did. I prayed they wouldn't, but knew that was unrealistic. They wouldn't want Willem to know they had let a prisoner, escape.

Morning found me high up on a plateau, cold, wet and hungry. The opportunity for me to escape came unexpected so I was not totally prepared. The only weapon I had was a hunting knife I'd found – probably lost by one of the guards. It had a six inch blade that was none too sharp. I had no food, and only the clothes I was wearing.

During my trek, I found it was not all, dense forest. There were large places where the ground was filled with large boulders instead of trees. And because of the heavy rain, there were small pools of water, which gave me hope.

I was sitting with my back leaned up against a boulder, sipping on water from a small pool next to the giant rock, when out of nowhere, a rabbit hopped out into the opening and stopped. He had very long ears and a large body. His nose was twitching – searching for danger, but apparently not finding any. I sat very still, unsure what to do, but in my mind, I could see him cooking over a fire, which was foolish since I had no gun to shoot it with and even if I did, the sound would carry for miles and the guards, if they were searching for me, might hear it.

I eased my hand over and put my fingers around a good sized stone, then sat there, wondering how I could throw it with any accuracy from a sitting position? Then to my surprise and good luck, the rabbit hopped a short distance away and stopped behind another large rock.

With the stone in my hand, I eased my way back up into a standing position, moving ever so slowly so as to not make any noise or sudden movement that might spook the rabbit.

The hand with the stone in it, was held above my head, in a throwing position as I held my breath and waited.

I didn't have to wait long before he hopped out into view, again and stopped.

I got lucky with my throw. I pulled a tin of matches from my pocket and started a fire. Fresh rabbit was the best meal I'd eaten in quite some time. I think it tasted so good because I was eating it as a free man, not an indentured slave.

Rabbits and small game seemed to be in abundance and I fashioned a slingshot like the one, David, from the Bible had, and found I was quite good with it. Because of wanting to put as much distance between me and the mining camp as I could, I only stopped once a day to eat – at night before I needed to rest. Most of the time I was able to find a rabbit or two for my evening meal.

By the time I was a week away from the mine, I was getting tired of rabbits and hoped I might find bigger game.

I always tried to find a place where I could hide the smoke from my campfire – filter it through trees and also, if I could, next to a pool of water. On my eighth night, I got lucky and found a large pool of water and was able to refill all three of my water gourds.

Even though I dreadfully needed it, a good night's sleep was never to be – at least not while I was on the run. As one would guess, I slept with my ears in tune with the sounds of the night, and if I heard anything unusual, it woke me up.

One night in particular, the cool breeze that normally blew through the trees, suddenly stopped. My eyes came open and I lay there, listening for any sound, but there was none. The silence was eerie and I felt my nerves tighten. Trying not to breathe, I listened as my hand slowly reached for my knife and held it close to my side.

Then, off to my right, I heard the low growl of something. I had no idea what animals of prey lived in this part of the world. Ever so slightly, I turned my head in the direction of the sound and less than ten feet away, by the light of the moon filtering through the trees, I could see the shape of something about the size of a dog. I didn't know if there were wolves in these hills, for this was not, truly a mountain – but too large to be called a hill. No matter. Danger, of the predator type, was only a short distance away and I had to do something.

Without giving it thought, I leaped to my feet, waving my arms and screaming like I'd been set on fire.

Whatever it was, gave a yelp, turned and disappeared into the trees. At this point I was still so rattled I knew I couldn't go back to sleep, so I added fuel to the coals and made some warm water to go with the leftover rabbit – never realizing that a few miles behind me, three men sat up and looked at each other, with one of them saying, "That's him."

TWELVE

As soon as daylight made its appearance I was up and ready to go. No tea or coffee to drink, just tepid water. Before leaving, I realized having just my knife and my slingshot as my only weapons, was not enough. I cut a long branch, then peeled the bark off to use for wrapping and tying off. I laid the handle of my knife next to the end of the stick and wrapped it with enough bark to make it solid, then tied it off. It made a credible spear to use should I happen to come face to face with anything like what I faced last night.

At noon, I reached the summit of a distant hill and looked out across the land. My shoulders sank and I gave a sigh. All I could see was a vast desert, and in the far distance, another small plateau. But no sign of a town or civilization of any kind.

Looking over my shoulder, I knew going back was not an option. There was no doubt in my mind that they had not given up searching for me. No, they would want me brought back and made an example of.

Going down the backside of the hill I found my spear/stick came in handy as a support in many of the steep places where I had to cross rough ground.

Finally, after several more days of eating rabbit and having only tepid water to drink, I reached bottom land and stood facing the vast desert in front of me. The sun was high in the sky and the heat was nearly unbearable.

Turning, I walked back into the trees and cut off several limbs and stripped them of the bark. I knew I couldn't try to cross the wasteland ahead of me without some protection for my head. I had no choice but waste precious time weaving a hat for myself.

Admittedly, it would never win a fashion design, but it had a broad brim and kept the sun from burning into my brain.

At every waterhole, I made sure to fill my gourds and as I stood there, I knew it might be several days, or longer before I found water, again, if at all. From where I stood, the likelihood looked slim.

The necessity to escape was stronger than the alternative, and I took my first step into the burning inferno.

The soles of my shoes were thin from wear and after less than a mile I could feel the heat burning into my feet. All the moisture was being sucked from my body and with each step, I felt myself getting weaker and weaker. I stopped and took in a large breath

of the scorching air that burned all the way down into my lungs, making me put my hand against my chest, and taking shallower breaths. I lifted one of the gourds to my split and bleeding lips and took a small portion, swished it around inside my mouth, then slowly swallowed it. I needed to conserve what water I had for the grueling days ahead.

I could feel the heat from my feet, creeping up my legs and I knew I needed to keep moving. Giving a sigh, I lifted my foot and continued on toward the small plateau in the far, far, distance. By the time the sun disappeared I wasn't sure I could take another step. I was depressed and feeling sure I was going to die out here, alone in this God forgotten piece of the world, where the only things that survived were biting insects, mean looking lizards and deadly venomous snakes.

I stopped and leaned my hand against a large outcrop boulder, then drew it away. The rock was still scorching hot.

From somewhere in the distance, I heard a voice that sounded human but I couldn't understand the language. "Aiee! Upghghil, yigumma, chuillie!" or something like that.

Whatever language it was, I knew it was someone in trouble and calling for help.

My eyes were dry and it was hard to see, but not too far away I thought I could see a small firelight and the shadow of someone dancing around, swinging a stick. And in front of the stick, it looked like the person was being attacked by a pack of wild dogs! Much like the one the one I had recently encountered.

On feet that felt like I was walking on hot coals, I hurried as best I could toward the snarling dogs who were bent on having whoever it was, for their evening meal.

When I got close, I yelled as loud as my parched throat would allow, which wasn't much and began stabbing the closest ones with the point of my knife, still attached to the stick.

CHASING THE NEXT SUNRISE

The injured dogs yelped, and apparently, the others could smell the blood from their wounds and in their frenzied state of mind, they attacked the wounded dogs and began dragging them away.

When they were gone, I stood panting from the exertion. "Umama Ipoulda cayaya," The words caused me to turn and look at the person who I had helped drive away the wild dogs.

Standing only a few feet away was a young man I judged to be no more than fifteen years of age. He had the blackest skin I had ever seen on anyone. I had heard the people in Africa had black skin, but I knew nothing of the people of Australia. And for sure, I couldn't speak their language, nor, it quickly became apparent, could he speak the Queen's English.

But the one thing we had in common, was survival. With what I'm sure was a great deal of fear and trepidation, he waved for me to come into his camp. It was not really a cave, but a bunch of large rocks piled on top of each other, leaving an open place, similar to a cave.

There was a small fire burning with something cooking on a spit. And to my surprise, I could see where he had dug a small pit in the ground that was now filled with water!

He pointed to where I was to sit and when I did, he pulled whatever it was from the spit and tore off a chunk of meat and handed it to me, pointing to his mouth, indicating I should eat.

I nodded my head and said, "Thank you," then bit off a piece and chewed. It was tough, like a piece of chicken breast that had set out a little too long. Tough, but not bad and better than rabbit, again.

The night passed without further incident, but when morning came, the boy pointed toward a far mountain range and with his fingers, made a sign of us walking, which I took to mean he wanted me to go with him.

I felt a little bit stupid, but I couldn't stop staring at him. He was short, but not like any of the wee little people I'd read about and seen pictures of. Plus, it was hard for me to conceive how a person's skin pigment could be so dark. His only clothing was a pair of pants that looked to be made from canvas, but I wasn't sure, and I wasn't going to try and examine them.

I looked toward the mountain range and came to a decision. First, I would need to be far, far away from the mine before I felt comfortable at not looking over my shoulder, and wind up seeing one or more of the guards. And secondly, traveling with someone who might know where he was going, was much better than stumbling around, going in circles. And third, he just might lead me into a town where I might find passage back to civilization. How I would pay for it was another thing, all together. But as pa always said, "Where there's a will, there's a way."

Once again, the day was hotter than the hubs of hell, and the boy was setting a fast pace, with little or no concern about the blistering sun beating down on us. It was almost as though he was oblivious to the heat, even though he had on no hat nor shoes, nor shirt.

We stopped when the sun was directly overhead and ate more of that tough meat, and drank warm water. There was no shade, which, again, didn't seem to bother him. I on the other hand, was spent from the heat and my energy level was very low. All I wanted to do is lie down and sleep, but I knew that would not be an option. If I did, I would more than likely never wake up – probably be eaten by those wild dogs.

Suddenly, the young man turned his head and looked back the way we came and then stood up from where he was squatting. He said something in that language of his that sounded more like gibberish than actual words as he pointed toward the mountain we'd been walking toward. I didn't understand what he'd said, but I did understand the urgency in his voice.

I turned my head and looked back across the desert and in the far distance, I saw a cloud of dust rising in the air. Someone was coming! And at a rapid pace! Instantly, I knew it had to be the guards! They hadn't given up and now here I was, out in the middle of the open desert with no place to hide and not much in the way of weapons to fight with.

They were still too far away for us to see anything but the cloud of dust, but I was sure they were riding horses and they would catch up to us long before we could reach the mountain and trees, where we might have been able to hide.

I jumped to my feet and was ready to run, but instead of running, the boy motioned for me to wait.

He turned and walked back a short distance, then turned and came back, wiping out our tracks with what looked like a piece of skin he'd taken from his pack. And when he got back to where I was standing, he pointed off to his left.

He followed me, wiping out our tracks behind him.

What good was that going to do? Okay, he'd wiped out our tracks, but we'd still be standing there in the wide-open desert when they arrived.

What he did next was something I would never have thought of. He began digging a shallow trench with his bare hands and motioned I should do the same – which I did and when he figured it was long enough and deep enough, he motioned for me to lay down in the trench, face down with my hands over my face.

And when I did, he commenced to cover me up!

I hoped and prayed a scorpion or some other biting insect didn't crawl into my mouth or ears and decide to take a bite of me.

I'm not sure how long we laid there, but it wasn't long before I felt the ground begin to rumble and I could hear their voices.

"Where did they go?" one of them asked.

"Well now that's a dumb question if I ever heard one," another voice said.

"Well, they couldn't have just vanished into thin air. We saw 'em through the binoculars and now they're nowhere ta be seen."

"They're here somewhere. They have to be," the other man said.

Suddenly, it became silent. The horses were no longer stamping around and the two men were no longer talking. After what seemed a long time, one of them said, "See anything?"

I assumed they were searching for us with the binoculars he'd talked about.

"I've covered ever speck of ground between here and that mountain, yonder, and I didn't see hide nor hair of anybody."

"They must 'a somehow gotten to the trees. I don't know how, but it's the only thing that makes any sense. C 'mon."

I felt the ground rumble as they rode away, running their horses, but still, I didn't move – and wasn't going to until the young man told me to.

The sun had been replaced by a half moon when I felt the dirt being brushed away from me and I stood up, shaking the residue from my face and hair. The sky was filled with at least a million stars or more, and the air had a bite to it, making me shiver.

He pointed toward the mountain and said more of his gibberish, then started off – with me only a step behind.

THIRTEEN

The moon was still hanging over the western sky as the sun came creeping over the eastern horizon and we left the desert and entered the quiet of the mountain, into the shade of the trees. During our entire trek from our near escape, to the mountain, not one word was spoken by either of us. Not that it would have done any good because neither of us could understand the other one.

A short distance inside the trees, the young man stopped and began preparing a fire that gave off very little smoke. From his pack, he took out a gourd that was filled with water, then sprinkled something in it and shook it up before placing it on the outer edge of the fire.

I sat down and leaned back against a tree, trying to regain some strength. I had been young and still quite strong before escaping from the mining camp, but at this precise moment, I felt old and worn out. Since my escape, I'd had no proper food to eat, or decent water to drink, and what sleep I'd had was done in short naps. I leaned my head back and closed my eyes – but only for a moment, or so I thought.

"Good morning Mister Courtney," said a voice that caused me to come instantly awake and climbing to my feet.

"Oh, don't be in such a rush to get up, Mister Courtney. It's still a long walk back you'll be doin'. But first, it looks like the lad has breakfast on the spit."

In the coming daylight, I could see Billy Barstow, one of the mining guards, sitting on his horse, not ten feet away from where I was. He was pointing a pistol at me and grinning.

"Gave us quite a chase, you did. But it will be worth it to see the skin taken off your back when we return. I'm thinkin' Mister Smit, himself will want ta do the honors," Tyrell Barnes, the other guard, said, chuckling.

He had stepped off his horse and was holding his pistol on the young black man, who had sat down next to the fire and was adding a few sticks, but keeping an eye on the two men, from the corner of his eye.

Billy stepped down from his horse and handed the reins to his partner, before walking over and staring down at me. "When did you tie up with this Aboriginal pup?"

I looked over at the young man. "Aboriginal?" I asked.

"Yeah," Billy said. "Ain't you never seen an Aborigine, before?"

"Can't say I have," I said, still looking at the young man.

"They ain't blacks, you know, like them from Africa. They're just dark skinned like 'em," Billy informed me. "They say the Aborigine people been around here in Australia for more'n forty or fifty thousand years. Keeps to themselves mostly and speaks ah language nobody but them can understand."

"Ain't good for much, neither," Tyrell added. "Sulky and lazy ah bunch as you've ever seen. Turn your back on 'em and they disappear quicker'n ah spooked deer; they do."

"But you do seem ta like the young females for a quick go, eh?" Billy said with a grin.

Tyrell got a look of anger on his face and changed the subject. "What're we gonna do with this whelp?"

Billy thought for a moment, then said, "No use takin' him with us, nor can we turn 'em loose, either."

After another moment, Billy said, "I say we tie him to one of these trees and leave him for the critters ta feast on."

I saw just the hint of reaction in the young man's eyes. He can understand the white man's language! I wondered if he could speak it, too?

I got slowly to my feet and asked Billy, "Can I have a drink of whatever it is he is heating up in that gourd?"

"Sure, if you're brave enough," Billy said with a grin. "And while you're at it, fill your belly on that bat meat he's got cookin' over the fire."

Bat meat? Is that what I'd been eating?

"I thought it was chicken," I said as I kicked at the fire, sending hot coals in the direction of the two guards.

"Run!" I yelled and didn't have to say it twice. In the blink of an eye, while the two guards were jumping away from the hot coals, the young man disappeared into the trees and was gone.

"What 'ya go and do that for?" Tyrell yelled.

I could see the anger in his eyes and the next thing I knew, he pulled a whip from his belt and lashed out at me, catching me around the throat.

While I tried to get it loose, I felt the sting of Billy's whip against my stomach and when I was able to step back, there was blood running down into my pants.

"Don't try nothin' like that again, or Mister Smit won't get the opportunity to punish you, himself," Billy told me, with a snarl.

"That's right. We can always say you fought back and got yourself accidental killed," Tyrell added.

After they rekindled the fire and fixed tea and some kind of cakes, they didn't share with me, they ate their morning meal – then with my hands tied in front of me, attached to a lead rope, we started off.

Even with them walking the horses, it was difficult to keep up and I stumbled and fell a few times, which didn't stop them. Rolling around, I had planted my heels in the dirt and was jerked back up on my feet.

By the time they stopped for the day, it was all I could do to put one foot in front of the other.

I dropped down on the ground, gasping for breath and begging for some water.

Billy poured half a cup and handed it to me. "Drink wisely, sport. This is all you get til morning."

I stuck my finger in the water then rubbed it against my cracked and bleeding lips – then took just a sip – savoring the taste. Even though it was warm and tepid, it felt good on my, dry, swollen tongue. It took all my willpower to not gulp it down. "Do I get anything to eat?" I asked, looking Billy in the eyes. "Or do you plan to tell your master that you starved me to death?"

I was given two, round, cakes made from flower and pieces of dried meat. I didn't ask what kind of meat it was, not after learning I'd been eating bat meat. Even so, I had to take small bites and soak them with sips of water to be able to swallow them. Every bone and muscle in my body hurt, especially my feet. They had taken my shoes and made me walk, barefoot.

Once I'd finished my meal and the water was gone, I lay down on my side on the ground and closed my eyes, hoping a snake or scorpion didn't find me attractive, during the night.

I don't know how long I had been asleep, but when I felt someone shaking my shoulder, I took my time opening my eyes. I was in no hurry to wake up – at least not until I heard that gibberish language speaking to me.

I opened my eyes and sat up, looking around. The first person I saw was the young man I'd helped to escape. He was smiling down at me with a mouth full of yellow teeth.

And standing just behind him were ten or twelve adult men, who were also staring at me.

I cringed from the pain as I slowly got to my feet. My feet were swollen and bleeding and I flopped back down on my rear and stared at them. They were all, much shorter than me, maybe a little over five feet.

To say I was confused would be stating it lightly. I looked around to see if I could see the two guards, but it was still too dark and the moon was partly hidden by the clouds.

The young man I'd helped escape turned and spoke to an elderly looking man who was holding a long, spear. He nodded his head and stepped up close to me. In what light there was, he seemed to have salt and pepper hair and a scruffy beard that was also salt and pepper.

He pointed to the boy and said, in English, "Boy's name Birrani. I am called, Kuparr. I am chief of our people.

Being able to converse with him was a pleasant surprise. I stuck out my hand and said, "I am called, Jubal. Jubal Courtney."

He took my hand and shook it once and said, "Hello, Jubal, Jubal Courtney."

I grinned as much as I could and said, "No, Jubal is my first name and Courtney is my last name. It's just, Jubal Courtney."

This seemed to confuse him some, so I waved my hands in front of me and said, "It's okay. It's just, Jubal. Understand?

He nodded his head up and down, then looked at the others, pointed at me and said, "Jubal," which got shouts of approval.

"Where are the guards?" I asked, which got another confused look. "The two men who held me prisoner?"

"Ah, two bad men?" Kuparr said, grinning and nodding his head, while pointing off beyond a blazing fire.

I still couldn't see them from where I sat, but with the help of several of the men, I was hoisted onto Billy's horse. From there I could see them. They had been stripped of their clothes and were tied, spread eagle out on the desert floor.

"Help us, for gawds sake. We're white men, same as you! Don't let these heathens do this to us," Billy cried out.

A part of me wanted to do something – to try and convince these people to let them go, but another part of me remembered the punishment the two of them liked to inflict on the slaves back at the mine, and the whipping they'd recently given me.

I shrugged my shoulders and said, "What do you expect me to do? I'm one man and there is at least a dozen of them, and they all have weapons. Why don't you tell them you work for Willem Smit, maybe that'll scare them into turning you loose?"

I looked down at Kuparr and asked, "What do you plan on doing with them?"

He looked at and said, "Nothing. The Gods will decide. We go, now."

And with that, he swung up behind me and started out, with the rest following him.

I was too tired and weak to protest. I felt bad for Billy and Tyrell, but in all honesty, I had watched many times as they whipped men so bad, they begged to die, and laughed all the while they did it. I had little compassion for them. They were evil men and deserved whatever the Gods decided should be their punishment.

As I rode away, I could hear their curses, ringing in my ears.

I knew I would hear those screams and curses for years to come, but with the condition I was in, there wasn't much I could do, or if I'm completely truthful, that I wanted to do.

FOURTEEN

We traveled for two days, with me mostly tied to the saddle. Then, on the third day we came to a large group of trees sitting in among some giant boulders, and somewhere I could hear water running. I was half delirious and barely hanging on. I remember being pulled off the horse, but nothing after that.

They later told me it was another two days before I opened my eyes and saw the woman looking at me. I remember being confused because her skin was as black as coal. She was smiling and her eyes showed kindness, which helped my confusion.

"You wake, now. Good," she said in broken English.

She helped me sit up, then handed me a bowl of something that looked like potato soup, but didn't taste like it. No matter, I was hungry and guessed whatever it was, it wouldn't kill me. I ate every spoon full, and in my eagerness, I didn't notice until I was finished, that the spoon was made from a piece of bone.

The woman took the bowl and spoon from me and left. And when I was alone, I looked down at my chest and arms. They were covered with slash marks from the guard's whips, but they didn't hurt. And upon further inspection, I could see the whip marks were covered with a salve of some kind.

I leaned my head back as memories came drifting back to me and I felt myself shudder when I remembered the two guards staked down on the ground and their screams.

Maybe I should have tried to talk to the chief. Maybe he would have let them go. And maybe they would have left me there with them.

After close to half an hour, I gingerly, got to my feet and stood for a moment to gain my balance. My feet were wrapped in strips of cloth and I was able to walk, if I went slow. In a shuffling motion, I moved toward the opening of the hut.

The opening was small and I had to duck to get through - and when I got outside and stood up, I saw at least forty, short, black men, women and children staring back at me.

CHASING THE NEXT SUNRISE

I identified Kuparr right away. He was smiling broadly as he walked up and stuck out his hand. And when I reached out and took the hand, the chief pumped my hand, once - then let go. "Good to see you alive," Kuparr said. Turning he looked at the people and asked, "Is good, yes?"

They cheered, with many of them pumping their fists in the air.

For a long moment, I stood there, looking over the heads of the people who I guessed, had saved my life, then finally looked down at Kuparr and said, "Thank you for saving my life."

By now, Birrani, had made his way through the people and stood next to his chief. "And thank you, too," I said, reaching out my hand.

Birrani grinned and said, "Come, you eat, get strong," which took me by surprise, since I didn't know he too, could speak the Queen's language. I later found out most of them could, but preferred their own language. One, older lady, said, "English be hard to learn and harder to speak."

I just smiled and thought to myself, 'Lady if you only knew what your gibberish sounds like...'

Over the next few days, I came to understand they were a tribe of Aborigines, called, Koori. I met a man so old that no one knew his exact age. His name was Burnum, which meant, Great Warrior, and he was their ex-chief, and still considered to be the wisest man in the tribe. The women who took care of him were called, Arika – Blue Water Lily, Orani – Moon, and, Jedda – Little Wild Goose. Arika had a son, Omeo, who was just a year younger than Birrani. Arika's mate had been killed by whites who raided their village and set fires to their homes.

Omeo carried water and did other chores his mother told him to do. And in his free time, he split his time, training to be a warrior and asking me more questions than I could answer. He and Biranni were a great source of information for me to understand more about the Aborigine people. There was also a time every day that was set aside for Burnum to teach the history of their people to the young children. I would have liked to sit in, but I still knew only a few words in their language.

For the most part they were a kind and loving people. But cross them and even though they were short in stature, they were not to be taken lightly as I found out one afternoon when a group of white men came, thinking to burn their village to the ground.

76

They saw the dust trail coming from several miles away and, shortly, a runner came in and told us the news.

When the white men arrived at the camp, they found it, empty. It was when they tried to set fire to the huts, that they ran into more trouble than they could handle. From out of nowhere, the Aborigine people appeared with bows and arrows, rock throwing slings, and spears, taking several of the men out of their saddle within seconds after the fight began.

Enraged by these white men who had no reason to invade these people, other than they were different, and the white men didn't like them, I joined in, defending my new friends. With a large club in each hand, I knocked a man from his horse, then swung up on the horse and rode into the battle, swinging my club and yelling at the top of my lungs.

It didn't take long before the white men turned their horses and rode for safety, taking their injured with them, but leaving the dead where they lay.

That night they held a huge feast and I was made an honorary Koori. "From this day forward, you shall be called, Warragal, which means, Wild Dog. Stories of how you fought against your own kind to help the Koori, shall be told over campfires for many years to come."

I had been with the Koori people for better than a year and had learned their ways, but now that I was healthy, again, I longed to go back – not to the mines and slavery, but to a town that sat on the coast; hoping I could get a position on a ship, going somewhere, anywhere away from Australia.

When I told them it was time for me to go, Burnum got very upset. "Why you go?" Burnum asked. "Stay here, marry one of our beautiful women, have many babies, be happy."

I was touched by the offer, and knew I had a home with them for as long as I wanted to stay. And there were at least half a dozen young women who had made eyes at me, but I knew it was time to go.

The night before my departure, they threw a party. And what a party it was. There were at least half a dozen fires going, and hanging over each of them was, a deer, a wild hog, fish, several large birds and what looked to be the hind shank of a water buffalo. And of course, there were huge jugs of the brew they made, which, one sip would put the toughest Irishman on his knees.

The following morning the only ones up and about were the children, who couldn't understand why their parents were still sleeping like they were dead.

For some un-godly reason, I was awake, with a mouth as dry as the desert. I staggered out to the well and pulled up a bucket of water and drank and drank and drank until I thought my stomach would burst. I poured the rest over my head and sat down and leaned my back against the well.

An older woman who had not participated in drinking the brew because she and two others abstained so they could watch over the children, came up to me and offered me something in a gourd.

I waved her away, saying, "I'm sorry but my stomach is far too upset."

She just nodded her head and extended the gourd closer to my mouth, motioning for me to drink. "This helps your stomach and head. Drink."

It was the most putrid thing that had ever passed over my lips and it was all I could do to swallow it. But as soon as it hit my stomach, the flip-flopping began to subside and my splitting headache began to lessen.

Another woman stepped up and handed me a freshly cooked bird of some kind. I never knew what kind of bird it was, but it helped settle my stomach, and the chunk of bread another of them gave me, did the trick. My stomach settled and my headache went away.

By then, the others were waking up and women were serving them the same as I'd had, and by the time the sun reached its apex, we were feeling human, again.

After packing up what things I had acquired during my stay, I walked outside my hut and was met by the whole tribe.

To show my appreciation, I spoke in their language. "I thank you for all your kindness and all you've done for me, but I must go back to people of my own kind. Even though many of them are bad, many are good, like you of the Koori, and I will never forget you."

The chief nodded his head and grinning like the cat that ate the canary, he said, "We will hate to see you go." Then, raising his hands in the air, he said, "Know all who can hear my voice, the man known as, Warragal, shall always have a home with the Koori!"

Cheers erupted throughout the tribe and I felt the love of these people. It's something I can't explain. You have to live it to understand.

Loaded with food, water and pelts to help keep me warm at night, Arika's son, Omeo, along with Birrani - headed off toward the northeast.

Omeo and Birrani had both volunteered to take me as far as the ocean, then point me in the direction where the whites live.

On the third night of our travels, we were attacked by a small band of Aborigines from a different tribe.

With a club in one hand and a sword left by the invading whites, in the other, I ran into the band of Aborigines, screaming like a wild man.

At the sight of a giant coming at them, screaming like a wounded banshee, silhouetted in the moonlight, they turned and ran for their lives.

No one had been injured or killed and we all got a good laugh. And when the laughter subsided, Omeo said, "My friend, you have given Birrani and me a wonderful story to tell when we get home. Thank you."

For the next two weeks we traveled in peace. The weather was warm in the daytime and cold at night.

On the sixteenth day since leaving the Koori tribe, we topped over a large hill and there before us the ocean lapped onto the beach.

Down on the beach, the three of us dropped our belongings and ran headlong into the water, letting the saltwater cleanse our bodies and clothes.

We romped and played in the water until finally, Omeo pointed at Birrani and said, "If you will make camp by that overhang, I will catch us some fish for supper."

While Birrani and I set up a camp and started a fire, Omeo, with a spear in his hand, waded the shallows, and soon came walking into the camp with four, good size fish.

After our meal, we talked long into the night, mainly about the good I had brought to the people of the Koori tribe, which in truth, I thought was the other way around.

CHASING THE NEXT SUNRISE

At the first sight of daylight, Omeo and Birrani said goodbye, and began their trek back to their people.

I packed up my few things and began walking north, along the beach, hoping to find a town. I stopped and looked back, but the beach was empty. To many, the Aboriginal people may be un-godly heathens, but to me, they were family.

I'd only gone a few miles when six, ugly looking white men rode down onto the beach and pointed their pistols at me.

I was back, among the civilized whites.

FIFTEEN

"Who are you and what are you doin' here?" one of them yelled. He was a man nearing middle age, with a thick, brown, beard, that hid pock marks. In his hand, he held a five-shot pistol.

I thought for a moment, trying not to panic, then found myself, relaxing and saying, "Hello, friend. What am I doing here, you ask? Why, just walking along, I am. My boat sank a few miles off the shore and my dingy smashed against the rocks as I came in, it did. So, I'm just following my nose in the direction where I'm hoping to find civilization. Am I headed in the right direction?"

"You don't look like you've just come in from the ocean," he said, looking at me with prying eyes. "Where'd ya get them pelts? They ain't from sea creatures, that's for sure."

Still trying to run my bluff, I said, "Found 'em back up the beach a few miles. Started to leave 'em where they lay, but decided they might bring a quid or two. You interested in buying 'em?"

One of the other men rode up and stopped, then leaned over and whispered something in the man's ear, then sat back on his saddle and nodded his head back and forth.

"Found the pelts just lying on the beach, did ya? And I'm sure they didn't come from one of those Aborigine tribes in the outback, did they?"

Still pointing his pistol at me, he yelled to his friends, "Check 'em!"

Knowing what they were about to do, I knocked the first two to the ground and went for one of the horses, and was just swinging my leg up when I felt the butt of a rifle slam against the back of my head.

When I came to, I was trussed up like a pig on a spit, still lying on the beach. The six men were standing nearby, passing a bottle of whiskey around. This was not good. I had been stripped to the waist and the slave number tattooed on my left shoulder stood out like two black eyes. They knew I was a runaway.

CHASING THE NEXT SUNRISE

When one of them noticed I was awake, he nudged the one who I suspected was the leader – the one who had done most of the talking, earlier.

He walked over and looked down at the whip scars on my neck, chest and back. "Looks like you've been disobedient. You got ah smart mouth, do ya? That it? Plus, since we found you out here on the beach, I'm bettin' you're ah skip-along – a runaway."

I held my tongue and said nothing, until he reached inside his shirt and pulled out my money belt, saying, "What I'm wonderin' is where you got all this money? You rob your lord and master before you skipped out, did ya?' Or, maybe you killed somebody for the money and then lit off on the run… That it, chap?"

"That's my money, earned fair and square, back in England and I'll be obliged if you give it back," I told him.

"Well, now, you ain't in England no more, mate. So, I don't reckon their laws will do you any good, here.," he said with a grin.

One of the others stepped up and looked at me, then said, "I recall some time back, seein' ah poster with this chap's face on it. Offerin' ah reward for his return, they were."

"You got ah price on your head, mate?" he asked.

And when I said, nothing, he yelled, "Speak up, Lad! You, ah wanted man with ah price on your head?"

When I continued to remain silent, he and two others hauled me to my feet, then they held me while he drove his fists into my stomach until I spit up blood, and one of the men took him by the shoulder and said, "That's enough. If there is still a reward, we want him healthy enough to collect it."

I was thrown back down onto the beach and left there to gag and try and get my breath back.

"We'll camp here tonight, then take him out to Smit's mine. Shouldn't be more 'n two days ride from here.

"Two days ride," I whispered to myself. I wasn't yet sure how I was going to do it, but there was no way I was going to let them take me back to the mine. The only thing I could expect there would be a slow, torturous death.

I closed my eyes. I needed to conserve my strength.

They were up and moving as soon as the sun came up, grumbling about not having anything to eat. While the horses were being saddled, one of them jerked me to my feet and put a noose around my neck and led me off a little from the others and with my hands tied in front of me, allowed me to do my business.

With the noose around my neck, I was led into a small town about five miles from where they found me on the beach. They paraded me down the main street for everyone to see, then stopped at a small café at the far end of town.

I was led inside and sat down at a table, and told not to move.

When the serving woman looked at me, all trussed up and a rope around my neck, one of the men said, "E's ah runaway slave. Caught him on the beach yesterday. Takin' 'im back, we are. But it's ah two day walk for 'em, and we need ta keep 'em healthy, so bring us some breakfast. And be quick about it, we need ta be on our way."

"And just ah spoon for him. Nuthin' sharp," one of the others said.

The woman served the others first and when she brought my food, she sat a cup of tea in front of me, then with the plate hiding her hand she opened it and I saw a small piece of metal that she dropped onto the table and sat the plate on top of it.

Her eyes had a sad look to them as though she knew more than she let on, and I got the impression she might have had or known someone who had been indentured into slavery.

I smiled and said, "Thank you."

"Quiet over there," came the sharp reply from one of the men.

As I ate my breakfast, I wondered how I could get the piece of metal from under my plate without getting caught? If they caught me, not only would I be in trouble, but I was afraid for the woman who gave it to me. Who knew what they would do to her for trying to help me? I dreaded to think about it, so I ate slowly, and waited.

I need 'in have worried, though. In just a few minutes she brought a steaming pot of tea to refill our cups and when she got close to the others table, she stumbled and spilled a few drops in the lap of one of the men.

He yelled and jumped to his feet, creating just the diversion I needed. I slid the piece of metal from under my plate and with a bit of difficulty, I was able to put it in the front pocket of my pants.

After getting everyone settled down, she filled their cups, then turned and filled my cup, giving me a sly smile and a wink.

I gave a slight nod of my head.

Except for a short break to have cakes and tea for lunch, they rode at a steady pace – them sitting astride their horses and me stumbling along as best I could.

That night, one of them put together a stew of some kind that was nothing to brag about. Even I was a better cook, but I said nothing – although, there was plenty of snide remarks from the others.

Clouds passed back and forth in front of the moon, giving short periods of darkness that allowed me to retrieve the piece of metal from my pocket. One edge of it was quite sharp and I cut my finger, before getting it out of my pocket, which had to be done slowly so I wouldn't draw any attention.

I made short order in cutting through the bonds on my wrists, keeping one eye on the sleeping men.

They had left one man on guard, but he was snoring like a drunken sailor.

I lifted the noose from around my neck, then got slowly to my feet – and with great caution I made my way over to the guard. He was sitting on the ground with his head bent over - his chin resting on his chest.

Luck was with me and I picked up a good size rock that I used to smash against the back of his head.

As he was falling off to the side, I grabbed the rifle that was laying across his lap. Then, as quietly as I could, I removed the holster belt and gun from his waist and strapped it on.

Again, I was lucky. Hanging on the belt was a good size knife. It gave me only three weapons against the remaining five men, but it would have to do.

With great stealth, I was able to collect the rest of the rifles and stood them up in a sort of tee-pee, off to the side.

Just as I turned back, one of them opened his eyes and looked at me with a confused look on his face. And before he could say anything, I smashed the butt of the rifle down against the top of his head. He fell back, unconscious. That left four to deal with.

I quickly moved to the next man, intending to knock all of them out, but this one gave out with a huge grunt that woke up the other three.

I stepped back and pointed the rifle at them and said, "Don't do anything stupid, unless at least two of you wants to die.

They stared at me with hate in their eyes, but didn't move. I motioned for all three of them to stand up and when they did, I pointed the rifle at the one who looked the most scared and told him to tie the hands and feet of his two comrades, or die. It was his choice.

In short order his two friends were tied, hand and foot. Next, I made him tie up the other three, then I had him step away and lay face down on the ground with his hands behind his back.

When they were all bound and I felt safe enough, I walked over and saddled a spotted gray horse who I believed to be the strongest.

"How'd you get loose?" one of them shouted at me.

Knowing I couldn't tell the truth and get the woman in trouble, I turned back and grinned, showing a lot of teeth, then said, "I chewed through the rope like it was soft bread, which you won't be able to do because, before I leave, you will each have a gag in your mouth."

SIXTEEN

As I rode away toward the rising sun, I laughed at my good luck. Not only had I gotten my money back, but also what they had in their pockets, and once I got to a town along the coast, I would sell the horses, giving me a bit more to hide away.

I truly wanted to go back through that town, if for no other reason than to let the woman know I had escaped, but I knew that wasn't an option. Too many people had seen me and I had no idea how they would react.

I veered off to the northeast and a little before nightfall, I could see the lights of a small town in the distance and veered off a little to bypass it.

I rode into the night, trying to put as much distance as I could between me and the six men who were hellbent on taking me back into slavery. I had no doubt they would get loose, eventually. I hadn't tied them that tight. But they would be afoot, which should give me some added time.

Two days later I saw the outline of a town up ahead of me and the ocean! The name of the town somehow escapes me… not that it's all that important, but it had something with, 'pine', in it. Like I said, the name doesn't matter. What matters is, it was a coastal town with ships sitting just off the shore! And a long pier jutting out into the water.

First thing I did was go to a livery stable and put the horses up with grain and a good rubdown. If I could find a ship, I wanted them in good shape for a sale. Next, I took the rifles and pistols I'd collected, and went in search of a gunsmith.

He was short and a good thirty pounds overweight. He was nearly bald, but had a fine set of muttonchops. He was wearing thick glasses and was bent over a table, working on something, with a lit candle, close by.

"Names Silas Franklin," I said as I walked up to him. "Sign on the front says you buy guns. Is that right?"

"Maybe," he said, eyeing me suspiciously.

I laid the six rifles and six pistols, along with holster belts on the table, then added a bag with ball and powder.

"Where'd you get these weapons?" he asked.

"Does it make a difference?" I asked.

"Does if they were stolen from somebody here in town," he said, looking the weapons over, carefully.

"I can assure you they didn't come from anyone here in town. Just so happens, I was way-laid over a hundred miles from here by some ruffians looking to take what is mine and I didn't take too good with that. So, when the scuffling was all done, I wound up with these rifles, pistols, powder and shot." I hoped being somewhat honest would do for him.

"Over a hundred miles from here, you say." He was staring at me with a slight gleam in his eyes. They were good guns and he wanted them; I could tell.

After a long, hard session of bargaining, I walked out of his shop with a goodly amount of money in my pocket that I didn't have when I went in.

Down, close to the wharf, I saw a sign that said I could get something to eat, and since it had been several days since I ate a regular meal, that was my next stop. I was powerful hungry and ordered the biggest meal they had, along with two pints of ale.

I was sitting there, enjoying my meal when this tall, raw-boned man walked in and stood looking at me. He had a star pinned on his shirt.

Next, he walked over and without a by your leave, he pulled out the other chair and dropped down on it. "You look to be new in town," he said with a gravelly voice, like he'd been injured at some time or other.

"Any law against being a newcomer?" I asked, between bites.

"Depends," he said, eyeing the plates sitting in front of me. "Looks like it's been a while since you've eaten."

"So?" I said.

Could be you might be a runaway slave. They're usually pretty hungry if they make it this far. "You a runaway slave?"

I stopped eating and looked him in the eyes and said, "I'm a free man. Always have been, always will be."

He stood up and put his hand on the butt of his pistol which was holstered on his right side. "Then you won't mind me checking your shoulders for a tattoo that says, 'Criminal,' he said, stepping closer to me.

The last thing I wanted was to have a problem with the police, but I wasn't about to let him look at my shoulders. I would be put in chains and sent back to the mine before I could spit.

I looked around and saw the other people in the café were staring at us. I looked at the sheriff and said, "Why don't we go to your office. I don't want to undress here."

I stood up like I was going to comply, then grabbed his arm, whirled him around and pulled his pistol out of his holster and tossed it on the table. "As a matter of fact, I do mind. I'm not looking for trouble. I just came in here to eat, and like I already told you, I'm a free man and I don't cotton to people putting their hands on me."

He turned his head and looked back over his shoulder. "You just got yourself in a whole lot of trouble, Mister."

About that time, the gunsmith came into the café and stopped short. "Hey, Mister Franklin, what are you doing, manhandling the sheriff?"

"You know this man?" the sheriff asked.

"Well, sort of," the gunsmith said. "I just bought some guns off 'en him, maybe an hour or so, ago. Why's he got you trussed up like that?"

I'm guessin' he's a runaway slave. I was about to check him for a tattoo, when he jumped me," the sheriff told him.

"Well, I'll be," the gunsmith said.

I'd had enough, and decided to continue running my bluff. "I'm not a runaway slave. I'm a free man who came in to get a bite to eat. I just can't abide folks putting their hands on me, that's all. I'm not looking for trouble. The sheriff brought it on himself."

About then, one of the men who had been sitting at a back table, stood up and came to where we were standing. He looked at me and asked, "Did you say your name is Franklin?"

Not sure where this was going, I said, "That's right. Silas Franklin."

The man looked at the sheriff and said, "I think I can clear this up. Mister Franklin and I have been in correspondence and he's just arrived to come to work for me. My name is, Captain Horacio P. Hollingsworth.

I'm the captain of that ship out there, The HMS Buckshire. I was in need of a helmsman and Mister Franklin applied for the job by mail."

The captain looked at me and asked, "Isn't that right, Mister Franklin?"

As I released the sheriff, I patted him on the shoulder saying, "That's right, Captain."

Then I turned to the sheriff and said, "I'm real sorry about the misunderstanding, but like I said, I'm a bit touchy when people want to put their hands on me."

The captain looked up at me and said, "You go on now. I'll catch up to you out on the wharf, just as soon as I've cleared things up with the sheriff."

I nodded and headed for the door, just as the captain pulled a wad of money out of his pocket.

Out on the wharf, the captain walked up to me and said, "I do hope you're a sailor. I'd hate to think the sheriff was right and that you are a criminal or a runaway slave."

I looked the captain in the eyes and said, "You're in luck. I'm a free man, a sailor, or a helmsman, whichever you need, and I'm looking for a ship. Name's, Jubal Courtney."

We shook hands and I told him I needed to go down to the stables and finish up some business, and he told me he would go along, just to make sure his investment didn't skip out on him. I don't know how much money he gave the sheriff, but I figured I was in debt to him.

After selling the saddles and six horses, the captain and I walked back down to where he had a long boat tied up. He sat in the aft part of the boat and gave directions while I sat in the middle and manned the oars. Where the horses came from was never brought up and I didn't say, nor did he ask about my experience.

SEVENTEEN

I was given a tour of the ship and introduced to the rest of the crew. He truly did need a helmsman and after I told him I'd singlehanded the open waters of the Atlantic between Ireland and England, and without going into details, said I had sailed the roaring forties, he immediately gave me the job. The one thing I didn't mention was how I wasn't too good at reading a map.

They were still loading the ship, which, I was told would take two and a half to three days. I wasn't crazy about hanging around that long in case, somehow the guards showed up. But it did give me time to familiarize myself with the ship. I was given a small cabin of my own, next to the captain's cabin, and thanks to the Gods, there were books on navigation – which I dove into.

After the evening meal, I stood on the bow, looking out to sea and wondered about all the twists and turns my life had taken, and why? One minute I was doing just fine and the next, I was fighting for my life, one way or another. "Out of the frying pan and into the fire, then out again," as pa would say.

I smelled pipe smoke and turned to see Monk Devers; the ships chief boatswains' mate, as he approached. He was a big man – as tall as me, with broad shoulders and thick arms – and an easy gate about him. He stopped and looked at me for a long time, blowing smoke into the night air. Finally, he knocked the pipe's ashes against the heel of his hand, allowing them to fall into the water.

"Good evening. Mister Devers, isn't it?" I asked.

"Just Devers, or Monk, if you prefer. I'm no officer, so there's no mister attached to my name."

"Monk, it is then," I said, sticking out my hand.

He took it and we stood there for a moment, staring eye to eye at each other as he squeezed my hand, taking all the circulation away.

I squeezed right back until we'd both had enough and released our grips at the same time.

"Kinda young ta be a helmsman, ain't ya?" he asked.

Most helmsmen were, indeed, older, with years aboard a ship and lots of book learning, so rather than trying to run a bluff, I said, "I'm older than I look. I tried to explain to the captain that I didn't think I had enough experience to be the helmsman for a ship like this, but I guess his hearing isn't so good."

That got a chuckle out of him and he said, "I like you, mate. Maybe me and the others can give you a bit of advice from time to time."

I nodded my head and said, "It will be greatly appreciated. Any idea where our first destination is?" I asked, hoping he would know.

With the little finger of his hand, Monk scratched something inside his ear, then wiped his finger on his pants. "Year ago, or so, a man called, Captain Cook discovered some islands north of here. He called them, the Sandwich Islands. Ain't never been there, myself but I heard from the cook, that's our first port to put into when we leave here. I hear they got some kind of fruit called pineapple, that folks thinks is right tasty. Reckon we'll be pickin' up a load of 'em, then head for North America."

I gave a sigh. None of the maps down in my cabin would help because those islands hadn't been discovered when the maps had been drawn.

As I stood there, wondering what to do, next, I saw the captain come topside and speak with a man who'd just come aboard. And after a few seconds, the captain waved for me to come to them.

The man was introduced as Captain Kryton Hill, who had just come from the Sandwich Islands and would be happy to give me the coordinates.

We went down to my cabin where he took a pen in hand and drew the route for me to follow.

My heart sank a little when I found out our destination was more than five thousand miles across the vast Pacific Ocean, to the north, northeast and had to navigate through a bunch of islands and atolls to get to open water. To stay on course for such a long journey with only the sun, the moon and the stars to guide me, was at the very least, very daunting.

I thanked him, and that night, by the light of a candle, I charted our course and came to the conclusion that the trip would take at least forty seven days – a little over a hundred miles a day - that is, if all my calculations were correct.

The following morning, I went ashore and hunted down Captain Hill who was having his breakfast. He invited me to join him. I was too excited to be hungry, but there is a thing called, protocol, and I couldn't say no. While we were waiting for the food to come, I presented him with my calculations. He studied them for only a few minutes, then smiled and handed the paper back to me, saying, "I'd say you're spot on, lad. With those coordinates, you should do just fine."

I was awed by his statement, but held my tongue. After thanking him, I tried to calm down enough to enjoy my meal. During our breakfast, he invited me to his ship to sample the fruit that was called, a pineapple.

When he presented it to me, I could see it was covered with what appeared to be thorns, and they were, of a sort. When pressed, they lay down against the body of the fruit, which was much larger than I expected it to be.

With a large knife, the captain cut off the butt end of it, then made another slice and handed it to me. "Tell me what you think, lad."

The meat was course, but chewy. It was the juice that caused me to grin. It was as sweet as anything I'd ever eaten. I looked at the captain and said, "And you say they grow these things in those Sandwich Islands?"

"Aye, they do, and other fruit, too."

He went on to explain to me about the people and their easy way of life, and how it was always warm there. I couldn't fathom such a place. I went back to my ship with my head spinning. There seemed to be a whole world out there I knew nothing about.

Shortly after getting back, I found Bosun Devers tending to some lines for the mainsail, and told him everything I'd just learned. He grinned and said, "You don't say. And you say these pineapples are as sweet as anything you've ever eaten?"

Grinning like a small boy at Christmas time, I brought my hand from behind my back and handed him a slice.

When he'd finished and tossed the prickly part over the side of the ship, he wiped his mouth on the sleeve of his shirt and said, "Good gawd, man, you could make a fortune selling those things. They're that bloody good!"

The ship was finally loaded and the captain said we would sail on the morning tide.

I was up early, checking my charts, and I'm here to tell you, I was a bit nervous. I was about to embark on an adventure that more than twenty lives depended on.

I watched the water and as soon as it began to head back to the open ocean, I weighed the anchor, and stood at the wheel, guiding the ship away from land – and as soon as I felt the first bit of breeze, I called to the bosun to haul up the mainsheet, followed by the other sails as we got further from shore.

I was concentrating so hard I didn't see the captain come up and stand next to me. He could see the whiteness of my knuckles as I held onto the wheel, my eyes intent on the compass.

"Relax, lad. You're going to be fine. Your heading is correct and you have the wind at your back." He patted me on the shoulder and left to walk among the crew, chatting it up. Today was my thirty-ninth birthday, but I didn't say anything

Monk came up and slapped me on the back. "Good job, lad. You keep us on the headin' ya want, and me and the crew will keep the sails trimmed so's we get the best speed."

The first three days were spent weaving in between islands and trying not to run into small atolls hidden just beneath the surface.

We were four days out before I began to relax. The weather had been perfect and the wind was steady. I glanced back over my shoulder and could see nothing but ocean. And that's when it hit me. I was truly, a free man. There would be no more mining guards or bounty hunters breathing down my neck.

On the tenth day, we weathered out a squall that dropped a lot of rain on us and the crew was ready for it. With barrels, they collected fresh water as it ran down the sails, and with bars of soap they washed themselves and the clothes they wore – some of them while they were still in them.

Although I could see nothing but water in any direction, I had held to the course I set and was beginning to feel a certain amount of confidence when on the morning of the twenty second day I came topside to find the ship bobbing leisurely on what looked to be an almost flat ocean. I licked my finger and stuck it in the air, but could feel no wind.

"Doldrums!" Monk shouted. "We're in the bloody doldrums!"

When he saw the confused look on my face, he said, "Happens from time ta time out here in the middle of nowhere. The wind just stops and we sit here bobbin' around like ah cork on ah pond."

"How long does it last?" I asked, looking around.

He looked around, shrugged his shoulders and said, "A few hours, a few days, maybe a week. Nobody knows. One minute the wind is blowin' just fine, then just for no reason a body can figure out, it stops, and then ya wait. And it don't come back til it wants ta come back and not a minute before."

Suddenly, I got a panicking feeling and ran up on the poop deck and asked the night man at the wheel, "How long has it been since the wind stopped?"

He thought for a moment, then said, "Maybe two hours or so."

I ran back down to my cabin and grabbed my charts. What waves there were, even as small as they were, to the best I could figure, had drifted us southwest, two, maybe three degrees. On a long voyage, such as we were undertaking, even one degree off could cause us to miss our target by hundreds of miles.

There was a tap on my door and when I called out, "Come," the captain came in and walked over to my table.

I jumped to my feet but he waved me back down and asked, "Have you figured out how far off course we've drifted?"

He studied my figures and said, "Four degrees. Not bad, not bad at all, but according to my calculations, we've only drifted three degrees. And as you know, even one degree off can put us a long way from where we want to wind up.

I had followed the book to get my findings and showed him. He grinned and said, "Yes, that's how I used to do it, too. But now, there is a new way. Have you heard of a sextant?"

"A what?" I asked. New to being a helmsman meant there was a lot of things I needed to learn, and this sextant, thing seemed to be one of them.

"Don't worry about it. Very few have, yet. It was just invented a few years ago and I happened to learn about it and took a class from the inventor on how to use it.

The captain took me up on deck and taught me how to take a sun sight by bringing the sun down on the horizon and writing down the finding. We started at eleven thirty in the morning and repeated doing it for an hour, and then calculated the middle finding, which gave us our exact location.

It was an amazing tool and my head was spinning on how someone could come up with the idea to make it in the first place.

The captain also taught me how to use it at night to navigate by the stars. And from that day on, my confidence grew like a young colt eating alfalfa.

Because of losing time due to the doldrums, we were three days behind in reaching our destination. On the morning of the fiftieth day since leaving Australia, the man in the crow's nest, high above the deck, yelled, "Land ho!"

I lifted the telescope from where it rested near the wheel, and put it to my eye. Sure enough, I could see land! As I laid the telescope back down in its cradle, I crossed my fingers and prayed the land we were seeing was the land we were searching for.

As we got closer, we could see at least fifty or more canoes coming out to meet us. One was decorated with flowers and an elderly man sat in the rear on a chair like affair. It was the largest of all the canoes and it was obvious he was the chief – or, king as I found out. They all had names I couldn't pronounce, but such lovely people I had never met before! Especially the beautiful young women with their brown skin, dark eyes, coal black hair and open arms.

I ate food that to this day, I still can't pronounce, but there was also a lot of fish and fruit. And they made an ale that would knock a bull to his knees. Besides pineapples, I was introduced to bananas, papaya and several other succulent dishes.

CHASING THE NEXT SUNRISE

When we left, a week later, I had put on at least ten pounds or more. But in truth, I hated leaving. And it wasn't just the people. The weather was the best I'd ever been in – warm, with balmy nights. And I loved swimming in the ocean.

My biggest worry was figuring out a route to our next destination. A week after landing in the Sandwich Islands, the captain informed us we would be returning to Australia with our load of fruit, but was concerned because we still had a good many items from Australia, still in the hold.

The thought of returning to Australia and the bounty hunters made me consider staying in the Sandwich Islands, which, by the way, may have been what I should have done. But it so happened that the captain met a man who had just come from a place he called, Alaska. He was Russian and told the captain the Russians had recently established a few villages along the western coast of the North Americas. He went on to say they would gladly trade for the fruit and other things he had aboard the ship.

And so it was, that the captain changed his plan and told us we would be going to this place called, Alaska.

Since there were no maps or charts, my only recourse was to hunt down this Russian captain and get some coordinates from him. He was a big man, well over six feet tall and weighed close to two hundred and fifty pounds, and as it turned out, a great lover of a drink called, vodka. And having drinks was the only way he would talk to me or help me in any way.

Monk later told me the crew carried me back to the ship and tossed me on my bunk, where I remained for the next thirty-two hours. And even then, I was weak and my head felt like it was going to bust wide open at any second.

Our cook, Elmer Sinclair, made up a concoction that he said would cure all my troubles, or kill me, whichever came first.

First, I hung my head over the side of the ship until there was nothing more to give to the ocean, then slid down and sat, leaning against the railing, knowing for sure I was living my last minutes on this earth.

Secondly, the cook brought me a bowl of stew of some kind with a small loaf of bread. Two hours later, I was able to stand up without feeling dizzy.

Fortunately, we weren't due to leave for another two days, allowing me to become normal again. And down in my cabin, I vowed to never let vodka cross my lips, ever, again. And I haven't. Gawd, that stuff is awful. I don't see how the Russians can drink it like they do. I would have been dead, years ago.

I got a lot of jibes from the crew, but it was all in fun, so I didn't let it bother me.

I'll never forget our sendoff. Again, fifty or more canoes came out to see us off, waving and asking for us to return. One of them had four young ladies, all waving with big smiles and blowing kisses in my direction. At least I hoped it was me they were waving at because I was waving back with the same enthusiasm.

I never made it back to the Sandwich Islands, but the pictures of the people and the islands, along with some wonderful memories, have stayed in my head all these years.

EIGHTEEN

Once again, I was sailing by the seat of my pants into the unknown. I had only the chart the Russian had given me and the hope that he knew what he was talking about. I was sailing north, northeast with only the sun and the stars to guide me.

Using the captain's sextant every day, I did my best to stay on the course that the Russian had given me, but once again, Mother Nature and I went head-to-head in battle.

This time it wasn't the doldrums – just the opposite. The wind came from behind us, pushing a blackened sky. Rain fell like lead pellets, smashing onto the boat and the men, who ran for shelter, anywhere they could find it. The wind tore at the halyards and several times broke the lines, whipping the sails and snapping the ends like a bullwhip.

While trying to make repairs, the men had to tie themselves together to keep from being washed overboard. The sea had swells twenty-five to thirty feet high that smashed down on the deck, washing anything not tied down, over the side. The bow of the ship would climb the swell, push its nose through the green water, then slide down into the trough and back up again to do it all over, again. I had Monk tie me to the wheel post where I stayed for thirty-six hours as the storm raged and tried to send us to the bottom of the ocean, over and over. She was sturdy built and sailed proudly through wave after wave.

Several crew members tried from time to time, bringing food, along with hot tea or coffee to me but the conditions were so rough they couldn't make it to the bridge. My only savings was I could open my mouth and in just seconds, it was filled with rainwater, so I didn't go thirsty and the cook was able to bring chunks of meat.

When the storm finally moved on, my first priority was to make sure we were on course. Then and only then, did I go down to the galley and eat my fill – after which I made my way to my cabin and slept for sixteen hours.

When I came up topside, I received a rousing cheer from the men and the captain, who was standing at the wheel. "You did well, lad," he told me, then stepped aside and I took the wheel, checking the compass.

With a following sea, helping to push us along, and with the storm pushing us even faster, on day twenty, the man in the crow's nest yelled out for all to hear, "Land ho!"

No one was more excited to hear those words than me. Leaving the wheel to Monk, I climbed the mast to the crow's nest and looked forward.

What I saw, was a small island with smoke rising into the air. I scrambled back down onto the deck and ran over to where my chart was rolled up, standing in a holder next to the wheel stand. To the best of my calculations, the island was at 51 degrees north and 176 degrees east.

The captain approached me and said, "Well done, lad. Well done indeed. Head straight for that island and let's see who we find."

From what I could see from the crow's nest, the island was fairly large. I guessed it to be around the same size as the largest of the Sandwich Islands, but more somber. And the people, while they weren't as friendly as the people of the Sandwich Islands, they weren't unfriendly – just more businesslike.

We anchored just off shore and they came out in boats and came aboard the ship.

They were a hardy bunch of people who called themselves, Aleut Indians and their island, Adak. They were short in stature and a darker brown than the people of the Sandwich Islands. Most of the men sported beards and mustaches. They spoke no English and communication was done through hand jesters and pointing.

During the two days we stayed there, the captain felt like he'd struck a goldmine. Their boats were loaded with skins that shed water, furs that would keep you warm in the coldest weather, and several kinds of fish. One called, Salmon, which the men liked.

While they didn't have a need for the lumber or other building materials we had, they did fall in love with the fruit we had loaded, back in the Sandwich Islands.

It soon became apparent this island was only one in a long string of islands coming out from a large land mass to the east. Since the people called themselves, Aleuts, I wrote on my chart, Adak Island, part of the Aleutian Islands, in the northern part of the Bering Sea.

We bypassed most of the rest of the chain of islands until we came to another, very large island, the natives called, Kodiak Island, because of the large white bears that inhabited the island. On this island, we met our first Russians who were there, trapping these huge white beasts for their fur, which the captain traded for, but this time, it was the building materials they wanted.

The captain spoke with limited and broken English, and did the negotiating. From him, we learned the main Russian site was on the mainland – a place called, Sitka.

In Sitka, things didn't go so well. From the time we dropped anchor in the large bay, in amongst several other Russian ships, that sported cannons, we were looked at with a lot of suspicion.

When we went ashore, we were met with men with rifles. The head man; a man who spoke fairly good English, introduced himself as, Major Ivan Abramov, and immediately asked who we were and what we were doing there, like we were hostiles, wanting to steal something.

I leaned close to Monk and said, "I've got a bad feeling about this guy. Keep your eyes and ears open."

Monk nodded his head and said, "I have the same feeling, mate."

The captain, however seemed to take the whole matter in stride and explained we were but travelers, trading as we went along, exploring new lands. "I'm told this is the main site where the Russian people are in the process of establishing a town – and I'm hoping we can do some business."

The major stared at the captain with fire in his eyes and after only a moment, he yelled, "I don't believe you!" He looked at the men with the rifles and said, "Take these men into custody until I can inspect their ship to find out why they are really here!"

Without hesitation, I turned and drove my shoulder into the nearest man with a rifle, sending him sprawling onto his back, then dove off the pier into the ice-cold water and doubled back underneath before coming up for air. My head had barely cleared the top of the water, when Monk's head came up close to mine.

We could hear the men on the pier running around, yelling loudly in Russian.

The water was freezing cold and I thought for sure the men on the pier could hear my teeth rattling. The truth was, they didn't hear Monk when he asked me if I could swim under water from the far end of the pier to the patch of weeds some two hundred feet further down the shore.

I knew it was either that or stay here and possibly be shot by the men on the pier. I nodded my head yes, and began moving down toward the end of the pier where there was deeper water.

I took a deep breath and followed Monk as he dove deep into the frigid water and swam with evaporating strength, toward our destination.

When we came up in the middle of the weeds, I was gasping for breath and felt numb from head to toe.

"C'mon, we have to get out of this water," Monk whispered as he started for the bank.

We had no more than belly-crawled onto the bank when we heard, "Spppst! Spppst!" coming from the nearby trees. I looked up and saw a woman, wrapped in furs, waving for us to come to her. I looked at Monk, who glanced over his shoulder in the direction of the pier. I too, looked toward the pier and saw they were all facing the other way.

Wasting no time, we belly-crawled the short distance into the trees and stood up.

There were four women inside the trees. They wrapped warm furs around us and motioned for us to follow them – which we did.

Close to half an hour later, we left the trees and walked along the beach to a group of large boulders sitting out in the water.

Without hesitation, the women went out into the water that was only knee deep and around one of the boulders, then back toward the land.

In among the boulders was the opening to a large cave. The ocean water flowed into the cave, maybe fifty feet, then it was dry. The cave itself, was at least sixty feet across and maybe seventy five feet deep. There was evidence of old fires here and there, along with pallets where people had slept.

One of the women bent down and began building a fire, while another dropped a sack on the ground and began removing food. The woman who had "Spppsted" at us, motioned for us to sit down. And when we did, she and the fourth woman made motions for us to take off our clothes.

Monk grinned and I told him I thought they only wanted to dry them by the fire while we stayed wrapped up in the fur robes.

"Oh well," Monk said as he pulled off his pants and shirt, wrapping the fur tightly around him to stop his chattering teeth.

While our shoes and clothes were drying by the fire, a second fire was made right in front of us and pieces of fish were cooked.

I would like to have asked questions about who they were and why they were helping us, but my first question, "Do you speak English?" was met by shrugged shoulders as some gibberish came from her lips.

I made a hand jester from the heart area of my chest, then pushing my hands in their direction, as a way to say, thank you. She got the idea and smiled. Next, she frowned and pointed toward the opening of the cave and made repeated stabbing jesters with her fist, which I took to mean they didn't like the major and his army.

Once our clothes were dry, and we had eaten our fill of fish, Monk and I strategized over how we might be able to rescue the captain and the rest of the crew. But before we could come up with a plan, from far off, we heard someone yell, then several rifles being fired.

We jumped to our feet and shucking our robes, ran out of the cave and stood near the edge of one of the boulders. There were no more sounds, so we went back into the cave, harboring some very bad feelings.

One of the women motioned for us to sit down and pointed to more fish cooking over the fire, and when we sat down, all four women turned and left.

The following morning, the women returned and when Monk asked what had happened to our friends, one of the women took a stick and drew men in the sand, and then she drew men with rifles pointed at the men. She made a loud sound, then, with the stick, she made the men disappear. It was plain enough; we wouldn't be needing a plan to rescue anyone. They had all faced a firing squad.

"So, what 'a we do now?" Monk asked. "We can't sail the ship by ourselves, can we?"

"We'd never make it out of the harbor," I told him. "They probably think we drowned in the icy water, but in case we didn't, I have no doubt they have armed men aboard the ship in case we try something stupid."

"Well, it's for sure we can't stay around here, now, can we?" Monk asked.

I walked over to where the women were standing and made motions with my hands, indicating Monk and I needed to leave – to get away, but didn't know which direction to go.

The woman with the stick, drew the opening to the cave, then drew a line pointing down along the shoreline, indicating the direction we should go.

I nodded my head and again, made the hand jester from my chest to them, then made the motion that we would be leaving.

Shaking her head, no, one of the women held both hands up, her palms toward me. She took the stick and drew a line in the sand, then what looked like the sun going down.

I got her meaning and nodded my head. She wanted us to wait until evening and leave when it was dark.

The women left again, and we spent the day, resting and eating more fish.

The opening of the cave was turning dark and I had just told Monk we should be leaving soon, when we heard a noise. We both grabbed a piece of firewood to use as a weapon and turned to face whoever was coming into the cave.

Monk and I sighed when we saw the women, motioning for us to follow them.

We were surprised when they kept going deeper into the cave. At what we thought was the back wall, there was a turn and a tunnel led off to the right. The tunnel was pitch black and one of the women took my hand and another woman took my other hand, and Monk's hand. Linked together we entered the darkness. It was cold and damp and it seemed like we walked for quite a long distance before we emerged onto a hillside. The entrance was hidden by trees and brush. We were, for sure, a good distance from the town.

I heard a horse snort and stamp its hoof. The woman who'd led us through the tunnel, pulled on my hand and said something I couldn't understand, but I followed her.

There, maybe twenty feet away, stood two short legged horses with a coat of long hair. They were saddled and had a large roll of something tied behind each saddle.

With hand jesters, she indicated we get on the horses and leave. I couldn't believe our luck.

Before I realized what I was doing, I pulled the woman close to me and hugged her. I felt her arms go around my back as she hugged me, too.

Finally, she released me and said more of her gibberish, pointing toward the horses.

Why or how they knew we were in those weeds, I'll never know, but you can bet I'll never forget them or what they did for us. And through the years, I've hoped and prayed they didn't get in trouble for helping us. Back in Ireland, stealing a horse was a serious offense.

There was no road, only the ocean on our right to guide us south.

NINETEEN

We rode as hard as we dared, trying not to wear the horses down and as it turned out, they were hardier than we were. When the light of day appeared, we were a far piece down the trail, but we rode off a short distance and hid in a grove of trees. While Monk made a small, smokeless fire and began putting together something to eat, I unsaddled the horses, gave them a rubdown, then hobbled them so they could move around and eat the nearly knee-deep grass.

When that was done, I went down to the trail and walked back close to a mile, then began wiping out our tracks, all the way down to where we were camped, which took the better part of an hour. When I got back to camp, Monk was nursing a cup of chicory coffee, which wasn't my favorite, but it was hot, and went along with the dried fish and pot of beans.

We'd just finished eating breakfast when Monk raised his hand for silence and in the distance, we heard horses running. They passed where we'd turned off the trail and to our relief, kept going.

After making sure there was no trace of our camp, we rode deeper into the woods for nearly a mile before turning south, again.

Come noon, we stopped for more of that chicory coffee. "No tea, I suppose?" I asked Monk.

"No. Chicory coffee is all that is in the packs they gave us," he said, shaking his head.

Over the years, I've come to like coffee, but the regular kind, not chicory.

We rested the horses for around an hour, then mounted up and continued on south, still staying within the forest, using my compass to guide us.

After three days of this, we turned west and rode back to the coast where we found a tribe of Indians who were camped on the shore next to the ocean. They were friendly enough, but kept an eye on us, as we did on them.

CHASING THE NEXT SUNRISE

We spent two days with them and went out on their boats, pulling at the nets, bringing in large amounts of fish. What they did with them, I'm not sure, but they had what looked to be pack horses, so I guess they had a market for them.

When we left, they waved and yelled a different gibberish at us – and we waved back. The horses were rested and we had plenty of dried fish to eat, along with another sack of beans.

They also showed us wild greens to pick, which, if their hand signals meant anything, the greens would be good for us.

After two weeks, we came upon a large town, or at least the makings of a town.

We were riding down the main street when I turned my horse and rode down an alley, with Monk right behind me.

"What's this all about?" he asked, riding up next to me.

"Saw two of those Russians from back up north. They were riding right toward us and looking around."

Monk swung around in his saddle and looked back down the alley, searching for the Russians, but didn't see them.

"C'mon," I said as I tapped my heels against the side of my horse to urge him into a faster pace – and at the next street, I turned back to the left – hoping to be going still in the opposite direction the Russians were.

At the south end of the soon to be, town, we found a general store where I was able to purchase real coffee and other supplies we needed, along with some grain for the horses and a packhorse to carry it. I hadn't wanted to dig into my money, but if we were to continue on south, we needed the supplies and extra horse. At least, the horse could be sold, if need be, to recoup some of my money.

We had no idea where we were going. The man at the general store was French, and spoke a broken English. He told us an Englishman by the name of Vancouver, started the village, and had high hopes for growth as a trading port.

As I think back, I believe it would have been a good place for Monk and me to settle down for a while, if not for those Russians looking for us.

Two weeks later we rode into another fishing village that had a mixture of English, Dutch and Indians. It was good to talk to someone I could understand and who could understand me. We hired on as crew on one of the fishing boats, but after finding out we would be going back up north, we abandoned ship and headed south, again.

There seemed to be an Indian village every few miles as we traveled south until we got to a place called, Seattle.

Seattle was a booming town with wagon trains from the east, arriving every few weeks. It was bustling with growth and Monk took a shine to the place, but not me. By now, I'd gotten used to chasing the next sunrise.

There was talk of a couple more places down the coast that sounded interesting. One was called San Francisco and the other one, Los Angeles. The first one was said to have people from several cultures and Los Angeles was mainly Mexican, with a few whites, here and there. Both were said to be booming, which didn't excite me much, but I did want to see them.

So, I said goodbye to Monk and headed south on a long legged chestnut mare, who made me feel like I was sitting on a rocking chair. I had a new packhorse, too. And not one red cent came from my stash of money. No-siree, not one red cent.

Before leaving, Monk and I happened to be down along the edge of town and saw several large tents and a whole bunch of people. As it turned out, it was a carnival show. They had this fella who could swallow a sword, and this other fella they claimed was a wild man from some place called, Borneo. But I reckon he was just a man who had a lot of body hair who jumped around and growled at folks for the dime they gave to come see him.

Monk saw a large crowd of men and a few women, standing in front of this platform that was just outside a huge tent. The front side was rolled up, and inside, there was a boxing ring set up. A man dressed in fancy clothes was standing on the platform, betting fifty dollars against ten that no man could stay in the ring with this fella he called, Battlin' Jim, who he claimed to be the toughest man in the world, for three, five minute rounds.

There was a giant sized fella standing off to the side, who had no shirt on and had his arms folded across his chest. He was glaring at the crowd. He looked to be the bully type and I guessed him to be this, Battlin' Jim.

Right away, three men offered to give this Battlin' Jim a go, and of course, the rest of us wanted to go see how tough he really was.

As we headed for the entryway of the tent, two men lowered the side so you couldn't see inside from out where we were. And there was a man at the entryway telling us it would cost us a dollar each to go in and watch the fights, which seemed a mite steep to me.

Curiosity got the best of me and I paid for me and Monk to get inside. We got right up close to the ring where we could see good and held our ground.

Sure enough, that giant of a man from outside climbed inside the ring and danced around on his toes, throwing punches at an invisible opponent.

"He sure looks tough enough," Monk yelled in my ear to overcome the noise all around us.

And as we waited for the place to fill up, there was a man going around taking bets on the fight. I figured he was with Battlin' Jim and the other man, and I said, "No," when he asked if I wanted to place a bet. I had other ideas.

When the tent was full and the betting all taken care of, the man in the fancy clothes called for quiet, then yelled for all of us to hear.

"The first challenger, standing in the far corner is, Sven Johansson! He's put up his ten dollars and says he can stand against my man, Battlin' Jim, the heavyweight boxing champion of the world!"

Well now, that would be quite the title to hold, wouldn't it? Of course, I didn't believe a word of it, but I think Monk did because his next statement was, "Ain't no way that Sven fella can stand up to the champion of the whole world. I knew I should 'a put some money on the champ."

I didn't say anything for I believe a man has the right to believe as he chooses.

The man in the fancy clothes raised his hands in the air, again, and said, "This is to be a straight, bare knuckled boxing event. There will be no, biting, kicking or ear pulling. Any infraction of the rules will immediately be declared a loss, and the fight will be over!"

The man in the fancy clothes looked over to where a man sat next to a bell. He had a hammer in his hand, and at fancy pants' nod, he rang the bell and the fight began.

This Sven Johansson was nearly as big as Battlin' Jim, but it was obvious he was no match for the champ. He threw several punches that hit nothing but air, while the champ threw four quick jabs to Sven's face and followed it with a right cross that dropped Sven in less than two minutes of the first round.

The second contender was of German descent, and also a large man. I believed him to be in his mid-twenties. He held up better than Sven because he could take a punch, which the champ gave him on a constant basis. The big German made only one hit on the champ's jaw, which he shook off, and gave back better than he got.

I didn't know the nationality of the third man, but he knew something about boxing. He was as tall as the champ, but not as heavy. He danced around, keeping just out of the champ's reach and threw quick jabs that every now and then, caught the champ on the chin. But as I watched, none of them had much power behind them.

Halfway through the second round, the champ must have gotten tired of being hit, and waded in, throwing lefts and rights at the man's head, sending him back against the ropes. I knew it was all over for the man and just waited to see him fall.

The champ walked around the ring with his fists in the air like he'd just done something extraordinary.

"Is there no one here tough enough to stand up against Battlin' Jim?" the man in the fancy clothes, yelled. "C'mon, there must be at least one among you…?"

I had been watching the champ's moves and he was easy to figure out if you paid attention. I looked at Monk and said, "Hold these."

I had taken off my hat and coat before climbing into the ring, holding ten dollars in my hand. Thinking I was crazy, Monk tried to pull me back, but I was already inside the ring and standing up.

The man in the fancy clothes looked at me and almost laughed, and would have if not for the money he believed he was about to make.

As he took my money, he leaned in close and said, "You won't last the first round."

Of course, I took that as a challenge and yelled so the crowd could hear. "So, you don't' think I'll last through the first round, do you?" Well, Mister Fancy Pants, let's up the wager then." I reached into my pants pocket and said, "I've got another ten against a hundred, that I will be the one standing at the end of the fight!"

The man grinned and said, "We have a bet, my friend." And as he reached for my money, I pulled it back and looked at the crowd. "You heard him. He's taking my bet on top of the fifty dollars he'll owe me when I put this tub of guts on the mat!"

The crowd cheered and yelled, "Go get 'em mister! We're with you!"

The man who had gone around making bets, was once again moving through the crowd, taking bets against me, offering five to one odds.

I walked to my corner and turned back and smiled at Battlin' Jim, then made a bow, to the delight of the crowd.

The betting was finished and the fight was about to begin when from behind me I heard Monk say, "I hope you know what you're doing."

"Me too," I told him. The truth was, back in Ireland, I was known as quite a scrapper and I had been watching Battlin' Jim's moves, and was betting I could out maneuver him. At least I hoped so, or I would not only be a laughing stock, but more than likely, tarred and feathered by the men who had bet on me.

The bell rang and I walked out into the middle of the ring, then began dancing around, taking short jabs to distract him, and when I saw an opening, I drove a hard right into his kidney area and watched him grimace.

There was no doubt about him being a bruiser, but I was counting on skill and a steady number of punches to the right places, while doing my best to keep just out of reach of his hammerlike fists.

Several times during the first round, he tried to wade in close and throw his hammer punches at my head, but I ducked away from them and danced around and drove my fist into his kidneys, time and time again. By the end of the first round, I knew my punches were having the effect I wanted.

"Good job, kid," Monk told me as I sat down on the stool, he provided me. He rubbed my face and head with a towel he got from somewhere and said, "Keep doin' what you're doin' and don't let him get close to you."

I nodded my head at him as the bell for the second round began. I stood up and headed for the center of the ring, but I didn't need to wait for him. He came running into the center of the ring, swinging both fists at me like a windmill. His first blow caught me on the left shoulder that caused my arm to go numb. Next came a fist against my cheek that staggered me backward against the ropes.

He followed me, throwing those hammerlike blows that felt like a mule kicking me. In defense, I raised my arms to block his blows and shook my head to get the ringing out of my ears.

I'm not quite sure how I did it, but I slipped under his blows and danced away from the ropes and as I did, I drove my right fist into his kidney area, again. I heard him groan and saw him stagger. But being the professional fighter he was, he shook it off and turned toward me. "That all you got, kid?" he asked, throwing a right at my jaw.

I jerked my head back and felt the wind off his fist as it went past. I danced away and said, "You ain't seen nothing yet, fat boy. I'm just getting warmed up."

The second round ended in what I believed to be a draw. My right eye was swollen and I could taste blood inside my mouth. And my left shoulder, hurt. But I wasn't ready to give up – not yet. I could see the man in the fancy clothes, and he had a frown on his face and was speaking to the champ in an unpleasant manner. The champ nodded his head and stood up just as the bell sounded for the last and final round. I knew I would need to take him down or I was going to lose the fight.

This time it was me who ran into the center of the ring, waving my arms in the air, then pointing at the champ, yelling, "It's time for you to go down, old man. There's a new champ in the ring!"

The crowd cheered, loudly and I hoped my strategy was working. I wanted him to be unsure of himself, giving me the advantage.

I danced around, throwing short jabs at his jaw that landed but did no harm to him. I started to move to my right, and when he started to follow, I stopped and stepped back in the other direction, driving my right fist into his stomach, three quick, hard blows.

I heard him suck air and then with my right leg to help, I threw an upper cut to his jaw and heard it break.

He staggered back, his eyes wide with pain, as I followed with more blows to his gut, doubling him over.

I didn't want to cause more suffering by hitting him in the jaw, again, so, instead, I drove my right fist into the side of his head.

He landed on his back and lay there, sucking in air. I looked down at him and said, "Don't get up. You're finished and I don't want to hurt you more."

He looked up at me and I could see the defeat in his eyes. With his broken jaw, he couldn't speak, so he raised both hands in the air, indicating I had won!

The crowd went wild and I saw fancy pants trying to sneak away. I pointed and yelled, "Don't let him get away!"

In less than a heartbeat, fancy pants was surrounded, and he stood there looking ever bit the broken man. Someone had the forethought to grab onto the man who had been taking the bets and dragged him up and stood him next to fancy pants. Both were brought to the ring where I collected my one hundred and fifty dollars, to pats on the back and men saying it was the best fight they'd ever seen.

While they were collecting on their bets, Monk and I slipped away into the night.

TWENTY

Even in a town as large as Seattle was becoming, we knew we needed to move on. Fancy pants wouldn't take kindly to what I'd done to him and his champion of the world and he would be looking for my hide. With a broken jaw, the champ's fighting days were over.

Once again, following the ocean, we traveled south, stopping here and there at Indian villages. I was having a hard time believing so many different tribes could be living so close to each other.

From what I could gather, their biggest thrill was stealing from each other. Using hand jesters, one of them told me a certain horse he had, had been stolen from him nine times, from three different tribes. Each time, he stole him back, along with as many other horses as he could get.

Three weeks later, we paid our fee to the ferryman and crossed a huge river that led out into the ocean and found ourselves in a town called, Portland.

Portland was making a name for itself with the influx of pilgrims coming in from the east in wagon trains, along with establishing a large port for ships coming from faraway places.

After boarding our horses and renting a room, we went down on the wharf to get a bite to eat and look around. And while we were having our dinner, a sailor Monk knew, came up to our table. Monk invited him to sit with us and in a short space of time, the man was asking Monk and me if we were looking for a ship? He went on to say the captain was looking for a few good men to sail with him.

When asked where the ship would be sailing to, the man looked at me like I was daft, and asked, "What difference does it make? A sailing man goes wherever the ship goes without questions about where it's going."

The sailor looked at Monk and said, "I could put in a word for you with the captain if you're interested," leaving me out of the equation.

Monk handed the man a coin and told him to go have a beer, on him, while he and I had a talk.

When the man had gone, Monk looked at me and said, "You're not interested, are you?"

I looked out the window and could see several ships sitting at anchor and others tied up to the wharf, and realized they presented no desire in me. I turned back to Monk and said, "No, my friend, but I see the lust in your eyes."

Monk pushed his plate away, saying, "Aye, the thought appeals to me. I'm a sailor. It's in me blood. Aboard a ship is where I'm most comfortable, don't 'cha see?"

I smiled. We'd been together for some time now and I'd gotten used to seeing his face every morning, and knowing he had my back when things got tight. But I also knew I couldn't ask him to stay. The sea was where he was meant to be. Me? I had a thirst to know what this land, this, America, was all about as I chased the next sunrise.

I stood up and stuck out my hand. "We've had some times together, and I'll not forget you, my friend. But it's time we parted ways. You back to the sea, and me? I'm not sure just yet. There's a lot of land out there that seems to be calling my name."

We shook hands and before he went to be with his friend, he said, "And I'll not be forgettin' you, either, Irishman. But remember what I'm tellin' you, right here and now. Keep a sharp eye out, and never leave your back unguarded. I don't know where you'll end up or what you'll be doin', but I'm guessin' it will be quite the adventure. And when your time comes, may you be in heaven half an hour before the devil knows you're gone."

And with that we parted ways. I was never to see my friend, again, but his words were to ring in my ears sooner than I expected.

I didn't wait around to see Monk off. The following morning as the sun came up, I was riding south, again – alone, this time. The cliffs along this part of the country sat high above the water and I could see the waves lapping against the shore. Far out over the ocean I could see dark clouds coming my way and knew a storm would be upon me in a short while. The incoming storm forced me to ride inland a short distance to take advantage of the trees for a little protection.

That first night, it seemed strange, making camp by myself, and as I sat eating my evening meal, I began to chuckle, then I leaned back and laughed out loud. I had just realized Monk was a better cook than me. I never cared much for cooking and kept it simple, whereas, Monk liked spices and went out of his way to search the woods to find whatever was available, and he almost always found something. And if he didn't, he carried a sack of dried peppers that he would use. Fortunately for me, Monk had slipped a good sized bag of peppers into my saddlebag.

Back in Portland, I had purchased a book written by a man called, Homer. It was a book of poetry. Now, ma always liked poetry, so that's why I bought it. The title seemed a bit odd to me, but what did I know about poetry. It was called, The Iliad and the Odyssey.

That night I found out what ma found interesting about poetry. The stories had highly developed characters, along with some fascinating settings. The Iliad, came first and the Odyssey was a sequel, coming sometime later. This Homer fella, had a way with words, for sure, and I spent several nights reading by the light of the campfire.

The next three weeks were for the most part, uneventful, except for the time when I saw a large buck deer standing with his head dipped in a small creek, taking his fill. I hadn't had any fresh meat in some time and the thought of a deer steak, sounded mighty fine to me.

I pulled my rifle from over my shoulder, where it rode most of the time, then took careful aim and pulled the trigger. And that's when the fun began. I quickly realized that my chestnut mare had never been fired off of and she took to bucking like the devil himself had landed on her back.

I dropped my rifle and grabbed for the reins that were hanging over the saddle horn, then pulled back with all my might, trying to get her head up so she wouldn't buck. As I said before, I don't believe in putting a bit in a horse's mouth, but right about then, I surely did wish I had some leverage. She went high in the air, kicked her hind legs out and twisted – and somewhere in all that, I went sailing into the air. I came down hard on my left shoulder and head.

I laid there for a good bit, trying to get my wind back and the pain in my neck, head and shoulder to go away. Once I could breathe, again, I climbed to my feet and looked around. The chestnut was standing a few yards away, cropping grass like nothing had happened.

After hobbling my horses, and unloading the pack, I walked over and picked up my rifle. It seemed none the worse for wear after being tossed onto the ground. I wiped it off, then propped it up against a nearby tree.

Still feeling pain in my neck and shoulder, and now my lower back, I went down to the creek to skin my deer and cut off a good size piece of flank meat. I'd earned it, for sure.

After putting a pot of beans on the fire to cook, I hung the piece of deer meat over the fire and watched as what little fat there was, dripped into the flames, making a cackling noise.

I cut some strips for jerky and hung them up to dry. The rest, I bundled into the skin and hoped I would run into some Indians to give it to. There was just too much meat for me and I hated wasting it.

I savored every bite and for the first time in quite a while, my stomach was bulging full.

I was sitting propped against a tree, enjoying a final cup of coffee when I heard the sound of soft footsteps, like someone wearing moccasins had stepped on a stick. And that someone was very light in weight. I stood up and picked up my rifle and stepped back into the shadow of the trees, and waited.

Within seconds, a man, woman and small boy stepped into the firelight, The man carried a rifle, and had a knife strapped to his side. They sort of looked like Indians, only different. I met my first people who called themselves, Mexican.

When I stepped out from the trees, he raised his hand in the air, palm forward – the sign of peace. I returned the salute and motioned for them to come closer to the fire. I could see them eyeing the deer meat and knew they must be hungry.

"I don't have much but you're welcome to what I have," I said, thinking he didn't understand a word I'd said. But to my astonishment, he said, "Thank you."

"You... you speak English?" I asked.

He smiled and said, "Yes, we all learned the white man's language from the nuns down in the mission in San Francisco. They have a small school there for any of us who want to learn. Mexicans or Indians."

When I told them they could have the rest of the deer meat and some beans and coffee, without a word, the woman began immediately to prepare their meal. And without being told, the boy, who looked to be about ten, went off into the forest and returned shortly with an armload of firewood.

As it turned out, his name was Carlos, and hers was Carmalita. The boy, they called, Tomas.

When I asked about San Francisco, Carlos frowned and said, "It is not a good place to go if you are not staying at the mission."

Carmalita had made some round, thin bread she called tortillas, which she offered some to me, and after I had taken one, filled with beans, meat and peppers, she said, "There are many bad people there. We barely got away."

I wasn't sure what to make of this news. I'd heard San Francisco was a boom town, but I'd not heard it spoken of as a place to steer clear of. "So… what's so bad about it?"

The boy, the one they called, Tomas, looked at his mother and father, obviously wanting to speak. Carlos nodded his head.

"They tried to capture us and make slaves of us. Mother would have been sent to one of the many houses where men go to find a woman. Father was to be sold to a ship's captain as a deck hand, and I was to be sent to work in a mine, somewhere far away."

I guess my jaw must have been hanging slack because Carlos spoke up, saying, "Tomas overheard them talking. We had been captured and they did not know he could understand their words. When one of the guards came to get us, I overpowered him and we escaped. We've been running for the past two days with no food or water."

Just then, I saw the boy's head turn and look into the trees. He'd heard the same thing I had – the sound of horses.

"Quickly, get into the trees!", I told them, grabbing up my rifle.

In the blink of an eye, they were gone, taking any and all evidence of them being there, with them. I grabbed a piece of brush and began sweeping the area to wipe away any footprints. I had just finished and was squatting next to the fire, pouring myself a cup of coffee when they rode into my camp. There were four of them – all, mean looking, men.

"Howdy," I called out. "Step down. Ain't got much in the way of grub, but the coffee's fresh."

They sat their horses and stared at me. Finally, one of them said, "We're looking for some runaways – Mexican man with his woman and brat. You seen 'em?"

I shook my head and said, "I haven't seen nor talked to anyone in over a week, til you fellas showed up."

One of the men in the back rode up and whispered something to the man who had been talking, and after a moment, he nodded his head and turned back to me. And I for sure didn't like the look in his eyes.

He pulled his pistol and pointed it at me and said, "Guess we won't go back empty handed, after all."

Well, that was all the information I needed to know. They planned to take me captive. I raised both hands in the air, saying, "Now just wait a minute." Then before they could react, I pitched my hot coffee at them and waved my arms, yelling, "Yaaaaa! Yaaaaa!"

That spooked the horses and they commenced to start jumping around, spilling their riders on the ground.

By the time the dust cleared I had my rifle pointed at them asking, "Which one of you wants to die, first?"

Carlos came out of the woods and went to them, collecting their sidearms, then took control of their horses. He then tied them up.

"What're you plannin' on doin' with us?" one of them asked.

I looked at Carlos and winked, then said, "I've been giving that some thought and the way I see it; I have two choices. First, I could tie each of you to a tree, and let Carlos here have a little target practice for what you intended to do to him and his family... But I'm kinda leaning toward my second choice, which is to stake each of you out on the ground, spread eagle and pour some honey on you, then leave you to the wild critters. But since I'm a man who believes in fair play, I'm going to let you choose your fate. Who's gonna speak up first?"

Carlos turned and walked back into the woods so they wouldn't see him grinning.

One of the men looked up at me and said, "You won't get away with this, mister. You don't know who you're dealin' with."

"And just who am I dealing with?" I asked, pouring another cup of coffee.

"Blackjack Dawson, that's who," one of the others said.

"And this, Blackjack Dawson, he supposed to be a real bad hombre, is he?" I asked nonchalantly.

"You'll find out, soon enough," one of them said. "If you know what's good for you, you'll let us go."

I shook my head and said, "I don't recall that being one of the options."

One at a time, we walked them over, sat them down next to a tree, then tied each man to the tree.

"Get a good nights sleep boys. The official court and sentencing will be in the morning right after we have our breakfast."

"What about us? Don't we get a last meal?" one of them asked.

I looked at him and said, "Now why would we do that. It would in the end, just be a waste of good food."

The four of us took turns, keeping the fire going and watching over our prisoners. I took the first watch, Tomas the second, Carlos the third and Carmalita taking the last watch so she could cook the rest of the deer meat and have coffee ready when we woke up.

When morning came, I woke up to the smell of coffee. Carlos and Tomas were already up and ready for whatever I had in mind.

After breakfast, we gathered in front of the prisoners and I held court, naming them as men who were paid kidnappers, for which the penalty was a firing squad.

Their protesting sounded like a bunch of hens being chased by a fox. I raised my hands and they got quiet. "Since I had a good night's sleep and now have a full stomach, I'm feeling a little bit lenient."

With that, we stood them up and marched them down to the beach, where they were instructed to strip down. They protested because of the woman being there, but she giggled and turned her back to them.

Barefoot from head to toe, I made them lie down face first on the sand, about ten feet apart.

I said goodbye to Carlos and his family, handing him the reins to the men's horses, then mounted the chestnut, leading my packhorse, and headed south.

CHASING THE NEXT SUNRISE

A short distance down the beach, I looked back over my shoulder and saw the four men standing – looking at Carlos and his family as they rode hard toward the north, leaving them, naked and afoot.

TWENTY-ONE

Riding in from the north, San Francisco was a lot more than I expected. I had thought of it as not much more than a fishing village sitting on the shore next to the ocean. I must have sat on my horse for close to half an hour, looking the place, over.

San Francisco sat on a large group of rolling hills and the bay was filled with ships of all size and description. A cloud of dark smoke covered a section of the town down close to the waterfront.

As I rode into town, I could see building going on, and the area I was passing through looked to be the rich part of town because the houses being built were humongous in size that flaunted great wealth.

The closer I got to the waterfront, the dirtier the town became. The streets were littered with trash and drunken sailors. There were houses where scantily dressed women stood outside on the sidewalk, offering pleasures beyond your imagination. I could smell the pungent odor of something Carlos warned me about. He said it was called, opium, and you smoked it in a pipe. It was supposed to take you to a place of euphoria, but in truth, just made you sleep and dream weird dreams, along with making you addicted to it. It was definitely not a place I would be going.

There were more bars in one place than I'd ever seen before. San Francisco was without a doubt, a very large den of inequity, and my first instinct was to turn around and keep right on riding… Which, as it turned out, I should have done.

My problem was, I had spent over a year living on the back of a horse and I was tired of traveling. During that time, my thirty-ninth birthday had come and gone and I just wanted to spend a few days with plenty of food to eat and a bed to sleep on at night.

Not far from the water, I saw a place where I could board the horses and not far from there, a hotel that had a restaurant attached to it.

The man at the livery stable eyed me for some time before agreeing to board my horses for a week, which is the amount of time I thought I

121

would need to recuperate – and he wanted cash up front – which should have been a warning.

As I handed him money for payment in advance, he looked at me and said, "You don't look like the kind of man who belongs in a place like this."

"And what kind of man would that be?" I asked, with a grin.

"Thieves, sailors and no-goods," he said, nodding his head up and down.

I stood there for a minute, looking at him, before I replied. "I've done my fair share of sailing, and might travel that way, again, but only as a last resort. I'm definitely not a thief, and I'm hoping I don't fall into that last category."

He got a puzzled look on his face and asked, "You come here looking for work?"

I shook my head and said, "No, at least not in this town. It's a mite too wild for my taste. It reminds me too much of London. I just need a few days of rest and some decent food in my belly."

"Well, best of luck with that," he said as he checked over the horses. As I turned to go, he called out to me, "The chestnut has a loose shoe on the left rear hoof. You want me to fix it?"

I turned back and said, "They've had a long trip, and maybe a longer one, yet to go… How much to reshoe both horses?"

"Buck and a half, each," he said without hesitation.

I dug in my pocket and gave him four dollars, saying "Do a good job."

The hotel looked better on the outside than it did on the inside and I decided to only get a room for the night. I could look for a better place to stay, come morning. And when I went into the restaurant, it was dirty and stunk of fish and used grease. I was about to turn around and try to find a better place when a young, oriental woman came up to me and said, "You come this way, prese."

For some reason I followed her to a table in the far back of the room, close to a door leading outside. And when I sat down, the hair on the back of my neck stood on end as Carlos' words sounded in my head. "Beware of the Orientals. They're never to be trusted."

"I bring you the special," she said. "You rike, berry good."

And with that she turned and walked away just as a young oriental man set a pot of tea on the table, along with a fancy, decorated cup.

He had a sleezy look about him and a sing-song voice. "You drink tea. It, special. Take all cares and troubles away."

And before I could ask any questions, he was gone, and the young lady reappeared with a bowl of something that smelled good. "This, Won Ton soup. Berrie good. You eat while food cooking."

I tasted the watery soup, and it did taste good. I wasn't sure that it was because the soup tasted good, or that I was hungry.

She pointed her finger at me and said, "Don't forget to drink, tea. Berrie good tea – berrie good for you."

Now, normally, I pick up on warning signals right away, but for some reason, it didn't happen this time. I finished off the soup in quick order and poured myself some tea, and took a sip. It tasted different than any tea I'd ever drank, before, but not in a bad way. It had a hint of mint to it, along with the sweet taste of something I couldn't identify.

As I waited for my meal to arrive, I downed two cups of the tea and indeed begin to feel relaxed. So relaxed, in fact that I fell into a deep sleep.

Morning came with a splitting headache and the stench of dirty bodies mixed with salt air. I immediately identified the pitch and roll of a ship. I opened my eyes and saw that I was in the hold of a ship that was idly rocking back and forth. Another man, a little older than me was also just waking up and looking around.

"You have supper at the Chinese restaurant, too?" I asked.

"What? Ahh, yeah, I did. What am I doing here?" he asked, rubbing his temples.

"Looks like we've been shanghaied," I said with a sheepish grin. I couldn't believe I had been that naive.

He shook the cobwebs from his brain and stuck out his hand. "Rufus Dunhill," he said.

I shook his hand and said, "Jubal Courtney."

We told each other about what brought us to San Francisco, and as it turned out, Rufus was from a place called, Colorado, where he said he had a gold mine. He'd ordered a piece of equipment and had come to San Francisco to pick it up.

"Guess they'll be wondering where I am, when I don't show up today," he said, standing up and stretching.

After looking around, he asked, "So, what do we do about getting out of here? I've got no hankering to be a sailor."

I looked around and saw we were in a barred cage. "Not much we can do until we figure out how to get out of this cage."

"Dere might be a vey," a voice from the other end of the cage, said.

A barrel sized man walked up to us and said, "Lars Hollinbooster, is my name and I tink I know how vee can get out of here. Dat is if vee all verk together.

"If you've got a plan, I'd like to hear it," I told him.

"I been lookin' at dem bars and I tink we can pull 'em apart vide enough ta squeeze trough. You two on one bar and me on da otter."

So, with mine and Rufus' feet on Lars' bar and pulling on our bar and Swen doing the same, we put our backs into it and little by little the bars began to spread apart. After close to half an hour of grunting and straining, the bars were spread apart wide enough for us to squeeze through.

Lars came through the opening last and when we were outside the cage, we heard the anchor being pulled up and the boat begin to move.

"We need to do something and do it quick, or we'll be out to sea where there won't be any chance to escape," Rufus said.

I looked at my two new friends and asked, "Can you boys swim?"

Both of them nodded their heads, yes, and I continued. "Our best bet is to get up on the deck, undetected, then run for the side of the ship and jump overboard. Then swim as far, underwater, as you can so they can't shoot us before we get ashore."

"Goot plan," Lars said and started for the ladder leading up to the deck.

At the top, Lars held his hand up, indicating we hold up and wait.

After about two minutes, he put his finger to his mouth for silence, then pointed toward the opening that led out onto the deck.

Trying to look like we belonged there, we walked out onto the deck and began making our way toward the port side of the ship, which was closest to the shore. The ship was gaining speed as the sheets were being unfurled and tied off.

We were within ten feet of the railing when someone yelled, "You there! Hold up!"

"Run!" I yelled and ran for the side, diving head first into the water. I dove deep and swam as hard and fast as I could in the direction of the shore. Balls of lead were making long streams all around me as they shot at us. I could only hope my new friends had not been hit.

When I could hold my breath no longer, I rose to the surface and only put my mouth above water and took a deep breath, then sank down again, and began to swim.

By the time I was out of air, again, I was in shallow water and rose to my feet and began to run for dry land. I heard splashing and looked to my right to see, both, Lars and Rufus running for land, too.

Once we were out of the water, we ran between two warehouses before we stopped to catch our breath.

"Lars has been shot," Rufus said.

"Yust ah flesh vound, I'm tinkin'," Lars said trying to look over his shoulder at his wound.

After Lars took off his shirt, I did a quick examination and sure enough, the bullet had just grazed the backside of his shoulder.

Taking no chances, we left the area and headed away from the waterfront.

When we reached the summit of a large hill, we stopped and looked back. The bay, with its many ships, was like a panoramic view – something like you'd see in a painting that hangs in the entryway of a museum.

But most importantly, we saw the ship we'd jumped from, heading out to sea.

"Guess we weren't important enough for them to stop and come looking for us," Rufus said with a big grin.

What we heard next, caused both Rufus and me to turn our heads and look at Lars.

"Damnation! he yelled, patting his pants pockets. "Dey took my money!"

My hands went immediately to my waist and I felt the anger welling up inside me.

"And mine, too!" Rufus said, stomping his foot on the ground.

"Vell, dat just does it!" Lars said. "I've got ah goot mind ta go down ta that place wheere vee vas kidnapped, and demand my money back!"

"While that sounds like a good plan, I seriously doubt they will even admit to have stolen it," I told him.

"But what if there was another way? All three of us were robbed and are broke, right?"

Both Lars and I nodded our heads as Rufus continued.

"I don't know about you two, but they took more than a thousand dollars from me – money I was going to use to pay for that gold mining equipment I ordered from Germany."

"I didn't have that kind of money, but I did had a little over three hundred dollars that I sure would like to have, back," I told them.

We looked at Lars, who puffed air into his cheeks, then blew it out. "I had more 'n tree tousand dollars, and I vant it back, so, vatever plan you got, I'm in."

It was close to midnight when we eased in the backdoor of the Chinese restaurant, into a dark room near the hallway and hid so we could plan what we were going to do, next.

Before anything was said, Rufus pointed down the back of the hallway to where light was coming from another room.

The restaurant area was filled with the noise of people talking, and eating, but the hallway was clear, except for young women coming and going from the kitchen with food and orders. They were speaking in Chinese so we couldn't understand what they were saying, but since no one was looking in our direction, we weren't noticed. When the hallway became clear, we rushed into the lighted room and saw an overweight Chinese man sitting at a desk, counting money.

As I closed the door and propped a chair under the latch, he jumped to his feet, and yelled something in Chinese. I didn't know what he said, but it was pretty clear he was calling for help.

Lars and Rufus rushed the man as he was trying to pull a pistol from the desk drawer.

Like I said, earlier, Lars was a swede and a big one at that, and when the Chinaman stuck his hand into the drawer, Lars hit him alongside his head and he went limp. The box on the desk was filled with money, with more in piles on the desk.

"Looks like more than enough to recoup what they took from us," I said.

Rufus wasn't satisfied with just taking what was owed us. "For what they did to us we deserve it all. And as far as I'm concerned, it isn't near enough. I want revenge for what they did to us and who knows how many others. I say we make them pay where it hurts them the most…

Just then someone out in the hall crashed against the door and the door and chair came flying into the room.

Suddenly, the room got crowded, as four, very large Chinese men came rushing in with clubs in their hands.

Lars grabbed the first one and smashed his fist into the man's face, breaking his nose and sending him to dreamland.

The second man swung his stick at my head and I ducked under it and drove my fist into his stomach. I heard a whish of air as I followed with an uppercut to his jaw.

He staggered back only a step and I could see the hate in his eyes as he swung the club, again, and this time it landed against my left shoulder.

I reacted by grabbing his arm and jerking him toward me, and at the same time, bringing my knee up against the back of his arm and pushing down against the top. I heard his arm break and the scream that erupted from his mouth.

Instead of joining the fracas, Rufus reached into the desk drawer and pulled out the pistol, then shot the man closest to him, in the shoulder.

The sound of the pistol going off stopped the fight as Rufus trained the pistol on the others. "Just stand still!" he yelled. And when they did, he motioned for them to go to the far side of the room and lay, face down on the floor.

I rummaged around and found several more pistols, then slapped the Chinaman's face until he came back to life.

With a pistol in one hand and a sack, filled with the money, tucked under my other arm, we took the Chinaman and the four bodyguards in tow and marched them into the main room where Rufus told them to go stand with the people staring back at us.

CHASING THE NEXT SUNRISE

Brandishing a pistol in each hand, Rufus ordered everyone out of the restaurant, and as an enticement, he fired a warning shot into the ceiling.

Like a stampeding herd of cattle, they ran for the front door. And when the place was empty, Rufus went around dumping bottles of alcohol onto the floor and furniture.

When he was satisfied, he went behind the bar and found a box of lucifers and told Lars and me go to the back door and wait.

Rufus lit three of the matches and threw them into the pools of liquor, which immediately caught fire.

We must have run close to three miles before reaching the top of a steep hill, where Rufus called out for us to stop. And as we stood there, trying to get our wind back, we could see the flames shooting into the sky.

While I thought we had our revenge by taking the money and burning the place to the ground, making it difficult for him to go back into business anytime soon, I sincerely hoped none of the buildings close to the burning one, caught on fire. I would hate for innocent people to lose their property or their lives.

Come daylight, we ventured back down to see what damage we'd done and I was grateful to find out that a water brigade had come together and the only building damaged was the one that belonged to the Chinaman. And to our delight, it was completely gutted.

We eased back from our hiding place and went down to the stables. While everyone was concerned with the fire, I figured we could get our business taken care of without being noticed. I retrieved my horses and gear, while Rufus was haggling with the blacksmith over a wagon and four oxen to pull it. The smithy was glad to get rid of the oxen which made the dealing easier. I thought I could have made a better deal, but it wasn't my haggle, so I kept my mouth shut. With Lars, also buying a horse and saddle, the man could see a prosperous day and finally gave in.

Rufus mounted the wagon and we headed for the backdoor of one of the many warehouses.

We helped Rufus load all the things he'd ordered – lumber, a roll of heavy screen, bolts and nuts, two sledge hammers, two picks, four shovels, and several boxes of dynamite, along with an apparatus he called a shaker for separating gold from the dirt.

Rufus paid a man to watch over the wagon, oxen, and riding stock, along with the pack horse, while we went up the street to a small café and had breakfast.

It was during our breakfast that Rufus made us a deal we couldn't refuse.

TWENTY-TWO

"Gentlemen," Rufus said as he took a sip of coffee. We'd just finished a breakfast of steak, eggs, fried potatoes, homemade bread, with butter and jam, and a bowl of bright red strawberries that would melt in your mouth.

"I think the three of us make a pretty good team. I was going to see to this once I got back, but I've had a change of heart. Instead of hiring day labor back in Colorado – men who would slit your throat for five dollars, I would much rather take the two of you on as my partners. There's plenty enough for all of us. I know there is."

Rufus was grinning from ear to ear and I could hear the excitement in his voice.

"Whoa! Hold on, partner. I don't think either of us has the slightest idea what you're talking about," I said, pointing at Lars.

"Ya. I don't know, eider," Lars said, shaking his head from side to side.

Rufus looked at us like we must be dumber than a rock, and finally said, "My gold mine. I want to make you equal partners in my gold mine back in Colorado. What do you think all those supplies we loaded, are for?"

"You want to give Lars and me equal shares in a gold mine in Colorado? Is that what you're telling us?"

"Couldn't be no plainer than that," Rufus said, grinning like he'd just done the greatest thing in the world.

"And juss where in Colorado is dis golt mine?" Lars asked.

"A couple hundred miles north and a wee bit west of Denver – high up in the Rocky Mountains. It's there, boys, I swear on my mother's grave, it is."

"Well, if it's so gal-darned rich, why would you be cutting us in on it without us putting up some money? You aren't asking us for money, are you?" I asked. I couldn't see Rufus as a man who would hoodwink us, but truth be told, I didn't know him all that well.

130

Again, he looked at me like I'd just said the stupidest thing ever spoken. "What are you talking about? I don't want your money. I'm trying to make you rich!"

I raised my hands and said, "My new friend, this all sounds too good to be true. Now, why don't you start at the beginning so we'll have a better understanding of what you're talking about."

"You're right," he said. "I guess I got carried away. I apologize. Okay, I'm not originally from Colorado. I was born in the swamps of Louisiana and grew up on the streets of New Orleans. Four years ago, I lit out to seek my fortune. Up in St. Louis, I hired on as a wagon driver in a wagon train going to Denver. While I was in Denver, I heard about the fur trapping going on up in the higher elevations. I'm a born trapper, alligators and such, so… I bought a horse and some gear and headed off."

He stopped and took a drink of his coffee, then continued. "That first year, I trapped a whole slew of beaver and one bear, and came close to losing my hair to a Cheyenne warrior on more than one occasion. I was camped along a river and one afternoon when I bent down to collect some water for coffee, something caught my eye."

He grinned at us and asked, "You got any idea what it was?"

"I'm guessing… a gold nugget," I said.

"As big as my thumb!" he said. "Well-sir, right then and there I quit the fur business and went into the gold business. And for the next two years, I panned up that river, hunting for the source and when I found the place where the water came out of the side of the mountain, forming the river, I knew that's where I would find the motherlode. Oh, I had a sack full of nuggets I'd panned from the river, but the real gold is inside that mountain.

"I went back down to Denver and staked me a claim on that site, but didn't tell him why. I said I wanted to homestead the area. Course he thought I was nuttier than a fruit cake. Said the Indians would have my scalp in less than a month."

"But he filled out da paper for you ta own da land?" Lars asked.

"He did, my friend. He did indeed. I left his office feeling mighty proud of myself. Next, I went to the assayer's office to cash in some of my gold. And when the man asked where I'd gotten it, I told him I got it not far to the south. A place they called Cherry Creek, not wanting to disclose the real location. Well now, he got all excited and as soon as he gave me my money, he closed up the office and lit out like his tail was on fire. Funny thing is, I found out, later, there was gold in that creek. Anyway, I bought a couple of mules, a second horse and some pickaxes, and shovels, along with some food, blankets and other stuff I figured I'd need and went back up to my mountain."

He stopped again and took another drink of coffee before he continued. "The day after I got back, I started digging into the side of that mountain – my mountain. And I'm here to tell you, it's hard, back breaking work, but the further I went, the more gold I found. The motherlode can't be much farther in. But a mine needs to be shored up or it'll cave in on you. I knew I needed help, but who would I get that I could trust? I couldn't just hire anybody or I'd go to sleep one night and never wake up. Anyway, I went back down to Denver to buy a piece of equipment, called a shaker, and a drill, but there was none to be found. Fella that owned one of the general stores, looked through his catalog and came up with what I needed – but it would have to come from Germany and I'd have to go to San Francisco to pick it up. And there you have it, boys. Course you know the rest. So, what 'ya say, you want to be my partners?"

Lars and I looked at each other, grinning like a couple of schoolboys who'd just pulled one over on the teacher.

After handshakes all around, I found myself a one third owner in a gold mine. All I needed to do now, was go there and dig it out, which sounds easier than it is.

A man just never knows where his future might lie, or what fate has in store for him. Just yesterday, I was a shanghaied sailor on a ship, and today I'm part owner in a gold mine, back in Colorado – wherever that is?

Suddenly, Lars pointed toward the large window in the front of the restaurant and said, "Maybe vee shoot look fer da back door."

When I turned my head and looked, I got goose bumps – There were six, very large Chinamen coming toward the restaurant, carrying clubs.

It was a good thing we'd tied off the horses and wagons out in back of the restaurant, otherwise we might have had a serious problem.

We rode off in a hurry and turned away from the restaurant at the first alley we came to. I hung back a little to make sure we weren't being followed, and gave a sigh when no one came out of the back door of the restaurant.

San Francisco sits on a point of land and to get to the other side of the peninsula, you have to either, drive several days away from the city, or take the ferry. The ferry was our best option and we took it.

We were well into the night before we stopped in a grove of trees to give the animals some rest and get a little shuteye, ourselves.

I took the first watch, Rufus the second, and Lars the third – and when I felt someone nudge my foot, I opened my eyes and looked up to see Lars holding out a cup of coffee in my direction. "Bacon and pan bread is on da fire. Vee shoot leave soon."

After cleaning up and loading our gear, we headed, north by northeast at a steady pace.

The oxen were strong and had no problem pulling the wagon. Truth be told, they were better than horses. An oxen can go all day long, and with just a little rest, do it all over again.

We were a week and a half into the trip when the country began to change. The land ahead of us was beginning to rise and the land was covered with pine trees – some, quite large.

Then we moved into a forest that took my breath away. The trees were several hundred feet tall and some of them took a good five minutes to walk around. I had never seen anything like them. Rufus said they were called, Redwoods.

Whatever they were called, they were the biggest trees I'd ever seen, or ever would see. I guessed, just one of them would provide enough lumber to build more than a hundred homes, or maybe a small town.

By now, with the going much steeper, we were lucky to make seven miles a day. Up to now we'd made ten to twelve miles per day.

Rufus was insistent that we not push the animals too hard, saying, "The gold has been inside that mountain for gawd only knows how long, and it will still be there when we get back. It ain't going no place."

We'd been on the trail for a little over two weeks when we saw several trails of smoke rising into the air, not far up in front of us and we hauled up.

Rufus looked at us and said, pointing toward the smoke. "Paiute Indian camp. They're friendly enough. Met them on my way to San Francisco. They like to trade, so I brought along some trade stuff."

They were camped along the shore of a huge lake that had glistening, clear water.

The village was filled with cone shaped huts called Wickiups, that were made of willow boughs, and covered with branches, grass and brush. There was a small, smoke hole at the top and that's where the smoke was coming from.

None of us could understand their language, but when Rufus brought out knives, blankets, a few mirrors and some fishing gear, like – hooks and line, they smiled and the trading began.

Even though we didn't speak the same language, there was enough hand signals and head shaking to make the trading interesting. They smiled and laughed a lot as though they thought they were getting the better part of the bargain. And maybe they were? Who knew?

We stayed there only two days, but when we left, we had rice, dried fish, dried meat of several animals, and each of us, a fur robe made from rabbit skins, which Rufus said we would need where we were going. We also left with four large bladders of water, which Rufus was glad to get, and it wasn't long before we understood why.

The next three weeks were the hardest so far. We were crossing land that I guessed had never been inhabited since the beginning of time, which one day, would turn out to be untrue. We had stopped for a noon meal and water and feed for the animals. The temperature was scorching hot, with a strong, hot wind blowing across the land, forcing us to put masks over our faces. My shirt was drenched with sweat, but even so, I was in need of some exercise. Sitting astraddle a horse for several hours can cause your legs and feet to go to sleep.

I walked out a good way from our camp and was turning to go back when something caught my eye. And when I walked over to see what it was, I stopped and stared. "Hey," I called out and when Rufus and Lars ran up, I pointed down at the largest bone I had ever seen. It was a good nine or ten feet long. "What kind of creature do you think this came from?" I asked.

Rufus, the only one of us who had been through this area grinned and said, "One of them dinosaur bones would be my guess."

"Dinia what?" I asked.

Lars reached down and lifted one end up. It was a good bit longer than he was tall. He shook his head and said, "I voud not vant ta meet up vit dis one in the dark, nor da day time, eider."

We all laughed as Rufus went on to explain, "They say, thousands or maybe it was millions of years ago, giant creatures roamed this part of the country. I heard one fella say there were birds with a thirty foot wingspan that was a flesh eater. All kinds of weird looking animals. Nobody seems to know why, but all of a sudden, they just up and died – and from time to time travelers find bones like this one.

We went on, but I kept a watchful eye at the sky in case one of them huge flesh eating birds happened to be in the neighborhood.

"How did dey survive in all dis dry land vit no vater?" Lars asked.

"Maybe that's why they died off? Too hot and no water," I said.

Three days later, we saw the sun glimmering on a large body of water. Both Lars and I urged our horses into a trot, eager to reach the water where we could cool off and drink our fill, but Rufus put a halt to that.

"Hold on, pilgrims. That lake ain't for drinking or bathing, for that matter."

"What are you talking about. Look at it," I said. "It's a huge lake with enough water for everybody!"

"Not that lake," Rufus said, shaking his head from side to side. "It's saltier than the ocean."

"What?" That can't be. It's too far inland to be salty," I told him.

"Maybe so," he said, "but the fact is, it's got a higher salt content than the ocean."

I shook my head from side to side. I was having a hard time believing a body of water this far inland could be salty.

"Is dere any drinking vater anywhere near here? I'm almost out," Lars asked.

"There's an Indian village on the far side of the lake and they have a hand dug well and the water isn't too brackish to drink. But you'll have to pay to get it and I don't mean with money."

"What is it they want?" I asked.

"They're Utes, and they want rifles, powder and lead," Rufus told us matter of factly.

"And what if I don't have any of those things or don't want to let go of what I've got?" I asked.

"Then I guess you would need a good supply of water still in your bladders because if you don't, you're gonna get mighty thirsty. The next water is more than a hundred miles from here – across some very rugged country. Worse than what we've just come through."

"It would have been nice if you had explained this piece of news, before we left, so we could have come prepared," I told Rufus, my hackles up a bit.

"Lars nodded his head and said, "Ya, dat voud have been goot ta know."

"Relax, gentlemen. I didn't want you spending your money. I came prepared.

Just then, six Indians on horseback came riding toward us with rifles in their hands. Utes – the first I'd ever seen. There was no doubt, these were fighting men. "Are they friendly?" I asked reaching for my own rifle.

"Depends," Rufus said. "And I wouldn't draw that rifle out if I was you."

I lifted my hand away from my rifle, but kept it close to my handgun hanging on my right hip.

My next surprise came when they rode right up to us and one of them asked, in English, "You come looking for water?"

"We do," Rufus said. "And we come in peace, bearing gifts for the great Ute warriors."

"And what is this great gift you speak of?" one of the other braves, asked.

"Two rifles, and two bags of lead and powder – plus, a bag of sugar."

I saw their eyes light up when Rufus mentioned sugar.

"You good man. I remember you from last time you come through," the brave said.

They led us into the center of the village where a large hand dug well, with a covering over the hole.

Two white men were standing not far away, with sullen looks on their faces.

Rufus walked over to them and asked, "Where are you boys headed?"

The taller of the two nodded his head toward the northwest and said, "We're trying to get to the coast, a town called, Seattle, but we're in need of water but these heathens won't allow us to get near that well, and did you know that lake over there is salty?"

"I take it you don't have anything to trade for water, right?" Rufus asked.

"We got beads, some chocolate, a few small mirrors and some needles and thread," the shorter man said.

"But they want guns, lead and powder," Rufus said, in his all knowing way.

"That's about the size of it," the shorter man said.

Rufus turned and said over his shoulder, "Let me see what I can do."

Rufus and their head man spent some time arguing and shaking their heads, but finally we watched as they shook hands.

Rufus waved the two men over and told them, "Fill up you water bladders and leave all your booty for the women to sort through. I've thrown in an extra bag of powder from what we're giving them. Be quick about it and be on your way before he changes his mind."

They thanked Rufus and did as he said, and were soon riding west at a lope.

We too were quick about loading up with water and leaving the village. And I have to say at this point, I was happy to be away from them. I didn't like the way they looked at us, not knowing that one day in the future, the Colorado Utes and I would not see eye to eye.

TWENTY-THREE

For the next several weeks, we traveled over hills, across miles of barren land, only to have to find a way between or over as rugged terrain as I had ever encountered. We cut trees that we tied to the sides of the wagon to help support the weight when we crossed three, wide - deep rivers. First, Rufus swam the oxen across the river towing a long rope attached to the wagon, and when he got to the other side, he urged the oxen up the slope, dragging the wagon across the river. Lars and I rode our horses as they swam alongside the wagon to keep it from floating down the river. Not an easy feat, I assure you.

Each time, when we were on the far side of the river, we had to stop and make camp to rest the animals.

We were, little by little, gaining altitude and the air was thinner and much colder at night. I knew absolutely nothing about the mountains that would be my home for a good many years to come. But at first sight, they were both, terrifying and beautiful. The giant forests and snow-covered tops made them look unconquerable. But Rufus assured us they were not. So, on we went.

By the time we reached the mine, at least a foot of snow covered the ground and the wind had a mean bite to it that would make a normal man, weep.

The first thing we saw was the mouth of the mine – an opening in the side of the mountain no more than eight feet high and six feet across.

Not far from it sat a small, one room log cabin.

"Well, boys," Rufus said, grinning and pointing, "Here we are!"

When he saw the look on our faces, he said, "I know it's a bit small and we'll need to expand it some so you boys will have your own room, but that shouldn't take too long. It will be fine. You'll see."

It took a week of cutting down trees, trimming off the branches and notching the logs before setting them in place to make the cabin larger. Then we had to make mud to pack between the logs to keep the wind and weather out – and I came to believe that was the hardest part. The temperature was down around zero and the ground was frozen, which meant it would take picks and shovels, and dynamite to get enough to put in buckets that we added water to and set next to a fire we built. And we had to be quick about putting the mud into the cracks or it would freeze and we would have to reheat it.

I got frostbite on two of my fingers, which still bothers me, all these years later.

Then came the blowing snow that left close to four feet on the ground and to make things worse, the temperature plummeted to twenty below.

"Dis is not quite vhat I expected," Lars said one evening as we sat around the open fire pit that sat in the center of the main part of the cabin. "Too much like Sveden."

There was a smoke hole at the top, but even so, the room was still filled with smoke. At least we were warm and protected from the howling wind and blowing snow.

"How long does it last?" I asked.

Rufus rubbed his whiskered jaw and said, "Bout eight or nine months out of the year, but it isn't always this bad. Most of the time we can shovel a path to the mine and once we're inside, we're out of the weather.

"How long before vee can go inside da mine ta see da golt?" Lars asked.

Rufus thought for a moment, then said, "I'm hopin' as soon as the storm passes over."

"And how long might that be?" I asked. I was anxious to see this gold mine we'd come so far to work.

Rufus took a sip of coffee and shrugged his shoulders and said, "Hopefully no more 'n a week or so."

His week turned into ten days. But we kept busy, learning about dry mining from Rufus, along with building furniture for our rooms. I built myself a bed and chair out of lumber we had stacked to the side for that purpose. I hung pegs on the walls of my bedroom so I could hang up what few clothes I had. I wouldn't have a mattress until spring when I could get enough grass and leaves to stuff the large, mattress bag Rufus suggested we purchase before we left San Francisco.

CHASING THE NEXT SUNRISE

On the morning of the eleventh day, the clouds disappeared and the sun shone brightly. When we opened the door of the cabin, we all laughed. Our entryway was blocked by a good five feet of snow.

Before making any attempt to leave, we filled buckets with snow and sat them close to the fire to thaw so we could have drinking water, along with water to do other things such as washing our eating and cooking utensils, our clothes and our bodies. When Rufus had first come up to this place, he brought along a washtub from Denver.

Next, we took turns shoveling a tunnel in the direction of the opening to the mine – which took us three days of hard work.

But finally, in the late afternoon of the third day, we heard Rufus yell, "Yee Haw!"

Lars and I ran up the passageway and got our first look at the inside of the mine, which to be honest, wasn't very impressive. Rufus had gone maybe twenty feet into the side of the mountain and had shored it up with logs.

"Well, here it is, boys," Rufus said, pointing at some dull looking yellow stuff in the wall of the shaft.

Lars got a questionable look on his face and asked, "Dis is vhat vee come all dis vay to find? Don't look like much to me."

Rufus patted Lars on the shoulder and said, "Yeah, you're right. Most folks think it's supposed to be shinny but raw ore isn't shinny at all."

He pulled out his knife and dug into the side of the shaft wall, prying out a small piece of gold, and handed it to Lars. "Your first gold nugget, partner."

Lars hefted it in his hand and said, "It be much heavier dan I taught."

"What you have in your hand, my friend is probably worth at least twenty dollars."

Lars was astonished. "Dis little piece of gold is vurt dat much?"

Not knowing anything about gold, I asked, "How much does gold sell for?"

"Depends on the grade, but gold like this, sells for ten to twenty dollars an ounce."

"You mean, a pound," I said.

"Nope. Gold is sold by the ounce," Rufus said, nodding his head. "Why else would we be up here - digging into the side of a mountain in freezing weather?"

Trying to work a gold mine, high up in the mountains, in the dead of winter held many obstacles. First, we were not deep enough into the mountain to try and use dynamite to help us get deeper. Second, the ground, while not frozen, was very hard and filled with sometimes very large rocks that had to be pried out of the wall, then broken up and put in buckets to be hauled outside and dumped. Problem number three – with snow as deep as we were tall, there was no place to dump the rocks, which still needed to be crushed into smaller stones to look for the gold. We had to wait for the spring thaw to set up the shaker Rufus loaded up back in San Francisco. Fourth, we had to shovel the snow to make places to dump the rocks we'd dug out of the mine.

We also had to dig paths into the forest to be able to cut down trees to use to shore up the walls and ceiling of the mine shaft so it wouldn't cave in on us.

During that first winter, we were lucky to make three feet a month with our digging. From time to time, we found small veins of gold, but not the motherlode Rufus was hoping for.

Spring brought new problems. Indians. Utes and Cheyenne in particular. Although we were later to also encounter the Shoshone, who were friendly.

The first attack came shortly after the big thaw. The temperature had come up to shirtsleeve weather, which melted the snow and left the ground ankle deep with mud.

We were putting the shaker together when they came out of the woods, screaming and yelling like demons. The air seemed to be filled with arrows. We turned and ran for the cabin where our rifles were hanging on pegs stuck into the wall. But before we could bring them to bare, the Indians were inside the cabin and it was hand to hand combat.

Rufus and I, each pulled our knives and began defending ourselves as best we could, but not Lars. He grabbed one of the braves and jerked him off his feet, then using him as a battering ram, drove most of the intruders back through the doorway.

With a few seconds of breathing room, Rufus and I grabbed our hand guns and ran outside, firing into the crowd of yelling, screaming, red men.

When four braves went down, the Indians turned tail and ran back into the woods, taking their dead with them. Lars started to follow them, but Rufus yelled, "Let 'em go!"

"But von't dey be back?" Lars asked.

"Probably," Rufus told us. "But not for a while. They need time to mourn their dead."

"Are there many Indians up here, and how often will they all be attacking us?" I asked, needing to know how safe we were, or weren't.

"The ones who attacked us, today, were Utes," Rufus said. "There are also, Cheyenne and Shoshone up here. I sorta made friends with the Shoshone when I first came up here, but you never know about Indians."

"Vhat aboot da Cheyenne you said ver also up here?"

Rufus stared off into the woods and said, "The Cheyenne are the worse of 'em. They're a proud bunch, and brave warriors, ever one of 'em. And they don't care much for white people."

"So, besides the possibility of the mine caving in on us, we also have the Indians to worry about?" I asked.

"I never said it would be easy," Rufus said as he walked into the cabin and began putting a pot of coffee together.

"Vell, dat seddles it den. Vee keep our rifles and pistols vit us all da time, now," Lars said, following Rufus into the cabin.

Me? I just stood there, staring off into the woods, wondering what the future held? And how long would I stay up here with just these two men to talk to? And to be honest with myself, I was missing talking to or being around someone from the opposite sex. Rufus said we needed just a little more gold before we could go down to Denver for a bit of a hooray, and some supplies.

I walked back up to where the shaker sat and picked up a hammer and some nails and began working on the completion of the shaker.

That night, I sat outside for a long while, just staring at the different constellations in the sky, thinking about how small and insignificant we are and how we think we're doing big things, when in reality, in comparison to Mother Nature and the universe, as individuals, we don't amount to much.

I sighed and got up, then after a moment, I went inside and went to bed. That night I dreamed some tremulous dreams.

It would be another month before Rufus declared we had enough gold to go down to Denver.

Excitement was high as we covered the entry to the mine with lumber nailed together.

The following morning, we nailed pieces of lumber across the doorway to the cabin, but knew if the Indians wanted in, there would be no stopping them. All we could do is hope the cabin would still be there when we returned.

Rufus drove the team of oxen while Lars and I rode alongside on our horses, with our rifles across our knees. My forty-first birthday had slipped past, five months ago and I hoped to celebrate while we were down in Denver.

TWENTY-FOUR

Spirits were high. We were going to Denver!

After turning my gold into money, the first thing I was going to do was get a hot bath and a shave. Rufus said there were places where women bath you and give you a shave, while plying you with liquor. … That sounded mighty fine to me. I hadn't seen a woman in better than a year.

We were laughing and joking instead of keeping a sharp eye out and suddenly, we found ourselves surrounded by Indians, all pointing arrows, and a few rifles at us.

One of the braves we considered to be the chief or head man, rode up next to the oxen and stared at them, then pointed at them as he turned his head and looked at Rufus.

"Oxen. They're called oxen," Rufus said.

"Ox… in," the brave said.

"Close enough," Rufus told him.

He then made motions with his hands like he was eating, and Rufus shook his head, no – then made a motion with his mouth like he was chewing tough leather.

The brave nodded, then rode over and looked into the back of the wagon, and after a moment, he reined his horse around and rode up next to me.

"Don't make any sudden moves," Rufus said.

"Won't," I said back.

Next, he rode over and looked at Lars, then turned and said something to the others, and they all laughed. I'd never heard an Indian laugh and suddenly I had a whole new insight to them. They were just people like the rest of us. I was sure they had wives and girlfriends, and children. And while their homes may be made of skins, or sticks, it was still, a home.

He rode back over and stopped next to me and made a motion for me to get off my horse, then made another hand movement I didn't understand. "What's he want?" I asked.

Rufus sighed. "He's challenging you to a fight. He wants your horse."

"And if I refuse to fight him?" I asked…

"Then he'll kill you and take the horse, anyway. Fight him, but let him win, but not too easy. These are Shoshone and they respect bravery, but hate cowards."

"But what about my horse?" I asked. I didn't want to give him my horse.

"Reckon losin' your horse is better'n losin' your scalp, or your life," Rufus said.

I looked him over. We were close to the same size – him being maybe an inch or two taller than me, but our weight was about the same. I stepped down and stood there, wondering what to do next.

He walked out away from the wagon, then turned and motioned for me to come to him. And when I got close, he drew his knife and pointed for me to do the same.

I stood there, my gut doing flip-flops. I was about to be in a knife fight with a Shoshone brave over a horse.

"What if I just give him the damn horse?" I asked Rufus.

"Not a good idea. He would believe you to be a coward and then we'd probably all die," Rufus said, shrugging his shoulders.

I sighed. I really wasn't in the mood for a knife fight, especially one where I might be killed.

I drew my knife and went into a fighting stance. He grinned and began to circle me, and I moved with him.

Suddenly, he darted in and swiped his knife at my stomach.

I was caught off guard and barely jumped back far enough to only feel the tip of his blade as it made a thin slice across my belly, which by the way, hurt.

He grinned and continued to circle around, darting at me with stabbing blows from time to time that I was able to jump away from.

I didn't want to kill him, but he wasn't leaving me much choice. Little by little I began to understand his moves and countered by cutting him on both arms and the back of the hand that he held his knife with.

The grin went away and a serious look replaced it. He became more cautious and the intensity of the battle grew a whole bunch more serious.

Once, he pretended to slip and go down on one knee and when he came up, he had a handful of dirt, which he tossed at my face as a distraction, then rushed in and drove the tip of his knife toward my stomach.

With dirt in my eyes and barely able to see, I felt the pain as the knife made its way into my stomach, which I found out later, how lucky I'd been. I'd moved just far enough to the side that the knife only cut the right side where no vital organs were hit.

Shaking my head to be able to see a little better, I continued on to my left, and when he turned to face me, swinging the knife in a backward slash, I switched hands with my knife and drove my right fist into his jaw, knocking him backward.

He regained his balance and came at me, again.

This time, I tossed my knife from hand to hand, making him stop to see which hand my knife was in…

I could feel the blood running down my body from the two wounds he'd inflicted on me and I knew I needed to end this before loss of blood made me too weak to fight.

This time, when he lunged at me, I didn't back away. Instead, I grabbed him by the wrist and drew the knife hand, upward, and stuck my right leg behind his left leg, and shoved.

He went down, flat on his back, and within a blink of an eye, I had the sharp side of my knife against his throat.

Without taking my eyes off him, I yelled, "Tell him to surrender and I will spare his life!"

And to my surprise, he looked up at me and said, in good English, "I understand you, white man and I surrender."

I looked at him and asked, "Why didn't you tell me earlier that you could speak the white man's language?"

"It is better you do not let your enemy know all there is to know about you," he said, still staring at me.

"But I'm not your enemy," I told him.

"But you are white. All whites are my enemy," he told me with a snarl.

"Not this white man," I said, as I released his wrist and stood up, holding out my hand to help him up.

He took it, and when he was on his feet, again, he walked over and took the reins of his horse and led it over to me and held the reins out to me. "You have won the fight; my horse is yours."

Knowing it would be an insult to refuse, I took the reins and as he walked away, I called out to him, "Hold up, just a minute."

I walked over and unsaddled my horse and led it over to the proud Shoshone brave and handed the reins toward him saying, "I make this gift to you as a friendship between us."

He stared at me for a long time, making me a little nervous. I was trying my best to show him that all whites are not his enemy, but I wasn't sure what kind of reaction he would have.

Finally, he spoke. "When an Indian receives a gift, he is obligated to give a gift in return. You won my horse in battle, so that cannot be my gift." He walked over and picked up his bow and quiver of arrows and came back and handed them to me.

"My gift to you, in friendship."

I took them and felt a little pride at what was happening. I was making friends with an Indian brave. He pulled out his knife and cut the palm of his hand, then said, "Give me your hand."

And when I did, he cut a small slice in the palm of my hand, then we shook hands, mixing our blood together.

"From this day forward, you will be the blood brother of Screaming Cougar and shall be called, White Wolf, for the Shoshone respect the wolf for his bravery. I cannot speak for the Ute or Cheyenne dogs, but you will be welcome in my camp should you come back this way."

I gripped his hand and said, "Brothers, forever. And you will always be welcome in my camp, wherever it may be."

We released our hands and he swung up onto my horse, gave a wild yell, then raced away.

"Well, now, don't that beat all I've ever seen," Rufus declared.

"Ya, you haft done good dis day, I tink," Lars said with a big grin.

Saddling the Indian pony was an experience I hadn't expected. Not only did he not like having a saddle on his back, he bucked and threw me off three times before I got him to settle down enough to ride, while both Rufus and Lars laughed hysterically. It took a while, but I finally found the humor in it.

CHASING THE NEXT SUNRISE

TWENTY-FIVE

From where we sat atop a knoll, Denver didn't impress me, much. Of course, the day being cold, windy, with a steady rain falling, didn't help.

We rode down the muddy street into the middle of town until we saw an assayer's office sign. What few people there were on the street paid us scant attention – they were far too intent on getting in out of the rain. At the front of the assayer's office, we tied up the horses and went inside. A big calendar on the back wall, read, May 6, 1843, still a few years before Denver officially became a town.

We must have looked a mess because the man behind the counter eyeballed us from head to foot. He was a small man with a bald head on top, and bulging eyes that nearly touched the glasses perched on his nose.

There was a sign on the wall behind him that read:

ARTIMUS POTTS, ASSAYER

"Yes?" he asked as though we had the plague.

Rufus walked up to the counter and said, as he tossed our three sacks onto the counter. "We have gold that needs assayin', Mister Potts."

He dumped the contents of one of the bags out on the counter and stared at it before picking up one of the nuggets and looking at it through a piece of magnifying glass.

He set the nugget on the counter, then weighed it on a scale, and when he was finished, he looked at Rufus and asked, "Where did you get this?"

Rufus grinned and said, "Why, out of our mine, of course."

"And where might that mine be?" Mister Potts asked.

Rufus didn't like Mister Potts attitude and said, "That piece of landscape has been duly registered with the state of Colorado and that is all you need to know. Now, Mister Potts, what does the gold assay at?"

149

CHASING THE NEXT SUNRISE

It was obvious Mister Potts did not like the answer, but he also knew Rufus was right. "It will take a while, come back in say, two hours and I'll have everything ready for you."

Rufus didn't trust that he wouldn't skim a few nuggets off to keep for himself, so he said, "It's alright, we'll wait. Besides, I'd like to see how the process works."

Without another word, he went about his business and we watched. In just over an hour, we walked out of the office with a little over three thousand dollars, each. I felt like a rich man, but Rufus was convinced this was only a drop in the bucket to what was still undiscovered.

Rufus wanted to go get a drink or two before renting a room and getting cleaned up, so Lars and I told him to go ahead, but to not go running off at the mouth about how much money he was carrying.

He peeled off a hundred dollars and gave me the rest, saying, "Keep an eye on this for me. If I don't have it, I can't spend it."

Lars and I went to the general store to buy new clothes because the ones we had on were in no shape to go to the laundry.

It just so happened that the owner was Swedish and his daughter, who was just a year younger than Lars, waited on us, or I should say, she waited on Lars.

Lars took the bath that came with the room, at the Denver House where we rented three separate rooms, but I had seen a sign that said, "Enjoy the luxury of being bathed and shaved by a beautiful young woman."

After hiding mine and Rufus' money in the room, I went down to the bathhouse. The man took my money and said if I wanted a bottle of bourbon to be brought in it would be two dollars extra.

"Have her bring a bottle and a cigar," I told him, laying three dollars on the counter.

If you've never enjoyed a steaming hot bath and shave, given by a gorgeous young woman who, for five dollars would climb into the tub with you, you haven't lived.

By the time I left, I was ravenous for a steak and all the trimmings. I knocked on Lar's door but there was no answer and then I checked several bars, but Rufus was not to be found, either, so I asked the bartender where a man could get the best steak in town?

"Most any of the restaurants along Front Street serves a decent steak, but if you want the best in town, go over two blooks and look for Sally's Place. She serves the best food in town."

I had a beer and gave him a dollar tip for the advice.

Sally's was a small place, tucked in between a real estate office and a lawyer's office, and it seated only twenty people – and the place was full of men, women and children.

A sandy haired woman with big, blue eyes walked up to me – introduced herself to me as, Karla, and said, "It'll be at least thirty minutes before a seat at the counter becomes available, and if you prefer a table, maybe longer."

She was about my age, a little shorter than me, with freckles across her nose and cheeks. Her smile was infectious. "Are you the one who waits on the counter?"

"No, that would be, Lou Ann," she said, pointing toward an older woman who looked tired.

"In that case, I'll wait for a table," I told her.

The place was noisy with all the chattering going on and it made me feel good. Up at the mine, we might go long periods without any of us speaking, so the sound of talking and laughter sounded just fine to me.

I was looking out through the front window at a woman who was trying to cross the muddy street and had lost a shoe in the mire, when Karla tapped me on the shoulder and said, "Your table is ready."

I was about to mention the woman who'd lost her shoe in the muddy street, when I saw a man stop, lift his hat and offer his assistance.

The table was in the far back corner, where I had a full view of the other customers.

"What's the best meal in the house?" I asked.

She smiled and said, "You'll see," then turned and sashayed into the kitchen.

I guessed I would be getting the house specialty, whatever that was.

Shortly she sat a glass of dark liquid in front of me, and to my astonishment, there were pieces of ice in it.

"What is this?" I asked.

"Something new. And I think we're the only place in town that serves it. It's called, iced tea. And with your accent, I thought you might enjoy it. I think it's delicious."

Granted, I'm a tea lover, but never had I ever heard of it being iced. I took a sip and to my great surprise, it was very good.

"I like it too," I told her. "Thank you."

She seemed very pleased and hurried away, saying, "Your supper should be ready any time now."

And sure enough, in less than two minutes, she sat a platter in front of me with a huge Porterhouse beefsteak, fried potatoes and green beans on it. And on a smaller plate was two large rolls and a big hunk of butter.

"Hope you enjoy it. It's the house specialty," she said with a hopeful look in her eyes.

"I'm sure I will, and thank you," I told her.

Everything on the plate was melt in your mouth delicious, and I was just chewing the last mouthful when Karla returned, refilled my glass of tea, along with a chunk of ice, and said, "Well?"

"It was the best steak I've ever eaten," I told her, honestly.

"Well then, just wait until I bring your dessert," she said, grinning from ear to ear.

She was gone hardly any time at all before she returned with a large bowl, filled with an apple, cinnamon, creation of some kind, and topped with a glob of something white that looked like frozen cream.

"What is that?" I asked, pointing at the frozen white stuff.

"You never had ice cream before?" she asked.

I looked at her and shook my head, "no."

She handed me a spoon and said, "Try it."

Not wanting to seem cowardly, I took a good-sized portion and put it in my mouth. I almost swooned at the sweet, creamy taste of it.

When I'd swallowed, I said, "This has to be the best tasting thing I've ever eaten."

She grinned and said, "Wait until you mix it with the apple cobbler."

The combination of the apples, the cinnamon and the ice cream sent my tastebuds soaring.

I took my time and savored each bite, hating the thought of finishing it.

The following morning, I was there for breakfast and Karla ushered me to the same table in the far back, where she brought me a T-bone steak, three fried eggs, fried potatoes and four slices of fresh tomato, along with a cup of hot tea. And as I sat there, enjoying my breakfast, I wondered about my two companions, neither of which had I seen since we parted, yesterday.

After breakfast, I stopped by Rufus' room and knocked on the door, but again, got no answer. I tried the knob, but the door was locked. Next, I knocked on Lars' door and heard him yell, "It's not locked."

To my surprise, he was dressed in a suit and when I asked what that was all about, he said, "I haft somtin' ta tell you. I vill only be goin' up to da mine fer ah short vile – yest long enough ta get ah little more gold. Den I vill be comin' back to Denver and getting married."

Well, this news almost sat me on my ear. "The young lady over at the general store?" I asked, but was sure I knew the answer.

"Ya. Her name is Gretchen and I vill be buyin' da store from her papa so he can retire. You and Rufus vill always get discount."

I shook his hand and said, "Congratulations, my friend. I wish the two of you the very best."

"Ya, and I vant you and Rufus as my best man at da vedding. Ya, you vill come?"

"When is this wedding to be?" I asked, feeling honored.

"Taday. Dat's vhy I'm all dressed up," he told me, grinning like a schoolboy.

I looked down at my clothes. They were clean, but not fit to be going to a wedding.

He must have noticed because he said, "Der be plenty of suits at da store. Vee vill go ober dere now, and get von for you and von for Rufus."

"I think we may need to find Rufus, first, to see what kind of shape he's in," I told Lars.

"Okay, but vee need ta get yer suit, right avay - now, if you vil."

We knocked, again on Rufus' door and called out to him, but still got no answer, which brought a feeling of uneasiness, but I shrugged it off. He was a grown man and could go off on a bender if he wanted to. He'd earned it. Besides, how much of a bender could a man go on, with only a hundred dollars. He would probably show up tomorrow, broke, with a giant hangover and we'd all get a good laugh.

I met Gretchen and Lars' father-in-law to be and liked them both. The way Gretchen looked at Lars told me he was one lucky man. I had mentioned to Lars about the fact that it had been a very short engagement.

"Ya," he told me. "She said she knew I vas da von, right avay."

The wedding was held in a small church up on a hill overlooking Denver, then the four of us, me, Lars, Gretchen and her father, went to Sally's for dinner. My treat. Sally met us at the door and had a special table waiting for us, with a bucket with ice in it, that held a bottle of champagne – on the house. Her gift to the bride and groom.

I asked Karla if she could join us, but she apologized, saying she had to work. "But I'm very flattered," she said. "And by the way, you look very handsome in that suit."

I'm sure my face turned a burnt crimson or some such color and I stuttered out a, "Thank you."

As we were leaving, Karla caught up to me and said she would be getting off around six and if I was available, she'd like me to come with her to the opera house to listen to classical music."

I didn't have a clue as to what classical music sounded like, but if I could be close to Karla... "Should I pick you up here?" I asked.

She put her hand to my cheek. It was soft and warm. "No, I need to go home and change. I'll meet you in the front of the opera house at seven, if that is all right?'

"Front of the opera house, seven sharp," I told her.

Looks like you fount somebody, too," Lars whispered in my ear when we got outside.

I looked over my shoulder and said, "She's very nice, but I'm not up to getting hitched. Not just yet."

I spent the next couple of hours searching for Rufus. Several of the bartenders said they thought they knew who I was talking about, but couldn't be sure, and couldn't give me any information. The clerk at the hotel said, he'd not yet picked up his key, which caused me more concern.

I tried to shake off the ill feeling I was having. Afterall, he was a grown man and owed me no explanation.

I was standing in front of the opera house when Karla arrived and I almost changed my mind about getting married. She looked beautiful in a soft colored blue dress that had sparkles on it. And her bright blue eyes and radiant smile made me feel weak in the knees.

I handed her a small bouquet of flowers, which seemed to please her immensely.

I had never seen so many musicians in one place – playing music I had never heard before. They were playing songs written by this fella named, Mozart and another man Karla said was called Brahms.

By the end of the evening, it was all I could do to keep my eyes open, but she seemed to be enjoying it and squeezed my hand from time to time.

I offered to hire a cab to take her home, but she said, she only lived about five blocks away, so we walked, and enjoyed the cool night air.

She said she'd been in Denver for a little over two years and had worked for Sally from the first day she'd been open. She asked how long I was going to be in town and made a pout with her lips when I told her I would be leaving in a day or so.

Before she went inside, she patted my cheek and said, "If you make it back to Denver, come see me. I think you're very nice."

And with that, she kissed me on the cheek and went inside the apartment house where she lived.

When I got back to the hotel, I queried the clerk and he informed me Rufus still had not stopped by to get his key and asked if I knew when he would?"

Of course, I had no idea, and told him so.

I lay awake long into the night, wondering what could have happened to him. Even if he got stinking drunk, he would need a place to sleep it off, wouldn't he?

The following morning, when Rufus still hadn't shown up, I decided to skip breakfast and go straight to the sheriff's office.

The sheriff was a big fella, well over six feet and had the body of a lumberjack. He was having his morning coffee when I walked in and before I could ask about Rufus, he offered me a cup, which I turned down.

I introduced myself, then got straight to the subject – the whereabouts of my friend – giving him a full description.

He listened and when I finished, he stood up and told me to follow him.

Three doors down, I saw a sign that said, "Coroner's office." He opened the door and we walked in.

I felt the bile come up into my throat when I saw Rufus laying on the table.

"We found him in the alley. His neck had been broken. He had no identification on him, so we waited, hoping someone would show up to claim him," the sheriff told me.

I paid to have him buried the following morning, then went in search of Lars.

The service was short, with me, Lars, Gretchen, and the preacher in attendance.

I told Lars I would be going back, and he told me he would go, too. "Ve'll haft da honey moon ven I get back. By den I vill have enough money."

TWENTY-SIX

Gretchen and her father saw us off, the following morning, with Lars driving the wagon loaded with supplies from his father-in-law's store.

Rufus had told us he had no relatives, so we split his share of the money and the mine now belonged to me and Lars.

The going was slow and tedious since it was mainly going uphill and no roads; just a wagon track. We were lucky to make ten miles a day.

We were about forty miles from the camp, and camped along a stream when out of the woods, came a lone Indian I thought to be a Cheyenne. He walked with his palms facing us – the sign of peace. And being peaceful men, we invited him in. He spoke broken English and was curious why we were up there?

I tried to explain that we had a cabin further up the mountain. I didn't mention anything about the mine since gold was not important to the Indians. It was just a pretty rock to make jewelry out of.

He wanted to know what was in the wagon and while I was showing him, twenty or so braves walked into the camp, brandishing rifles and bows and arrows.

I shook my head for being so stupid.

We were taken to their camp, stripped naked and stood between two poles. We were tied to the poles with our arms and legs spread wide.

Children would throw rocks at us, and women would poke us with sharp sticks or beat us with saplings from trees. By the end of the third day, with no food and very little water to drink, neither Lars and myself were in the best of condition.

On the morning of the fourth day of captivity, a young brave walked up to me and passed his knife in front of my face, talking to me. Even though I couldn't understand him, he'd made his intentions quite clear.

Then he moved the edge of his knife down to my chest and very slowly, sliced off a strip of my skin, an inch wide and six inches long.

Knowing the Indians hated cowards, I willed myself not to scream, even though my brain was crying to. Grinding my teeth together, staring straight ahead, my silence did not go unnoticed.

When the young brave, angry that I hadn't screamed out in pain, decided to cut off another piece of skin, hoping this time to hear me beg for mercy, an older brave who had been standing nearby, called out to him and begrudgingly, he stopped and walked away, throwing my piece of skin on the ground.

The older brave walked over and looked me in the eyes, then nodded his head and walked away. I noticed he had several scars on his chest and shoulders.

Flies and other flying critters flocked to the wound, brought there by the smell of blood, and there was nothing I could do about it.

"Hold on, mine friend, vee vill get free ven it gets dark, I promise," Lars said in a low voice.

I turned my head and looked at him and saw the anger in his eyes.

"If we were free, I think I can get us out of here," I whispered back.

"I haft been vorking on it for some time and I tink I'm almost dere," he said.

I suffered the long afternoon of having rocks thrown at me and women switching me until red welts covered my body.

I had dozed off, trying to avoid the pain, when I heard, "Pfffssst, don't make any noise."

Lars was standing behind me, untying my hands. I looked around and saw that it was dark and everyone was asleep.

With what strength he had left, Lars had pulled and stretched the leather pieces we were tied with until he was able to break them and get free. His wrists were red and bloody, but we were free!

I motioned for him to follow me and we went to where a woman had been painting symbols on a piece of deerskin stretched between some sticks. There, on the ground, sat several gourds filled with various colors of paint.

I looked at Lars and said, "Do what I do." And with that I covered my body with red and white paint. Lars, without question, did the same.

When we were finished, I said, "You don't have to do the same thing I do, but do something similar."

With that, I went running through the camp, jumping up and down and screaming at the top of my lungs, while singing a bawdy song.

People rushed from their wickiups and stared at us in awe. And when the chief emerged from his wickiup, I ran over and jumped in the hot ashes of the dying campfire, and began to dance around.

At this, the chief and all the rest began running for their lives. They thought we had gone crazy and didn't want to be anywhere near us. I'd heard that Indians were afraid of crazy people and left them alone. And when the camp was empty, I had proved the point.

As quickly as we could, we hitched up the oxen, threw the saddles in the wagon and with Lars driving the wagon, and me on my horse and leading his, we escaped what would have surely been a painful death.

I kept watching behind us to see if they were following, but apparently, they didn't want anything more to do with us.

Four days later, we arrived back at our mine, tired, but very much, alive.

TWENTY-SEVEN

For the next two months, while we still had good weather, we shored up the cabin, stacked wood for winter, shot and dressed out deer and elk meat to eat during the long, cold winter months. We had canned vegetables and other things like, beans coffee, sugar and flour, so we wouldn't starve.

Besides working in the mine, searching for that allusive big vein Rufus always talked about, we built a covering over the walkway between the cabin and the entrance to the mine. We hoped it would make getting between the cabin and the mine, easier when the snows came. We also built a cover over the shaker.

From time to time the Shoshone brave, Screaming Cougar, would come by for a visit, or ask if I would go hunting with him. I always said yes, because I had come to enjoy his company and he was teaching me to speak Shoshone, while I helped him with his English.

We had plenty of meat for the winter, so whatever I shot, I helped Screaming Cougar by taking it to his village. At first, the people were a bit shy of me, but by my third visit, they had excepted me and spoke with me, freely. And from time to time, I spent the night.

Soon I was free to come and go as I pleased, and did so, more and more.

Screaming Cougar had a younger sister who was called, Calling Bird. She was shorter than me and when she smiled at me, it made me feel all funny inside. She wanted to learn to speak English, like her brother and I enjoyed teaching her. We went for long walks and very quickly, we were talking English for her, and Shoshone, for me. I learned a lot that summer, along with considering the thought of marriage – but not as long as Lars still lived in the cabin. If I were to approach her and she said, yes, I would need to speak to Lars about when he would be leaving.

Before I could get up the courage to ask her, the snows came. We couldn't get out and they couldn't get in, so, whatever the future would hold, would have to wait for spring.

During my time in Denver, I had purchased a scale so we could weigh our own gold and know if we were being cheated, or not. So, during the evening when I had nothing else to do, I weighed our gold and portioned it out, equally between myself and Lars.

The roof over the passageway helped a lot. We still had to shovel some snow, but not nearly as much and for the most part, could get back and forth to and from the mine with ease. While we didn't hit a huge vein, we did find several good size ones. And by the time the snow began to melt, I guessed we had about fifty thousand dollars worth of raw gold, each. Of course, I wasn't absolutely sure because I didn't know exactly what gold was selling for. But no matter how we looked at it, we were both wealthy men – thanks to Rufus.

Plus, we still had some of the money that had been left over from our first trip.

One night, Lars looked up from the book he was reading and said, "You are goot friend, but I vill not be coming back dis time. I vill haf enough money to buy da store and I know Gretchen vill vant me ta stay, too."

"I understand, my friend. And if I were in your boots, I would probably feel the same way."

"So, you plan to come back up here?" Lars asked with a questionable look.

I thought for a moment, gave a sigh and said, "I used to think I wanted to live in the city with all the people coming and going, and all the things there is to do – and all the young ladies, but no more. I guess I've come to like it up here."

"Ya, and yest maybe a certain young Indian voman," Lars said with a wide smile. "Ya, maybe I tink so."

I chuckled and said, "Yeah, maybe, my friend, maybe."

Lars was anxious to get back down to Denver and Gretchen, and to be truthful, I couldn't blame him. So… When the snow had melted low enough for us to travel, Lars suggested we leave. It was early April of 1844.

The following day, we boarded up the entry to the mine, and the door to the cabin and set off for Denver. Lars had been away from Gretchen for a year and was anxious.

CHASING THE NEXT SUNRISE

As a precaution, we painted our faces, stuck sticks with fresh buds on them in our hair and sang loudly as we crossed Ute and Cheyenne country. From time to time, when I saw them peeking at us from the safety of the trees, I would stand up in the wagon and begin to dance to whatever song we were singing.

Needless to say, we were not attacked.

This time, Denver was just coming out of a cold winter and there was still snow on the ground as we pulled the wagon up in front of the general store. And before we could get down, Gretchen came running out of the store, screaming like a wounded banshee Indian. She climbed onto the wagon and threw her arms around Lars' neck and kissed him right on the mouth!

I left them to their greeting one another and got down and tied the oxen to the hitch rail.

Lars' father-in-law came out and motioned for them to get down and come inside. "You are causing people to talk," he said, at their impropriety.

Lars loosened his bride from around his neck, picked her up in his arms and jumped down, then carried her inside the store.

Gretchen's father just shook his head and shrugged his shoulders, saying to the crowd of people who had been watching – "Newlyweds. What can you say?"

He patted me on the shoulder and said, "Come inside. It's still cold out."

I checked into the hotel and got my customary bath and shower but by a different young woman, this time, who more than earned her money.

The following morning, Lars and I went into the assay office expecting to face Mister Artimus Potts, but came to a halt just inside the door. The sign now read, Melvin B. Sawyer, Assayer.

Melvin was tall and rail thin, with a protruding Adam's apple. He was clean shaven and wore a suit that hung on his skinny frame like a feed sack.

He looked up and grinned and asked, "What can I do for you gentlemen, this morning?"

"What happened to Mister Potts?" I asked.

Melvin gave me a questioning look and asked, "Why do you ask? Are you an associate of Mister Potts?"

"No," I said a bit too quickly. "We're not even friends with Mister Potts. When we were here last year, he gave us a hard time and well, I guess we were expecting to go head-to-head with him again this year, and we weren't looking forward to it. I think the man was a cheat. I didn't trust him."

"I see," Melvin said, shuffling some papers and acting suspiciously – so I asked, "What aren't you telling us, Mister Sawyer?"

"Maybe it would be better if you inquired of the sheriff," Melvin said, raising his head to look at me.

"And maybe it would be better if you told us," I said with a stern voice.

After a moment of decision, Melvin said, "Very well, it's not like it's some big secret or anything. First off, Artimus Potts, was not his real name. It was Orville Snipes and he was wanted in several other western towns for the same crimes he committed here."

"And vat might dose be?" Lars asked, stepping up closer the to counter.

"It seems, if a person's gold assayed high enough and if the person seemed weak enough, Mister Potts would send some men to follow the person back to his claim to convince him to sign the claim over to one of Mister Snipes' many aliases, then the miner would have a fatal accident, leaving Mister Snipes the sole owner of the claim."

"And vot about you? Do you got men to help you do evil deeds, too?" Lars asked, leaning over the edge of the counter.

Melvin stepped back and said, "Indeed, I do not! I am an honest assayer, and I'll have you know, my record is impeccable."

"Goot," Lars said, stepping back. "Den vee haf no problem, ya?"

"Yes. I mean, no, we have no problem," Melvin said, sweat popping out on his forehead.

Like I said, earlier, I had weighed all the gold and had a list of each bags weight, and when Mister Sawyer finished and handed me the total, I compared it to my list and was gratified to find they matched, perfectly.

CHASING THE NEXT SUNRISE

Lars chose to leave his money in the Denver Bank, but I wasn't so sure. I didn't know much about banks, having never dealt with one, much, and told the teller I wanted my money in cash.

The banker became short of breath and I thought he might have a heart attack right there in the bank. My portion came to sixty-eight thousand dollars.

In the end, I left the money in the bank and put Lars down on the account to watch over it, and if there was a problem, he could pull it out and save it for me. I was given bank drafts, or, checks, as he called them, which meant I could write in the amount and then sign my name and buy things. People could present them to the bank in return for cash. It didn't make a lot of sense to me, but times were changing and I guessed a man needed to change with them.

The oxen were getting along in years and I traded them for a pair of tough looking draft horses, called Clydesdales. They were the biggest horses I'd ever seen and I had no doubt they could pull the wagon with hardly any effort. Plus, the livery man I bought them from, said I could ride them, if need be. I laughed. I would need a ladder just to get on one of them.

As big as the they were, I was surprised at how gentle they were. One was a male and the other one, a female, so I named them Buck and Becky.

I felt proud of myself as I wrote out the check and handed it to the livery man, who took it like it was an everyday occurrence – the same with Lars' father-in-law. What was this world coming to when a slip of paper was worth whatever amount you write on it?

For me, Denver was getting too crowded and I was anxious to get back up on the mountain.

So… after saying my goodbyes, with my saddle horse tied onto the back of the wagon, I tapped the reins on the rumps of Buck and Becky, and off we went, leaving Denver behind us.

The weather was fair and bright and a good day to be traveling. That night I camped under the stars and dreamed about the young lady from my bath.

TWENTY-EIGHT

The weather was fair and the scenery was spectacular as I pulled up next to a crystal-clear lake for my second nights camp. And even though we had been going uphill all day, neither Buck or Becky seemed to have broken a sweat. After hobbling them so they could eat the rich, green grass that was at least twelve inches high, I made my camp, started a fire and put a pot of water on for tea. I was alone and preferred it to coffee.

There was still some daylight and while the water heated, I cut a piece of tree limb and made myself a fishing pole.

I dug around and found a couple of worms and my hook had barely submerged below the water when I thought a whale had attacked my line.

That night, to go along with my beans and tea, I had a tasty brown trout.

Several days later, as I approached Ute territory, I checked the pistol I had purchased before leaving. Lars' father-in-law said it was the latest thing available. It was made by a man named, Colt and could shoot five bullets without reloading.

I had tried it in the field behind the general store and was amazed by its power and performance. I think it would bring a bear down at close range, and a man too.

I had also purchased a new rifle that fired the same ammunition as the pistol so I wouldn't need to make my own, any more – although, I kept them loaded, too.

As we went up the trail, I knew the Ute Indians could be hiding in the forest, waiting for me to pass before attacking, and I wouldn't know they were there until it was too late.

My only advantage was Buck and Becky. Horses have a great sense of hearing and smell, so they raise their ears at any new sounds or smells – and I was sure they would be able to smell the Utes. Therefore, I kept my eyes trained on their ears.

We were about a mile into Ute territory when their ears went up and they swished their tails.

My eyes went to both sides of the trail, trying to decide my next move – run for it, or try and shoot it out.

When I saw them emerge from the forest on horseback, I set my pistol back down on the seat and pulled the team to a halt. My friends, the Shoshone rode out and stopped next to the wagon.

I could see a stern look on Screaming Cougar's face as he climbed from his horse to the wagon seat and sat down next to me. "There's something wrong, I can see it in your eyes," I told him, and he nodded his head, yes.

"We talk as you drive. Not safe here," Screaming Cougar said, motioning for me to move out.

For a long time, he said, nothing, but kept looking from side to side as though he expected trouble. Finally, when the cabin was in sight, he said, "There is trouble. We are at war with the Utes. Blood has been shed."

"What can I do to help?" I asked as I pulled to a stop in front of the cabin.

"First, we unload wagon and get big horses in barn. Where you get such big horses?"

As we, meaning me and Screaming Cougar, and two of the other braves, unloaded the wagon while the remaining braves kept watch, I explained about the Clydesdales and how I thought they would be better than the oxen.

Screaming Cougar grinned and said, "They will also provide much meat during the cold winter months."

I looked him in the eyes and said, "They're not for eating."

He nodded his head, but said, nothing.

With the supplies unloaded, the horses put up in the corral next to the barn, I made a pot of stew so we could eat. Indians were always hungry, it seemed.

When we were finished, I looked at Screaming Cougar and said, "Okay, my friend, now, maybe you'll tell me whatever it is you've been holding back and what started the war?"

I had made a pot of coffee for my friends because they preferred it to tea. Screaming Cougar took a sip, then sat his cup on the table. "At first, we were just stealing horses from each other – just having fun. Then we found my cousin lying dead, where he had been standing guard and six horses had been stolen."

He took another sip of coffee, blew out some air and continued. "We went to confront them and found the man who killed my cousin and I shot him. Two days ago, while we were hunting meat, they raided our camp and took three women prisoners. Calling Bird was one of the women taken."

Instantly, anger began welling up inside me. My heart began to race and my blood was beginning to run hot. "We will get them back," I told him through gritted teeth.

"It will not be easy. They will be waiting for us. This is why we have come to you, my brother. I know you have feelings for my sister and she for you. We are hoping you will ride with us when we raid their camp."

As angry as I was, I knew raiding them was not the answer. They would be waiting for us and there would be a lot of bloodshed, and possibly that of the three women. There had to be another way.

I stood up and paced around the room while my brain cleared itself and I could think straight.

After maybe five minutes, I turned and looked at Screaming Cougar and said, "It is too dangerous for us to try to raid their camp to get the women back. I have a plan where, I hope, we can get the women back, without bloodshed."

"How can be?" Screaming Cougar asked. "You cannot just walk into their camp and take them back. They will kill you the moment you get there."

"Maybe not, my friend, maybe not," I told him with a grin.

First thing the following morning, while several of the braves were in the woods, searching for berries I wanted, I made up a paste I hoped would act as glue.

Later that day, I walked into the Ute camp, bold as brass. I was stark naked, with white ash spread across my body, a broken knife glued to my neck and a Shoshone arrow looking like it was protruding from my back and stomach, like it had gone all the way through. From both the

167

phony knife wound and the arrow, I had red berry juice running down my body like blood. I was shaking a gourd and talking like a crazy man, giving no regard to any of the Utes, other than shake my gourd at them and scream to the heavens.

The men, women and children ran like I was old Lucifer, himself, coming to take them.

I found the three women in one of the wickiups and it was only after explaining to Calling Bird, who I was and that I had come to rescue them that they calmed down.

Back at my cabin, after I washed and put my clothes on and had put some chunks of venison over the spit, to cook, did Screaming Cougar speak. He and two braves, along with Calling Bird, had come back with me. For what, I wasn't sure, but I knew he would tell me when he thought the time was right.

I poured us cups of coffee and was about to sit down at the table when Screaming Cougar walked over and took me by the shoulders and said, "You are truly, a brother, and have done something today, only a brother would do."

I tried to wave him off, but he wouldn't have it. "I have something to say and I want you to listen," Screaming Cougar said to me, a stern look on his face.

I could see he was serious, so I nodded my head, yes, and said, "There is no need for thanks, but if you must…"

Screaming Cougar took me by the hand and led me over to where Calling Bird was standing, then placed our hands together and said, "From this day forward, Calling Bird and White Wolf will be together. She will be your woman and you will be her man. Let it be so."

And just like that, we were married. I couldn't be happier, and I could tell by the look in her eyes that she was glad about the union, too.

Screaming Cougar and the two braves shook my hand, then sat down to devour the steaks and canned vegetables I'd fixed. Those boys sure could eat. It was my wedding night and I thought they would never finish.

While her brother and the two braves were trying their best to burst their stomachs, Calling Bird was going around, straightening and cleaning up the cabin, a coy smile on her lips.

Finally, when the food was all gone, they stood up, shook my hand, again, told me I was a lucky man, and then left, saying if I needed help with the Utes, they would come.

I closed and locked the door, then turned to see Calling Bird, smiling at me.

TWENTY-NINE

For the most part, life with Calling Bird was not just good, but really good. We didn't argue, but she had a stubborn streak when it came to something she really believed in, like going with me when I went hunting, to help protect me from the Utes or animals, like bears and cougars.

If I brought home a deer or elk I'd shot, she would tan the hide and make something of it. Most of the time, something for me, until I insisted, she make something for herself; then it was usually moccasins because when we went down to Denver, I would buy her store-bought dresses or a warm, winter coat. I also bought her heavy socks and a pair of boots, but she would rarely wear them.

Work in the mine didn't come to a standstill, but I only worked when the mood struck me. What did we need money for except once a year when we went down for supplies, and things her people might need?

The forest provided us with meat. The river gave us an abundance of fish, along with a place to swim together and play in the water. She had me buy seeds at the general store so she could have a garden. I think her thumb must have been dark green as big as some of the things grew.

We also bought books for reading during the long, cold winter nights. She came to love reading and couldn't get enough of learning. By now, she could read and write better than me.

There were a few incidents – like one day while I was working in the mine, and deep down in the shaft. I heard gunshots and ran as fast as I could to the entryway, only to find it blocked by half a dozen Ute warriors firing arrows, blocking my escape.

From where I stood, I could see at least twenty braves trying to break into the cabin, only to have lead flying at them. I could see three braves lying dead a few feet from the front door.

I pulled my pistol and fired at the ones blocking my way and saw one go down, but the influx of arrows increased and I couldn't get close enough to fire, again.

Not far inside the entrance was a box of dynamite, which caught my attention – but as I turned, an arrow caught me in the back of my leg. I fired three shots at the entryway, then, gritting my teeth, I pulled the arrow out and picked up a stick of dynamite. I pulled a lucifer from my pants pocket and lit the fuse, then ran to the entryway and threw the stick of dynamite into the middle of them. The burning fuse was very short, leaving no time for them to run.

The explosion created exactly what I wanted it to do. First, it killed three of them and stunned the others, causing a great deal of confusion. And second, it gave me time to light a second stick and throw it at the ones attacking the cabin.

By the time the smoke cleared, the yard was empty of Ute braves – even the dead were gone.

I ran to the cabin to find out how Calling Bird was doing, only to have her trying to get me to lay down so she could tend my wound.

Then there was the time the Utes came just as the sun was rising over the treetops. We were still in bed when Calling Bird jumped up and said, "The cabin is on fire!"

I jumped out of bed and we ran for the door, only to be driven back inside because of the arrows being shot at the doorway.

I honestly believe they thought if they couldn't have her, she needed to die – and me along with her. I'm sure they did a lot of praying before trying to kill the crazy white man.

So, there we were, trapped inside the burning cabin. And by now, the wood was dry enough that it burned like firewood. Smoke was getting thick, causing us to cough and our eyes to burn.

Over the years, I had bought several more pistols and rifles to ward off attacks with, but none of them were any good to us at this very moment. Even so, I grabbed them, along with the boxes of ammunition and dumped them into a gunny sack, while Calling Bird gathered up some food.

Good ole Rufus had foreseen this possibility and had provided for it. Before we knew each other, while he was up here, alone, he had dug an escape tunnel that went off into the forest out back of the cabin. It wasn't big enough for a man to stand up and walk, but, if you stayed hunkered over, you could do just fine.

CHASING THE NEXT SUNRISE

I had never been inside the tunnel, but Rufus had told us about it. The entryway was close to the far wall inside his bedroom.

With a lantern in one hand and the gunnysack in the other, I led the way. It was totally dark and had a pungent smell to it, but hopefully, it would lead us to safety.

At some point, I stepped on something that squealed. I jumped and bumped my head against the ceiling and was rewarded by my head hitting a rock protruding from the ceiling. "Damn rats," I said.

After what seemed to be a long distance, we came to an abrupt end. There was no way out! This was not good. Rufus had neglected to tell us this bit of news.

I set the gunnysack on the floor of the tunnel, and handed the lantern to Calling Bird – then began to dig with my hands. The dirt had its fair share of rocks, but all in all, the digging wasn't too bad, and after about eighteen inches, my fingers found daylight.

I stopped digging and listened to hear any movement or talking. Other than the wind moving through the trees and the faint smell of smoke, I believed we were alone. Even so, I dug the hole only big enough to get my head above ground so I could look around.

A rabbit hopped near my head, took one look at me and moved on. Other than that, we were alone. I finished widening the hole until it was wide enough for us to crawl through.

Hidden behind some bushes, we could see the Ute braves standing near the cabin, waiting for it to finish burning – which didn't take all that long.

When there was nothing but a pile of smoldering ashes, they walked around, looking into what used to be the interior of our home. The cabin had burned to the ground, along with everything inside.

Satisfied we had perished in the fire, they sang and danced around for close to an hour, then mounted their horses and left – I'm sure, rushing back to tell the others of their triumph.

We eased back into the forest and made our way to her people. The Shoshone camp was close to seven miles from the mine – located along the side of a river.

It was midafternoon when we approached their camp and were surrounded by armed warriors, holding drawn bows on us. Calling Bird called out to them and we were rewarded with smiles and welcomes.

But when Screaming Cougar heard about what had happened, he was ready to take his braves and rush their camp and wipe them out, once and for all.

Once again, I had a plan that would keep them away, I hoped, forever, without bloodshed.

The following morning just as the sun was coming up, I walked into their camp, stark naked, but covered from head to foot with red, berry juice, singing a sad song. Only this time, I carried several sticks of dynamite with short fuses. As I lit each one, I tossed it among the braves who came rushing out of their wickiups, ready to fight. I don't think any of them were killed, but without a doubt, they were injured and scared half out of their minds.

The sticks of dynamite did what they were supposed to do, and as far as the Utes were concerned, I was a walking dead man, shooting exploding fire from my hands.

Calling Bird was right behind me, also naked and covered with red, berry juice. But instead of throwing sticks of dynamite, she held her hands above her head and laughed a cackling laugh that even gave me the shivers.

Not only did they not bother us again for a long time, they packed up and moved away. Superstition is strong among the Indians and I'm sure we were talked about and the story handed down from generation to generation – the white man and his squaw who even fire could not kill.

My Shoshone brothers would also sing the praises of White Wolf and Calling Bird as the story passed along about how we had fooled the Utes.

I had avoided bloodshed, and maybe a war between the Shoshone and the Utes, but, unfortunately, I had not ended their desire to kill us. Afraid, or not, they still wanted us dead – even more so after what had happened. It would take them a couple of years before they figured it out, and tried again, but try, they would.

THIRTY

With help from my brothers and sisters, the Shoshone, a new cabin was built. And this one was even better than the old one. I hauled furniture up from Denver, along with pots and pans, blankets – anything and everything to make our lives comfortable. I also bought things for my Indian family. Rifles and ammunition for them to hunt game – blankets, pots, pans, buckets – anything they wanted. I had more money in the bank than I would probably ever spend because the only time I spent any, was when I went down to Denver to cash in what new gold I'd dug out of the mine.

I continued to dig gold from the mine when time afforded it. I preferred to hunt, fish and take walks along the river with Calling Bird, or sometimes, just sit and read. Life was once again as happy as I could ever hope for. One afternoon when I came back from the mine, Calling Bird informed me, I was to become a father.

I couldn't contain my excitement and knew I had to share the good news. I bagged up all the candy I'd brought from Denver, hitched up the wagon, loaded Calling Bird and the candy in the wagon and went to the Shoshone camp.

We told them the good news and I handed out candy to anyone who wanted it, which meant, every person in the camp, adults and children, alike.

After some argument, I convinced Calling Bird to allow me to bring one of the women from the tribe, home with us, to help with the chores.

Several months into the pregnancy, the weather began to turn cold and I decided we might have an early winter and we didn't have as much meat as we would need. So… off I went on a hunting expedition, leaving her at home with Cooing Dove.

Screaming Cougar also needed more meat and we decided to go together.

We each took a pack horse with us and headed up the mountain where no one lived except deer, elk, mountain lions and bears. We traveled for three days before making a permanent camp.

The morning of the fourth day, maybe half a mile above the camp, we came upon a bear stalking a heard of Elk and since the Shoshone were more partial to bear meat than either, Calling Bear, or me, I allowed Screaming Cougar to have the honor.

He creeped as close as he dared - then stood up and put his rifle to his shoulder.

The bear must have noticed because he turned, just as Screaming Cougar squeezed the trigger. The shot missed the heart and lodged itself in the bears right shoulder.

The bear, wounded and angry, charged Screaming Cougar, who in his haste to cock the rifle, dropped it.

The bear was on him before he could even pull his knife and went down, screaming.

I had stayed back a ways, to give Screaming Cougar his chance at shooting the bear, but when I saw what was happening, I raised my rifle to shoot but they were rolling around on the ground and I was afraid I might hit Screaming Cougar. In a panic and wanting to help my brother, I pulled my knife from its sheath and leaped on the back of the bear, locking my legs around its girth, then reached in and sliced my knife across his throat.

Bears are not easy to kill once they become riled up and this one was angry clear down into the marrow of its bones.

He stood up on his hind legs, trying to reach me with his claws, or shake me off, whichever came first. But I had my legs wrapped around his middle and with a handful of hair in one hand – I kept stabbing him in the neck.

The next thing I knew, Screaming Cougar was on his feet and running toward us, yelling, "Jump off!"

Without hesitation, I did and Screaming Cougar, who was very close now, raised his rifle and shot the bear in the chest, knocking it over on its back, where he finally took his last breath.

Screaming Cougar was bleeding from several places where the bear had clawed him.

I took him back to the camp and washed out the wounds as best I could and put some paste Calling Bird had made for cuts over each of his wounds.

I also made some tea and put in some herbs Calling Bird said would help prevent infection.

After much protesting, Screaming Cougar agreed to stay in the camp while I went to drag the bear back to camp.

As I was about to leave, I heard the snarling and knew there would be a problem. Wolves had smelled the bear's blood and came to feast. There were four of them.

They were just doing what came naturally, and I didn't want to kill any of them if I didn't have to. So, I fired a shot into the air, which startled them, but with such a meal, they weren't going to give up, easy. I had no choice.

I took aim and shot the one closest to the bear, and as I suspected they would, the others grabbed his body and dragged it off into the woods, to eat, instead of the bear.

I tied a rope around the hind legs of the bear and dragged it back to camp.

Screaming Cougar was sitting by the fire, drinking his tea. He looked up at me and said, "Wolves."

"Four of them," I countered.

"And you had to shoot one of them?" he asked, knowing the answer.

"Only way I could get them to leave the bear, alone," I told him as I loosened the rope from the bear's legs and tossed one end over a large tree limb, then got a second rope and did the same thing. With the two ropes tied to the bear's hind legs, just above his feet, I used my horse to hoist the bear in the air, just high enough so we could skin and butcher him.

The first thing Screaming Cougar did was cut out the liver and offer me a bite. I never cared much for raw liver, but he was my brother and it was a tradition, so I took a bite and handed it back.

After taking a bite of the liver, Screaming Cougar walked over and stuck it on the spit over the fire and watched for a moment, then turned to me and said, "Never cared much for raw liver, but it is my people's tradition."

"And I only took a bite because you are my brother," I told him.

Darkness was overtaking the forest by the time we finished cutting up the meat and hauling it high up in a tree to keep wolves and other meat eaters from coming into the camp to steal it.

Using my horse, again, I dragged the skeleton off into the woods, close to a mile before leaving it for whatever other critters there were, to find it.

Ordinarily, the women also came on a hunt and would save the bones to make things out of, but we were out here strictly for meat and hides. Besides, they now had store bought utensils and didn't really need the bones.

Over the next two days, we brought down four deer, two elk and a cougar.

With meat and hides we headed back to the Shoshone camp. He would take the bulk of the meat and hides. With what we already had, one elk and hide would do Calling Bird and me through the winter.

The women had taken custody of Screaming Cougar, much to his protesting, and were treating his wounds.

With spirits high, I said goodbye to the Shoshone and headed home.

I rode into the barn where I put up the horses, then packed the meat and hide into the cabin, calling out, "The weary hunter is home with meat, but hungry for the taste of your lips."

When I didn't get an answer, I called out, "Calling Bird?" And when I got no answer, I called out to the woman I had brought to help. "Cooing Dove?"

I dropped the meat on the table and went outside to look to see if they had gone to the river for water, and a cold fear washed over me.

I ran to the river and stopped. There, on the ground, in two pools of blood, lay, Calling Bird and Cooing Dove. Both had been shot with arrows and Calling Bird's stomach had been cut open.

With tears in my eyes and an ache in my heart, I did what had to be done. I dug two graves, wrapped them each in a blanket and buried them.

It was totally dark when I realized I was still standing at the foot of Calling Bird's grave. Never in my whole life had I known so much pain. And suddenly, a name jumped into my head. Utes.

CHASING THE NEXT SUNRISE

Mixed with the pain, anger engulfed me from head to foot. I wanted revenge and I wanted it now! Calling Bird and I had eleven good years together, but not enough. I wanted us to grow old together.

Back at the cabin, I was taking down a rifle and had just picked up a box of ammunition when reality hit me. Number one, I couldn't go down there alone, and number two, they would be expecting me. And number three, I didn't know which of them had done this terrible deed.

Going into their camp and killing everyone in sight, wouldn't necessarily get revenge on the one or ones who did this. Yes, I wanted an eye for an eye, but would I have gotten revenge on the guilty party? I would not give up on my revenge, but I needed time to think and to plan.

I put the rifle back on the rack and the ammunition back on the shelf, then went about curing up the meat.

The following morning, while I was saddling my horse, I heard the sound of an unshod horse approaching. I grabbed my rifle and stepped out of the barn, looking toward the sound.

There, coming toward me was a horse without a rider.

I guess instinct took over because I ducked back into the barn just as an arrow drove its way into the side of the barn, close to where I had been standing.

Looking toward the direction the arrow came from, I saw nothing – no one.

I eased myself down along the barn to a shaded spot close to the back door and waited.

I didn't have long to wait before the back door opened ever so slowly, and then, only wide enough for a man to slip through. Still, I waited.

He eased his way into the barn, a knife in his right hand. Just inside the door, he stopped and looked around. And when he saw me standing there, he grinned and said, "Now it will be your turn to die, white man. You stole my property from me and got her with child. But you will never hear the brat call out your name. I made sure of that. And now, I bring death to you, once and for all."

And with that, he lunged at me, knife raised up for the kill. With a calm I never knew I had, I squeezed the trigger on my handgun and saw the surprised look on his face.

As he sunk to the floor of the barn, he began to sing his death song, but got out only a few words before I shot him again, and again, and again.

Finally, when I heard the hammer slam down on an empty chamber, I stopped squeezing the trigger. I stood there, tears running down my cheeks, feeling the pain of my loss, all over, again.

My first impulse was to drag his body out into the woods and leave it for the wolves and other critters, but then, anger welled up inside me. I wanted them to know what I had done. I wanted to show them they couldn't bring me grief without me bringing my wrath down on them.

I finished saddling my horse, tied a rope around the brave's ankles, then mounted my steed and headed down the mountain.

Screaming Cougar had told me where they had moved their camp to – some ten miles to the west – and that's where I headed.

It was late afternoon when I neared their camp. Fires were burning and the squaws were making the evening meals. The men were sitting in a circle, talking, when I went racing into the camp - right in among the men – screaming profanities at them, then dragged the dead brave into their camp fire and left him there.

I raised my pistol into the air and fired it three times before racing away.

On the way back to my cabin, I stopped at the Shoshone camp and told them what had happened and what I'd done.

Knowing I had just started a war, Screaming Cougar and ten Shoshone braves rode back to the cabin with me, where we loaded rifles and prepared for their coming.

Sure enough, come daylight, they came swarming into the yard shooting fire arrows, but met with lead flying at them. Four Ute braves fell from their horses and the others turned tail and raced away.

Shortly, they came back, palms raised forward. It was a sign to let me know they were only there to get their dead.

None of the fire arrows had set the cabin ablaze, and the Utes left in defeat, once again.

CHASING THE NEXT SUNRISE

Like almost everybody else, Indians don't like defeat, and I knew they would be back. When, I had no idea, but I was positive they would make sure I was alone before they came.

Over the next two years, during the spring, summer and fall months, I fought them off each time they came – with a little help from ingenuity. I sat traps for them that cost them lives each time they came. But still they came. I was the thorn in their side that they couldn't pull out – not until I was truly dead.

So, here I sit with another winter upon me as I wait for the first thaw and their arrival.

I have plenty to eat and books that I've read several times and will read again to pass the time. I doubt I'll have time to set traps, so I'll rely on my rifles and pistols. Maybe this time, they will win. Hopefully, not.

THIRTY-ONE

I'm back. The winter is waning. The sun is out and soon they will come. The snow is melting and I have now seen fifty-four winters. Will I see fifty-five? Only time will tell.

I opened the door and windows to let in the fresh air. Although the air still has a bite to it, it is better than the ripe smell after being closed in for three and a half months.

Not knowing when they will come, I will need to clean and wash everything, along with going out and finding fresh meat. I still have enough canned goods to last for a few weeks, but not much longer.

I had just stepped outside the barn after feeding and watering the horses when I saw them standing at the edge of the forest, staring at me.

I continued on back to my cabin and went inside. They were in no hurry. They just wanted me to know they were there and that my time was short.

ADDENDMENT TO MY JOURNAL

I write this as a last will and testament, leaving the mine and this property to whomever finds this journal, and God have mercy on your soul if the Utes are still around.

With that said, I must now prepare myself for war.

THIRTY-TWO

It has been three days now since my last entry, and there is much to tell. They came – the Ute braves, and this time they had more than just bows and arrows, they had rifles.

They were of the old cap and ball, type, but still, more deadly than bows and arrows.

From inside the trees, they were able to fire their bullets at the cabin. Why they wasted lead on the wall of my cabin, I was, at first, not sure. Then through the peek hole in the window shutter, I saw four braves run out and shoot fire arrows at my cabin. Once again, they were trying to burn my cabin down, with me in it – or force me to come out where they could shoot me. I suppose, either way, they were going to burn my cabin down – again.

Lucky for me, while down in Denver, over the years, I had purchased several lever-action rifles and five shot pistols – which made me sort of a one-man army.

With a bucket of water, I stepped through the front door and doused out the flaming arrows, then ducked back inside as a hail of arrows slammed against the door and wall of the cabin, along with two pieces of lead ball.

Next, I flung the door open and with my rifle at my shoulder, I sent three braves to the happy hunting grounds – then ducked back inside, again.

For three days now, I have held my own against them, but I'm almost out of water and can no longer put out the fire arrows if they shoot them. I haven't slept for three days and I'm bone weary, tired. I can hardly keep my eyes open. If it wasn't for the coffee I've been swilling and the fact that I rubbed smoking tobacco in my eyes, causing them to burn like the fires of hell, I'm sure I would have fallen asleep, and prey to my enemy, the Ute Indians, a day or so back.

Through the peek hole, I saw two of them belly crawling toward the cabin. With what little strength I had left, I staggered to the door, flung it open and fired at the two braves.

I missed both of them, but the bullets came close enough to cause them to jump to their feet and run for the shelter of the trees.

I took a sip of tepid coffee, then went back and looked through the peek hole, trying to prepare myself for one last stand, because I know that is all I have left in me. I'm sure with this next attack, I am going to die, but not without one final battle.

The area around the cabin was clear, which made me think they were talking about what to do, next, and I would be safe to take a short break.

I went back to the table and drank more of the tepid coffee in the hopes it would help me stay awake for one last hoorah. I must have fallen asleep and woke up, coughing. The cabin was filled with smoke and I could hear the flames eating away the roof. I tried to stand up and go to the door but my legs gave out and I felt myself falling.

How long I lay there, I don't know, but somewhere in the distance I heard yelling, loud screaming, and gunfire, then everything turned black.

The next thing I knew, I was outside the burning cabin, bent over, with someone beating on my back. I coughed several times, then was stood up and given a drink of water.

When the world quit spinning and my eyesight returned, I was staring into the face of my Shoshone brother, Screaming Cougar.

"Good. You still among the living," he said with a grin on his mouth, but fear in his eyes.

Later with more water and a few good pulls on a bottle of whiskey I had in the barn, I began to feel like I just might make it.

"How did you come to be here?" I finally asked.

"We come to see if you want to go hunting, and when we got close, we could see the smoke and smell the fire, and we knew you were in trouble," Screaming Cougar said to the nodding of heads of the six other Shoshone braves.

"You look very tired. How long you fight with the Utes?" Swift Runner asked.

I thought for a moment or two before answering, "This is the fourth day."

"You were here alone, fighting with no time to sleep?" Screaming Cougar asked.

"How could I?" I asked. "Had I gone to sleep, I would have died."

I stood at the opening of the barn and stared at the burning cabin. Once again, I was without a home.

"You will come with us. We will take you back to our village, where you can rest in peace,"

I didn't have the will to argue, so I allowed them to hook up the team, tie the riding horses to the back, then help me lay down in the bed of the wagon.

I think I was probably asleep before we got out of the yard.

It's a funny thing; knowing you're in danger, you can go without sleep for days, but once the danger is over and you're safe, nothing you can do will hold your eyelids open.

They said I slept for two days, only coming awake to drink some water and take a little broth.

On the third day, after eating, bathing in the river and putting on clean clothes provided by Screaming Cougar, I was called into the main lodge, where, Screaming Cougar and four other tribal leaders, sat, staring up at me.

They indicated I sit down and I did – then, after looking at the others and getting nods of their heads, Screaming Cougar said, "During your time of sleep, we raided the Ute camp. The few braves we left alive, along with the women and children, were sent in search of another place to camp – far, far from here. They will not bother our brother, White Wolf, again."

I couldn't believe they had done that. I started to say something, but was stifled with Screaming Cougar raising his hand.

"We have further discussed the problem of your cabin and we believe you should come and live with us."

I was touched. I mean, really touched. To think they would take me in, meant a lot, but I couldn't do it – nor could I go back to live at the mine and build another cabin.

"Thank you, my brothers. You are generous and kind, to a fault – but I no longer have a desire to live up here," I told them.

They were startled by this news and mumbled among themselves until finally, Rusted Nail looked at me and asked, "Why you no want to live here where there is good water and plenty of game and those yellow rocks you like so much?

"Is it because Calling Bird is no longer here? There are plenty of our squaws who would be honored to share your bed. You can have your pick," Rusted Nail told me, pointing toward the opening of the wickiup.

"Again, I am honored at your generosity, but it is time for me to go back down and be with my own people," I told them.

"Then go down to Denver if you must, but when you get tired of them, you come back to live with the people and we will have several squaws to greet you and welcome you back," Rusted Nail said with a lot of assurance.

I didn't want to hurt his feelings by telling him I would never return or that I wouldn't be living in Denver. Where I was going, I didn't know, but from what I'd learned, there was a whole lot of this America still to see. So, I nodded my head and said, "It is good to know that I will always be welcome here, and if the whites get to be too much for me, I will always know I have a place to come to. Thank you, my brothers. And if for some reason, I do not make it back, know that you will always be with me in here," I said, pointing to my heart.

The following day, I hitched the team and tied my two riding horses to the back of the wagon, leaving four others for my brother, Screaming Cougar.

The entire village stood and waved goodbye to me as I left their camp and headed for Denver.

I was once again, heading into the unknown. Where I would wind up or where I would settle down, if I ever did decide to settle down, again, was still an adventure to unfold.

THIRTY-THREE

Before going down to Denver, I made a quick detour back to the mine and collected what gold I had hidden in the barn. It was a hefty sack and I had a twinge of guilt. Rufus should be here to share, and Lars, too.

I stood, staring around, one last time and chuckled to myself about writing that stuff in this journal about willing the mine to whoever finds this place and the journal. I didn't get killed, and I'm still writing in my journal, and to be honest, the mine isn't mine to give away. It should now go to Lars.

Just then a thought struck me and I tucked it into the hidden part of my brain, to be thought about, later, should the occasion arise.

As I drove the wagon away, I glanced over my shoulder for one last look. This place had been my home for many years – mine and Calling Bird's. And before that, Rufus and Lars. There would always be memories, but it was time to move on.

Denver had changed a lot since the last time I was here. It had grown. With all the mining and trading going on, it had spread out, and would soon be a thriving city. In fact, it was now being called, The Mile High City. In 1858, it would be changed to Denver.

After putting the horses and wagon up at the livery, I went to the bank and left the gold with the bank president, Randolph Samuels, who I had come to know and trust. "I need to get cleaned up, some, and put some food in my stomach. I'll be back in the morning," I told him.

"It will be right here when you return, "he told me, putting the sack of gold in the safe.

I purchased some new clothes – a suit, this time, with a white shirt, and some shiny new boots.

The little gal at the bath house, brought me a bottle of bourbon and a cigar and giggled and almost blushed when she climbed into the tub with me. I gave her a twenty dollar gold piece. I had a stab of consciousnesses. But Calling Bird had been gone for some time, and…

186

Dressed in my new clothes, I walked into the general store. It was crowded, so I just meandered around, looking at things.

Gretchen must have noticed me wandering around, but hadn't yet recognized me and came over to me and said, "May I help… Jubal! Is that really you!" And with that she threw her arms around my neck, kissing me on the cheek – right there in front of God and the whole world.

"Jubal? It is you. Vell I'll be," Lars said, taking me into a bear hug that nearly broke my ribs and backbone.

Lars turned and looked at the people staring at us and said, "Dis is Jubal Courtney, da man I haft tole you about. My partner who helped find da gold so I could buy dis store from my fadder-in-law."

I think I shook hands with almost everyone in the store. After they left and things quieted down, I asked if I could buy them some supper because I had something I wanted to talk to them about. They already knew about my losing Calling Bird, so they knew that wasn't it.

"Sure, sure," Lars said, nodding his head at Gretchen who was also nodding her head.

"Vee can go to da nice place up da street – Da Chicago House. Dey surbe goot steaks dere," Lars said, pointing.

"What's wrong with going down to the restaurant we always go to? Sally's place?" I asked.

"It burned down 'bout six months ago. Da Chicago House is goot. You vill like it," Lars said, nodding his head, again.

The Chicago House was impressive with all the frills a fancy restaurant could have, and the food was excellent. The menu was two pages long.

Lars and I had steaks with all the trimmings, while Gretchen had an Italian dish that had a lot of sea food in it.

For dessert, we had large pieces of pecan pie with ice cream, and cups of coffee - and that was when I broached the subject that had been rolling around in my head, along with telling them of my plan for the future.

"I've left the mine for good this time, and Lars, you are now the sole owner. We can find a lawyer and make it legal."

Both Lars and Gretchen were giving me a stunned look, and Gretchen said, "It's Calling Bird, isn't it? You miss her and don't want to be up there anymore."

"That's part of it. And I'm tired of looking over my shoulder all the time, expecting a Ute or Cheyenne brave to come sneaking up on me. Although, my Shoshone friends said they run them off after this last skirmish, I can never be sure."

"Vhat last skirmish?" Lars asked.

I took a sip of coffee and said, "This sure is good pie, don't you think?"

"Don't be changin' da question. Vhat skirmish?"

"They tried again a few days back. I fought 'em off for three days, but on the fourth day, I was so sleepy I couldn't keep my eyes open and they shot fire arrows onto the roof of the cabin. I would probably have died had not our friends, the Shoshone, ridden up and drove them away – then carried me down to their camp and nursed me back to health. Screaming Cougar said they raided the Ute camp and drove them away, telling them to never return, but who knows the mind of a Ute?"

"Are you saying they burned the cabin down, again?" Gretchen asked.

I nodded my head, yes. "And for the last time as far as I'm concerned. I'm done with the place – it's all yours," I told them.

"You're sure?" Lars asked. "You vill alvays be a partner if you vant ta come back."

"I'm more than sure. I'm positive. I have plenty of money to see me for many years to come and I'm told there is a lot of America out there for me to see, which is what I plan to do."

Lars had a funny grin on his face and I asked, "Did I say something funny?" I asked.

Lars shook his head. "No, it vas not vhat you said dat is funny. Yust da situation, I tink."

"And what situation might that be, Mister Hollinbooster?"

Lars wiped his mouth with his napkin and said, "You gift da mine over ta me, just as Gretchen's nephew, Albert Olsson and his vife, Astrid, come from da ole country and lookin' fer vork."

I must have had a puzzled look on my face because Gretchen said, "Don't you see? We will need someone that we can trust, to work the mine. And who better than our own family?"

I could see their point and said, "Well, I'm glad things are working out, and now I know what to do with the wagon, draft horses and riding stock. It will be my welcoming gift to them, to help them get started."

Lars looked at me and said, "You are goot man, Jubal Courtney. And ah goot friend. I vill tank you for dem."

I had another thought and said, "Before you start building a new cabin, I suggest you take them up to the Shoshone camp and introduce them to Screaming Cougar and his people. Otherwise, things might get a little dicey."

"Ya, I see vhat you mean. Maybe you could come vit us?"

I thought for a moment. I was anxious to start my new adventure, but the truth was, it would be better if I explained things to Screaming Cougar, so I said, "Sure. Why not."

I chuckled inside as I introduced Albert and Astrid to Screaming Cougar and his people.

With his eyes wide, Screaming Cougar looked up at Albert's face – and I said, up, because Albert stood six feet seven inches and was almost as thick as a Redwood tree.

"You are the biggest white man I have ever seen," Screaming Cougar said, nodding his head.

"Ant you be da first Indian I ebber met," Albert said.

Astrid was surprised that the Shoshone spoke better English than either her or Albert.

In less than half an hour, they were all chatting like they'd known each other for years.

I spent the night, but the following morning, I felt anxious to be on my way and said so.

"We will do what we can to help your friends," Screaming Cougar said, as we said our last goodbyes.

I rode into town and down to the livery stable to put up one of the horses I'd given to Albert and Astrid, then went to see my favorite banker.

CHASING THE NEXT SUNRISE

    With a thousand dollars in my pocket, and the knowledge of how to transfer money from the Denver bank to a bank wherever I wound up. There was a lot to see out there and I bought a saddle horse and a pack mule. The first place I was going to see was a place down in Kansas, called, Cow Town.

THIRTY-FOUR

The trip was comfortable. Kansas was flat, with miles and miles of nothing but miles and miles. The highlight was a herd of Buffalo that stretched out as far as the eye could see.

Cow Town was a cattle town and full of cowboys and action – in fact, more action than I liked. Within a minute of riding up in front of the hotel, I saw two men come out of a saloon and shoot each other down.

I vowed to not stay long, and I didn't, but I couldn't get a train going to Kansas City for two days.

After checking into the hotel, I went into the dining room and sat down and ordered a whiskey before my meal to calm my nerves a little. I asked the waitress what the special of the day was – expecting her to say, a steak, because of this being a cattle town, but she surprised me and said, "Fresh Catfish."

She pointed to a man standing at the bar and said, "He just brought them in less than an hour ago.

The fish was excellent, with fried potatoes, green beans and cornbread. I had coffee to go with my meal, and afterward, I walked over to the bar and introduced myself, and we struck up a conversation about fishing. He said, as far as catfish were concerned, there wasn't a better place in this part of the country than on the Arkansas River.

I spent the next day, fishing with him and never have I had a better time. I caught six, very large catfish, while he caught nine. I gave him my catch and he sold the whole lot to the various restaurants around town.

I left Wichita, with fond memories of my day of fishing and the fact that there were no more shootouts.

From Wichita, I traveled to Kansas City, where I caught a train up to Chicago. Chicago sits next to a huge lake and I charted a boat and went fishing, again. Chicago is a growing city, but it's not for me. I'm not sure what I am searching for, but I hope I will know it when I find it, if I ever do.

CHASING THE NEXT SUNRISE

I am still in the prime of life and have a pocket full of money, thanks to Rufus and his gold mine – a hundred and sixty-eight thousand dollars, to be exact. But, while I have more money than I ever thought I might have, I didn't flaunt it. Yes, I stay in nice hotels and eat good food, and even wear better than average clothes, but I don't live a lavish lifestyle.

When I arrived in New York City, I had mixed emotions about the city. It was already overcrowded, in my humble opinion. And there was far too much crime, but it was an important city with all its banks and big business, and the port was impressive. I even went to the opera. I didn't quite understand it because it was in Italian, and I don't speak Italian, but the audience seemed to like it very much because at the end, they stood up and applauded for a long time.

From New York, I boarded a ship that would take me down along the east coast of America, to a city called, Charleston. That would have been in the fall of1858. I celebrated my fifty sixth birthday aboard the ship with a widow lady from a place called, Boston.

Charleston is a beautiful city filled with southern charm and architect. Men and women stroll the promenade, dressed to the nines. Women with their large hats shading eyes that take you in from head to toe, inviting you into their world, and men who dare you to try. The most depressing thing I felt in Charleston was that they seemed to be in a big argument with the folks up north about slavery. Seems the people down south thought it was a good idea and some of them owned several hundred black people as slaves, along with a few white men and women - and the folks up north didn't like it. It seemed to be what everyone was talking about. The way things were going, it might escalate into a war, which is never good for either side.

The other thing I didn't care much for, was the humidity and the mosquitos. I did, however, spend an entire week in Charleston due to the fact that while admiring the ships in the harbor, I noticed a lady's hat rolling down the pier, coming toward me and a young lady, chasing it. I grabbed the hat before it went flying into the bay and stood, holding it as she ran up to me and stopped.

"Thank you," she said when I handed the hat to her. "It's brand new and I was just putting it on when the wind blew it out of my hand. What can I do to repay your kindness, kind sir?"

She had the most beautiful blue eyes I'd ever seen and a figure men dream women should have.

I put the fingers of my right hand to the brim of my hat and said, "I'm glad to be of service and as far as what you can do to repay me, I would be honored if you would have supper with me – a restaurant of your choice, of course."

"Oh my, you are the forward one, aren't you?" Then, after a moment she batted her eyelashes at me and said, "Before I could possibly think of accepting your most gracious invitation, we would need to be properly introduced."

I took off my hat and made a proper bow, then held out my hand and said, "My name is Jubal Courtney. I am new to your fair city and I know no one, but I would be honored to make your acquaintance."

When she offered her hand, I took it and gently pressed my lips on it - looked her in the eyes and smiled.

She made a slight curtsey, then said, "Mister Courtney, my name is Annabelle Sanders, the daughter of Colonel Harriman Sanders of Cotton Oaks Plantation, just outside of Charleston. I am most happy to make your acquaintance, and honored to accept your invitation to supper.

She took my arm and never released it for the following six days. The morning of the seventh day, I awoke to find a note pinned to the pillow on her side of the bed.

My dearest Jubal, this past week has
been wonderful, and I thank you from
the bottom of my heart… and I will always
treasure our time together, but…
I must confess, my father and
husband will be returning from their
trip up north, and as much as I would
love to stay with you, I must return to Cotton Oaks.
I will always cherish these past few days, but do
not try and see me for it will only end tragically.
With loving memories, Annabelle…

Of course, I honored her wishes, and caught the next train heading west for Atlanta, Georgia.

Like Charleston, Atlanta was most definitely, a southern town with an abundance of southern belles and men ready to fight a duel over them.

From Atlanta, I went to the famous city of New Orleans – a city I was told, was wide open to most anything a man could want. And I must tell you, never in my life have I seen more beautiful women than the Creole, with their dark hair and eyes. And even as passionate as Annabelle had been, the several Creole women I was fortunate to meet were even more so.

At one gambling house, I won eight thousand dollars in a poker game and when I left, two men followed me, hoping to relieve me of my winnings – but I was not the easily picked tenderfoot they expected me to be.

I ducked into the first alley I came to and waited, with my pistol in my hand. They came running into the alley, and hauled up seeing the pistol pointed at them.

To make a long story short, I made them strip down to their bare skin and walk back out onto the sidewalk, while I yelled out to the people staring at them. "These men tried to rob me of my money, so in turn, I took their clothes."

People were falling down with laughter as the two men tried to find somewhere to hide.

I saw a man burning some trash and dumped the men's clothes into the barrel and walked on down the street.

I didn't stay around New Orleans long after that. I had humiliated two, bad men and I had no doubt they would come looking for revenge.

I caught a paddlewheel boat heading north, which the man at the station said was going to a place called St. Louis. "It sits right alongside the Mississippi River. It's the stepping off place for folks going west. There are a few stops along the way and no problems with sandbars. You should be in St. Louis in a couple of weeks."

I was in no hurry and from what I'd heard, there was more to do aboard the boat than watch the banks of the river. The Princess Queen, was bigger than I thought it might be. I purchased one of the state rooms where I could stay by myself. As I walked up the gangplank, the captain was there to greet us. He was a jovial soul, with muttonchop whiskers and stood close to six feet, towering over most of the passengers. When he shook my hand, he held it long enough to give me the once over, as though he saw something he didn't like. "I don't hold to trouble on my boat," he said, looking me straight in the eyes.

"Not looking for any," I said in reply.

"I saw what you did in town," he told me of the incident with the two robbers.

"They jumped me, not the other way around," I told him.

He squeezed my hand a little tighter and said, "Just don't give me cause to dump you in the river. It holds its fair share of gators."

While I was putting my bag in my quarters, I felt the boat leave the dock. I walked out and stood at the rail, and was too slow to move back when I saw the two men that had tried to rob me. They were standing on the dock, staring at me with hate in their eyes.

I put my fingers to the brim of my hat in salute, then turned and went inside, searching for a poker game.

The room was quite large for being on a boat. There were a good twenty tables used for eating and playing poker. There was a large stage at the far end of the room, along with a bar against one wall. Most of the tables were already full and waiters were taking food orders – and since I hadn't eaten, I found a place at the bar and ordered beer and a bowl of fish stew.

After lunch, I strolled along the deck for a while, then went to my room and took a nap. The steady drone of the paddlewheel put me right to sleep.

I awoke sometime later when the boat grazed a sandbar and slowed it down some, but only for a moment or two. The boat had a bath and shave room and I went there to get cleaned up before going into the big room for some supper and maybe a little poker. I loved the game and had become quite proficient at it – along with having a large helping of luck.

I had a steak dinner and coffee. If I could get into a poker game, I wanted a clear head. Of course, I encouraged the others to drink up, if that was their desire. After eating, I walked around the room and in the far corner, I found a poker game going on with one space open. I asked if I could join and was offered the empty seat. "Twenty dollar buy-in for the house," the dealer informed me. I gave him the money, then bought five hundred in chips.

I excused myself before the first hand, saying I needed to use the privy before beginning. But in truth, I found the man who waited on our table and gave him a ten spot to bring me only sarsaparilla, no matter what I ordered. He winked at me and said, "As you wish, sir."

At the table, I ordered a whiskey, straight up, and took a long pull when it came. The sarsaparilla was sweet tasting and I licked my lips. "I do like a good southern mash," I told my fellow players, who all had drinks sitting next to their chips.

The cards were good to me and each time I won a hand, I bought a round of drinks.

Later, standing on the deck, enjoying a cigar and looking at the lights of homes along the shore, one of the players staggered up to me and said, "Tonight was your lucky night, but I fancy tomorrow, it will be my turn."

He was short, bald and very rotund – and well-oiled from the drinks I'd bought.

"You just may be right, my friend. You just might be right," I told him, patting him on the shoulder before turning and heading for my stateroom. I had won a little over thirty-five hundred dollars and was not planning on giving them a chance to get their money, back.

The following morning, I was standing at the rail marveling at how large the river was, when I saw two men coming toward me. I gave a sigh and wondered how they had gotten aboard. I knew the boat made a lot of stops along the way, for various reasons, like unloading and loading passengers, along with freight. They must have ridden hard and gotten on at the first stop.

I remembered what the captain said about being thrown overboard and didn't care for that idea, so, I turned and ran for the pilot house with them right on my heels.

When I entered the pilot house, the captain looked at me and was about to say something when the two men came rushing in. One of them grabbed for me, but I shied away and stopped next to the captain, who said, "What's going on, here?"

"These are the two men who tried to rob me, back in New Orleans," I told him and before he could reply, one of the men spoke up.

"That's a lie! We were just trying to get back the money he cheated us out of," one of the men said, well above normal volume.

"Are you implying he is a crooked dealer?" the captain asked.

"I never dealt. There was a house dealer," I said.

"Him and the dealer were in cahoots," the man said.

"How could that be when I was just passing through town? I had never been there before and I didn't know the dealer.

"Hold on just ah goldarned minute," the captain said. "Were the two of you playing at the table?"

They were stumped for a moment and I was sure the captain could see it. Finally, the shorter of the two said, "No, just me. It was my friend here who saw them cheating."

"And just how much did you lose?" the captain asked, stumping them, again.

"Ah… well now, let's see. I can't tell you exactly, but it was in the neighborhood of a thousand dollars."

I'd had enough, but kept my calm. "You are such a liar. Neither of you were playing cards at that table. You were standing against the wall, swilling beer while you watched the game, and the two of you followed me out of the place, then down the street. You're just mad because I caught onto what you were up to and one upped you. You're just mad because I embarrassed you in front of the people."

The bigger of the two men took a step forward with a pistol in his hand. "Don't matter that we weren't in the game. What matters is, you won a lot of money and we want it, so hand it over and I won't have to shoot you."

The captain looked at me and said, "Looks like I got my answer. You planning on giving them your money?"

I grinned and said, "Don't reckon I am."

The captain grinned at me and asked, "You thinking what I'm thinking?"

I smiled and said, "I do believe I am."

And with that, I rushed the one with the pistol, while the captain grabbed the other one.

With one hand holding the gun hand and my other hand around his throat, I backed him out of the pilothouse door and shoved him, backward over the rail. The captain came through the door with the other man by his shirt collar and the seat of his pants and pitched him over the rail.

As the paddleboat continued on up the river, we could see them swimming for the shore where there was no sign of life.

The captain grinned and stuck out his hand. "That was fun... And thank you for keeping your word and coming to me rather than taking them on by yourself."

The rest of the trip was a pleasant one. I ate well, had a few drinks, watched a few shows and got a lot of rest – all the while, with over a total of eleven thousand dollars in winnings from the gambling house in New Orleans and the high rollers on the boat. Life was good.

Even though I felt safe enough, at each place we stopped, I kept a sharp eye out for the two men we tossed over the side of the boat. They had been humiliated, twice, and if I was any judge, they would be wanting revenge in the worst way.

But once again, Lady Luck rode on my shoulder.

THIRTY-FIVE

St. Louis was a mixture of old and new. Construction was going on everywhere I looked. I found a nice-looking hotel near the docks and rented a room for an undetermined time.

St. Louis was loaded with hustle and bustle. People were running around like worker ants – many bent on going west to find gold in the mountains of Colorado.

While eating supper on my second night in town, at a hotel up near the center of the city, I got to thinking and calculating and figured I'd been gone from Denver a little more than two years. I'd seen the big cities and had me some adventures - I surely had. I knew that St. Louis didn't have anything keeping me here, and wondered where I should go next. I'd already been west, so that was out. Maybe South America?

I wandered into a bar for a cold beer and since I was early, there weren't many people in the place and I happened to strike up a conversation with the bartender.

He said he was from Cincinnati, Ohio, and had come west to make his fortune, but had gone bust without striking it rich and had come back this far. "Saving my money to lay claim to a piece of land about a hundred and fifty miles from here as the crow flies."

"Farm land?" I asked.

"Forest land," he said, "And it bumps up against the best fishing lake you've ever seen," he told me with a grin.

"Nice lake, you say?" I asked.

"You bet, and ah big 'in too. Close to a hundred miles long, I'm told."

"Fella that lives down there said he's caught fish outta that lake that was as long as he is tall," the bartender said, nodding his head up and down.

"Good land you say?" I asked… somewhat intrigued.

The more we talked about the place the more curious I was and asked him if he was going down anytime soon?

"Come next payday, I'll have enough saved to make the trip to find just the right spot and stake out my claim, then come back here to register it."

"When is payday?" I asked.

"Two days from now. Why you asking?"

I swallowed the last of my beer and pushed the glass over, indicating I wanted another one.

When he got back, I said, "If you don't mind, I'd like to tag along. Sounds interesting, and I'll share the expenses..."

"You looking for a place to settle down?" He asked.

"Could be, if the place strikes my fancy," I told him, wondering if that was so, or was I just curious to see this place that had fish as long as a man was tall.

Three days later we rode out of St. Louis, headed due west, on two horses we'd bought, along with two pack horses loaded with enough supplies for at least a month, or more.

It was late afternoon on the third day when we topped over a rise, and there it was, as pretty body of water as you've ever seen. The sun was making the water glitter like diamonds sparkling.

"That it?" I asked.

"That's it!" he shouted.

To me it looked like a long, wide river, which it turned out to be, but I held my tongue. We were sitting on a rise some six or seven hundred feet from the water and all around, as far as I could see, were trees of several kind.

I got down off my horse and scooped up a handful of dirt and let it sift through my fingers, then lifted it to my nose and smelled. This was good land – dark brown. It would grow most anything a man wanted to plant.

We rode down next to the water, near a small inlet - and made camp. I swam across and secured one end of a trout line on the far bank. Using worms I'd dug up, as bait, I set six hooks. After putting my clothes back on, I made a pot of coffee and set it on the fire to perk.

As we stood, looking out across the water, I asked, "Where are you planning to stake out your claim?"

"Why, right here looks good enough to me," he said, waving his arm around. I got enough money for twenty acres."

"How much are they asking per acre?" I asked, looking around, knowing the timber alone would be worth a fortune.

"Two dollars an acre," he told me.

After a moment, I said, "I'd like to see what's on the other side and if I like what I see, I'm thinking I'll file on some land too, but a whole lot more than twenty acres."

"You got that kind of money?" he asked.

Now I wasn't about to tell him about the money in the belt strapped around my waist, so I said, "Not on me but I can get it. I have a little put away in a bank in Denver."

"What are you planning to do with the land?" I asked.

He grinned and said, "I've got it all figured out. I'll cut down and sell enough timber to get me a stake so I can build a cabin and put in a crop. Then me and Audrey are gonna get hitched and move in. Audrey is my girlfriend."

I thought for a moment, then motioned that the coffee was ready. Over coffee, I asked, "What if you could buy, say a thousand acres?"

"Oh sure, and where would I get that kind of money – an angel loaded with cash gonna come down out of the sky and hand it to me?"

I scratched the back of my neck and said, "Maybe not an angel, but maybe a business partner."

He got a puzzled look on his face and over a dinner of fresh trout and bass, fried potatoes and canned tomatoes, I explained what I had in mind.

It took us several days, but we staked out more than a thousand acres along the shoreline and inland close to half a mile.

Next, we cut down some trees and made a raft big enough to take us and the horses across to the far side, where I staked out the same amount of land.

Back in St. Louis, at the age of fifty-seven, I went to the bank and had them wire Denver for ten thousand dollars, and two days later, we went to the registrar's office and filed our claims.

The deal was, I would provide the money to purchase the land on the proviso that he give me a third of the profits from selling the timber until the debt was paid off, then the land would be his, free and clear.

He'd talked it over with Audrey and as far as she was concerned, I was an angel with a pocket full of money. She was a nice girl, with a lot of spirit and a good sense about her. I liked them both.

We decided we would cut the timber and clear the land for their cabin, first, and then, build mine, but wound up only building theirs. I was in no hurry, but he was. I was to be the best man at their wedding and he could hardly wait.

It was a simple wedding, but nice. Audrey's parents owned a mercantile store in St. Louis, where we purchased, for a discount, all the things we would need, that they could supply. The rest, we ordered from a catalog. The newlyweds settled into the cabin and I set up a tent on the far side of the lake, on my newly acquired land. This was not only beautiful country but one of these days, when people found out about it, they would pay top dollar for the land, and I would be sitting on more than a thousand acres.

The young man's name was Charles Benson, but everyone called him, Charlie. So, every morning, Charlie would come over and help me until noon. Then I would go back across the river, where Audrey would have a nice lunch prepared.

Charlie and I would cut and stack timber in the afternoon on both sides of the lake.

After a month, we had a small, three-room cabin built on my land and I needed things from St. Louis.

Charlie promised to keep an eye on my place while I rode into St. Louis to see about the things I needed, along with a list of things Audrey wanted.

The first thing I did was buy a team of draft horses and a sturdy wagon. The draft horses weren't Clydesdales, but they were big and strong.

Next, I went to Audrey's parents store and hinted to Audrey's mother, what I needed in the way of furniture and such. She smiled, then patted me on the cheek and said, "Just leave it to me. Now, draw me a picture and tell me how big each room is. And don't forget to draw in the windows, if there are any."

As I left the mercantile store to go to the general store for canned goods and such, I saw a young woman running down the sidewalk in my direction. An older man, wearing dirty, ragged clothes, seemed to be chasing her. He was yelling, "Stop, you little hussy, you're mine, bought and paid for!"

Being taller, he took longer strides and caught up with her and reached out and grabbed her by the back of her dress and jerked.

Her feet came off the sidewalk and she landed on her rear with a loud thud. Next, he grabbed her by the hair on her head and slapped her face. "I'll teach you to try and run away from me, you little tramp!"

Indeed, she wasn't much to look at. Her clothes were nothing more than dirty rags and she had dirty hands, face and bare feet. And her hair looked like a bird's nest.

The truth was, no matter what she looked like, she was a girl and men just didn't go around hitting on women and girls. It just wasn't right.

As he raised his hand to hit her, again, I grabbed his wrist and jerked his arm back.

He swung around and stared at me and I could understand why a person would run away from him. His breath stunk of whiskey; his teeth were brown with tobacco stains, and he was in bad need of a bath. The man stunk to high heaven.

"You got no truck with this, Mister. Now get on down the street before I mess you up, bad."

"Where I come from, we don't beat our women," I said, staring him in the eyes.

"I'll do as I damn well please. She's bought and paid for, fair and square," he said.

"Where I'm from, we don't buy and sell our women, either. So, I'd be obliged if you take your dirty paws off her."

He glared at me for only a moment, then grabbed his knife and took a swing at me.

I stepped back and went into a crouch, watching his eyes and when he swung the knife, again, I was ready for him. I pushed the knife hand away from me and drove my fist into his gut.

A rush of air came out, then I hit him in the stomach a second time and saw him stagger backwards.

Turning, I grabbed his arm and drove it down across my knee, sideways, and heard it break. He dropped the knife and yelled, "You son of a…"

That was as far as he got before I drove my fist into his jaw with all the power I had.

His eyes went wide, then he toppled over backward and landed flat on his back, causing several of the sidewalk boards to break.

I took her hand, gently in mine and said, "We need to get you out of here."

I took her to the mercantile store and told Audrey's mother what had happened and after laying money on the counter, I asked her if she would see to helping the young lady get cleaned up and into some new clothes.

Before leaving the store, I peeked around the edge and saw the man, holding his arm and limping down the sidewalk in the direction of the doctor's office.

I rented her a room at the hotel, then took her to supper in the hotel dining room. Now that she was cleaned up and in decent clothes, she was beautiful. Auburn hair, brown eyes and a smile that needed a good teeth cleaning.

Two doors up the street, I paid a dentist to see what he could do. During all of this, she hadn't uttered a word.

When the dentist was finished, he gave her a brush and some powder to help keep her teeth clean. She took them, then followed me out of the office.

When we were once again, sitting at the table in the dining room, she finally spoke. "So, am I to be your property, now?"

I shook my head and said, "Nope. You're a free woman to go or do as you please. I was just concerned about your safety. Once we've eaten…" I left the statement hanging.

Her eyes softened and she looked at me quizzically. "I have no place to go. My father doesn't want me, that's why he sold me to Walter. I have no other family."

I thought for a moment then said, "I have an idea I'd like to run by you and if you like it, I can ask Charlie and Audrey if they like it too."

A look of distrust was written all over her face and who could blame her after what she must have gone through.

"Where did you live before your father sold you to Walter?" I asked, trying to get her to open up some.

"Deep down in the bayou of Louisiana. My father traps alligators and runs moonshine for a man not far from us," she said… "But I don't want to go back there! Please, don't make me go back there!"

Her voice was beginning to rise and her breathing became labored. "Whoa. Hold on. Relax. You don't have to go anywhere you don't want to. Like I said, you're a free woman. My idea is only to keep you safe, not to enslave you," I spoke to her with as much sympathy as I could muster.

"You said you have an idea?" she said, reluctantly.

I smiled and said, "If we're to continue talking, it would be helpful if I knew your name."

"You first," she said with a coy, smile.

"My name is Jubal Courtney and I'm originally from Ireland. How I got here is a very long story… Maybe I'll tell you, another time. I have a place three days from here, and yes, I have an idea that hopefully will help you get out of this situation you're in and keep you safe."

She looked at me for a long time before answering. I think she was trying to make up her mind if she could trust me, or not.

"My name is Ressie Mae Sterner. I'm the oldest of seven children and like I said, papa sold me to Walter because he didn't want me around, any more. Walter brought me up here to rent me out to men, but I ran away and you know the rest. So, what's your idea to protect me? I will not do what he wanted me to do."

"And you shouldn't have to," I told her. "My friends and I, each have a large piece of land, about a hundred and fifty miles from here. It's out in the wilderness, next to a large river. My spread is on the opposite side of the river. Charlie and Audrey are newlyweds and not much older than you. I think, since there is no town nearby, you would be good company for her. You could help with the place until such a time as you think it's safe to leave. No strings attached."

I sat back and stared at her – and she back at me. After a minute or so, she said she would give it a try.

If she slept at night during our trip, I would be surprised. She was awake when I curled up in my blankets and awake, drinking coffee when I woke up.

I stopped the wagon at the top of the rise where you could see Charlie and Audrey's place. It was clean and pretty as a picture.

Ressie Mae looked at the place, then all around her and for the first time, she smiled and said, "You weren't funnin' me… It's beautiful here and far away from St. Louis. Do you think the Bensons will like me?"

"Without a doubt," I told her. Truth was, I liked her.

"And you said your place is across the river? Is it beautiful like the one on this side?"

"Not yet, but one day, with a woman's touch…" I told her, and got a curious look in return.

The Bensons liked her from the get-go, and she them. Audrey was especially glad to have another woman to talk to and Ressie Mae pitched in and was a good worker.

After a week, she talked me into taking her over to my place, where she immediately began to fix up the inside of the house.

By the time winter was upon us, Audrey was with child and Ressie Mae was part of the family on both sides of the river. No longer was she untrusting. Audrey and Ressie Mae were as close as sisters… Better than many.

And as for me and Ressie Mae, well I guess we were getting pretty close. She was smart and beautiful, and not afraid to pitch in when needed. And as time went along, she spent more and more time on my side of the river.

I had decided that for the time being, I would cut down, mainly, only hickory and pine trees for selling. There was a big demand for both of them and I had an abundance of them – as did Charlie, on his side of the river.

There were plenty of fescue grass for the horses and the few cows Ressie Mae recommended I buy. Apparently, she'd had enough deer meat. Plus, one of the cows was a milker, so Charlie and Audrey's baby would have plenty of milk to add to the milk they got from their cow that Ressie Mae had also recommended they buy.

Besides the hickory and pine trees, I had maple, dogwood, oak and apple. Game was never a problem as far as meat went, and the river furnished all the fish we wanted. In fact, I was thinking that I might start a hunting and fishing business. I was sure if I bought a few more acres of wilderness, and put up posters, and ads in the paper, back in St. Louis, men would come to hunt and fish. And from there, who knew?

The lumber business became so good, Charlie and I, each bought another thousand acres – him on his side of the river and me, on my side. And I bought an extra five hundred for the hunting business I was planning on opening. I also purchased several canoes for people to go fishing in, along with fishing equipment to go in the small store I was about to build. I even thought of building some cabins to rent out.

Audrey had a beautiful baby boy and six months later when he was able to travel, we decided to celebrate, and take a trip to St. Louis.

Ressie Mae was reluctant to go because she thought Walter might still be there. I laughed and said, "It's been over a year. Walter will be long gone by now."

And that's how I convinced her to go. Big miscalculation on my part.

THIRTY-SIX

Charlie and I had both, been back to St. Louis several times with loads of timber, but neither of the women had and they marveled at how much it had grown. After checking into a hotel, Charlie and I had some business to attend to; getting new orders for lumber. The ladies went straight to the doctor's office to have little Amos, checked over, and from there, they were going shopping for new clothes for all of us, including little Amos.

Apparently, my thoughts about Walter giving up his search for Ressie Mae and going back down to Louisiana, were dead wrong.

Charlie and I had just concluded our business and were headed for the hotel dining room where we were to meet the girls for lunch when we saw Audrey hurrying toward us with a scared look on her face. And even before she got to us, I knew I had been wrong.

Gasping out the words, Audrey said, "We'd just left the doctor's office… and that awful man… Walter… came out of a store… and bumped into Ressie Mae. He… almost didn't recognize her, all cleaned up and all… but she recognized him - and that's how he knew who she was, I think."

Are you telling me, Walter is in St. Louis and took her?" I asked, my nerves growing tight.

Audrey nodded her head, yes, and I felt anger welling up inside me. Where would he have taken her? I was sure she would have mentioned me and he would hide her away until I gave up the search. Well, right then and there, I decided that wasn't going to happen. Ressie Mae Sterner had come to mean a lot to me, and if I was to admit it, I was in love with her.

While Charlie took Audrey and the baby back to the hotel, I went to see the sheriff, who said he knew who Walter was, and that he had several girls working for him but he'd never caught him doing anything illegal. He also went on to warn me to be careful because he had several thugs working for him who were real bad men. Plus, Walter was not afraid to bloody his own knuckles when he was in the mood.

For the next three days, I slept very little as I haunted every bawdy house in the entire St. Louis area, and was thrown out of several of them when I tried to talk to the women.

I didn't know Walter's last name, but as it turned out, I didn't need to. Just the mention of his name caused fear to light up in their faces. I even tried to talk to people on the street and still got no results. People were afraid of Walter and his goons and clammed up tighter than a jar of preserves.

I was lying on my hotel bed, staring at the ceiling, wondering how I would ever be able to find Walter and Ressie Mae, hoping and praying she was still all right, when there came a light tap on the door. I swung my legs over the side of the bed and jumped to my feet, rushing to the door, calling out, "Coming!" hoping it would be Ressie Mae.

When I jerked the door open, no one was there, and the hallway was empty. I turned and was about to go back into my room when a woman stepped from the doorway of the room next to mine, where she'd been hiding. "Mister Courtney?"

"Yes." I told her.

She ran up to me, handed me a piece of paper, then turned and ran back down the hallway, and disappeared down the back stairs.

I looked at the piece of paper and read the only thing on it -1012 North Walnut Street.

I walked down the hallway and tapped on Charlie and Audrey's door and when they let me in, I showed them the piece of paper.

"It's got to be the address where Ressie Mae is being held," I told them, which got an agreement from both of them.

"So... what's your plan?" Charlie asked.

"I think I should wait until around four in the morning before I go in and get her. They work late into the night and by then they'll be asleep. At least I hope so."

"Oh, no, you're not going alone," Charlie said, pointing his finger in my face.

"It's not your fight," I told him. "Besides, it might get rough and you have Audrey and little Amos to consider."

Charlie looked at me and said, "And you think she doesn't mean anything to us? Jubal, she's become family. And family takes care of each other."

"That's right," Audrey said, causing Charlie to smile.

The moon was hovering over the tops of the buildings when Charlie and I looked at the house at 1012 North Walnut Street. It appeared to be an old rooming house, with a lot of bedrooms.

There were no lights on and no signs of life as Charlie and I crept up next to a window on the side of the house and listened for anyone talking, but heard nothing.

"I think they're all asleep," Charlie whispered.

"I'll Injun up and try the front door. If it's locked, I'll try the back door. You keep an eye on the windows to see if a light comes on," I told Charlie, who nodded his head.

Indeed, both the front and back doors were locked, but I noticed the kitchen window was cracked open just a little.

With great caution, I pushed up on the window and it opened with ease.

Charlie nodded his head, indicating it was alright to go in, which we both did as quietly as we could. We stood in the kitchen, listening for any sound.

The sound of three people snoring came from the living room – and when we made our way in there, the three goons were each sprawled out on three couches, deep in sleep.

I was hoping to get in and out without waking anyone, but I still didn't know what room Ressie Mae was in, if indeed, she was here at all?

We searched the downstairs and found Walter, asleep in one of the bedrooms. Anger washed over me like a waterfall and I was tempted to kill him where he lay, but getting Ressie Mae out of that place was a stronger impulse, so I backed out and closed the door, making a slight clicking sound.

"What? Who's there?" we heard Walter say.

We froze, and waited until we heard snoring, again, then made our way up the stairs and down the hallway, opening each door and looking in. Charlie opened the fourth door and waved his arm at me.

We found Ressie Mae lying spread eagle on the bed, her hands and feet tied to the bed posts.

I put my hand over her mouth to stifle any sound as her frightened eyes popped open.

"Shhh, it's me and Charlie. We've come to take you home," I whispered.

When her arms and legs were unbound, she jumped to her feet and threw her arms around my neck and smothered my face with kisses, whispering, "I knew you would come. I just knew it!"

We left the room and tiptoed down the hallway. We were halfway down the stairs when Walter and his three goons stepped out in front of the bottom step, with pistols in their hands.

"Didn't think you could just waltz in here and steal my property, again, did ya?"

"She's not your property. She belongs with me and we're going to get married if she'll have me," I said, not believing I'd just proposed here in front of everybody.

Ressie Mae stepped behind me and said, "That's right. We're getting married, now step aside and let us through."

"Now ain't that sweet. You're planning on making my little money maker an honest woman, are ya? Ain't that a laugh, eeh, boys?" Walter said to his goons.

They laughed along with their boss.

"I don't want any trouble. Just step aside and let us leave. She's not the same woman you brought to St. Louis over a year ago. She has people who care for her," I told him.

Walter looked down at the floor, then back up at me and said, "None of those pretty words mean squat to me. Besides, you don't want a defiled woman, do you? Before you got here, me and the boys sorta broke her in for workin' the streets and bawdy houses.

"Easy," Charlie whispered, knowing my temper was rising. I also felt Ressie Mae tense behind me, before she said, "It's all right if you decide you don't want me anymore. I will understand."

And with that, she stepped up next to me and said, "Let them go and I'll do whatever you want. I'm spoiled now and no decent man will want me, so you've gotten your way. The only thing I'm good for is the streets."

She looked up at me and said, "Please, go."

Walter raised his pistol and pointed it at me, saying, "Not so fast, missy. They ain't goin' nowhere, cept in a hole out back of here."

Now, admittedly, I'm no gunman, but I practiced shooting rattlesnakes on my place and had become a fair to meddling good shot, and quick on the draw. My right hand flew down to my pistol and in the blink of an eye, I fired a bullet at Walter that took him dead center between the eyes, knocking him over backward.

At the sound of my pistol exploding, Charlie and the three goons began firing. I shoved Ressie Mae to the stairs and began shooting back.

In less than five seconds, the area was filled with smoke and smelled of gun powder.

Walter and his three goons lay, dead and bleeding on the floor. I took Ressie Mae by the hand and led her down the stairs and out the front door, as the women came out of their rooms to see what had happened.

After waking up the doctor to patch up Charlie's gunshot wound to his left arm, and him complaining it was only a flesh wound, we went to breakfast.

I had just finished telling Ressie Mae and Audrey to go pick out a dress for the wedding while I went to explain to the sheriff, what had happened – but I didn't have to.

The sheriff walked up to our table, pulled out a chair and sat down, signaling the waitress to bring him some coffee.

"Seems you boys woke up the whole north side of town. Want to tell me about it?"

As the sheriff sipped his coffee, I told the sheriff what happened, with Charlie tossing in his two cents worth, from time to time.

And when I finished, the sheriff said, "That's about what I figured, but we got us a town council who think up a lot of rules and one of them is that in a case like this, the judge has to hear what happened and then make his decision as to how it will end."

The sheriff scratched his ear, then his eyes lit up and he grinned, saying, "Well now this seems to be our lucky day, here he comes now. Comin' in for his breakfast."

We all moved to a larger table and he listened as I told him the whole story right from when I first rescued Ressie Mae and took her down to the lake to hide. I even told him the part about asking her to marry me, which drew a grin.

"So, you say this place of yours is the best fishing you've ever seen?" the judge asked.

"I'd be obliged if you could come down sometime and see for yourself. Plenty of room for you to stay… no charge," I told him.

He nodded his head and said, "I just might take you up on that. Now, as far as that hooligan, Walter, and his goons are concerned, I've suspected them of skullduggery for some time and always figured they'd end up like that. So, with that in mind, I'm declaring this case to be one of self defense."

I stood up and reached my hand across the table to thank him.

He put his hands up, palms forward, and said, "Not so fast, Mister Courtney. Didn't you two say you wanted to get married?"

"We do," I told him.

"Well, then, what's wrong with here and now. I'm available and I only charge two dollars. You got two dollars to spare?" he asked with a grin.

"But what about that dress you wanted?" I asked, looking at Ressie Mae, who was grinning from ear to ear. "And I don't have a ring." I said, my head in a daze.

Ressie Mae looked up at me and said, "If you still want me, right now is fine with me. Besides, I don't need a fancy dress, and Audrey said I could borrow her ring to get married with, and her papa sells rings down at his store. That's where Charlie got hers."

THIRTY-SEVEN

It's hard to believe that I've been living on this beautiful land for the better part of forty-five years. It's now 1906 and I'm now a hundred and four years old. Never thought I'd outlive Ressie Mae, her being so much younger than me, but she passed on five years ago, and Charlie and Audrey passed... must be fifteen years ago now.

Their son, Amos runs his parent's business now, and is married with children of his own. In fact, his sons do most of the running of the business since Amos broke his back a few years ago. He still gets around, all right, but can't do much lifting and his wife nags at him something awful if he tries.

For the most part, those years were some of the best of my life. Because of what Walter and his goons did to Ressie Mae, she could never have children which wore on her something terrible. But as the years rolled by, she came to terms with it – although, between you and me, I don't think she ever got over it... She just hid it well.

The judge did come down and was so impressed he told a whole bunch of people and before I knew it, I added the hunting and fishing business to my already prosperous lumber business.

In my almost three thousand acres was some pasture land that turned out to be good for raising crops. I had, cotton, corn and potatoes. In fact, while I was in St. Louis, one time, looking for someone to hire, I met up with this young black man and his new bride. Seems they were looking for work and after a half an hour of talking with them, I hired them and took them home with me.

We built them a cabin not far from our house and they pretty much took over all the work in the fields, and the timber cutting.

Shortly thereafter, I found out there was trouble brewing.

By now, I had six lumberjacks working the tree business and they didn't like me hiring blacks to live on the place, drawing wages and bossing them around.

One afternoon, we heard pistol shots and went outside to see a cross burning in the front yard, and at least a dozen or so riders sitting their horses. They wore long white sheets over their bodies and white hoods over their heads.

One of them rode up close to me and said, "We don't cotton to darkies drawin' wages like they was white. Get rid of them or suffer the consequences."

I stared at him for a long time, then said, "Take your cross and get off my property, and I won't tell you again. As far as who I hire and who I don't is of no concern to you. Now, get off my land!"

I yelled and waved my hands in the air and he almost fell off his horse when it reared up.

Ressie Mae stepped up next to me with a double-barreled shotgun in her hands and yelled, "You heard him… Get!"

They left, but not for long. A week later, during the middle of the night, they rode in with torches to burn us out, but we were ready for them. While I fired my rifle at them, Ressie Mae rang a big bell I'd installed, alerting not only the young man and his wife, but Charlie and Audrey, who came hurrying across the lake in a boat. Charlie came charging up from the rear, firing his shotgun, while Willy and Martha, the young black

Before a single torch could land on any of our buildings, they were turning tail and running for their lives. I'm sure several of them were injured, but I don't think we killed any of them.

Suffice to say, they never came back – but my six lumberjacks quit and never came back, which was fine with me. I hired six more men, who weren't prejudice, and gave not a whit about the Klu Klux Klan, as those men called themselves.

As I think back on it all, I've had a good life with lots of adventure. More than many I know of. And two women that no man could have done better. Calling Bird was always there, no matter what. And Ressie Mae, the same.

I've had a good life. It's 1906 and I'm a hundred and four years old. Over the years I've seen a whole bunch of changes. We have automobiles, electricity – even a phone that I can call Charlie, on. There is talk of building a dam and tying a couple of tributaries to the river to make the largest manmade lake in the world. The land and the river provided for me and I had friends - along with more money than we actually needed. How can a man ask for more than that?

I've never actually been sick a day in my life, but now, with everyone gone, the joy of getting up every morning to chase the next sunrise has lost its luster. I'm not sick or anything, I'm just tired. So, I'm thinking, this will be the last entry. I know, I said that, many years back when I thought the Utes were going to kill me, but this time it's for real. It's time for me to go be with Calling Bird, Ressie Mae and my friends, Charlie and Audrey, Lars and Gretchen, and maybe even, Rufus.

If you've spent time reading this, I hope, if nothing else, you've learned that no matter how hard you try, you can't predict what tomorrow will bring. You just have to take life one day at a time and live it the best you can.

Jubal Courtney

EPILOGUE

Jubal Courtney's journal was found by Charlie and Audrey's son, Amos.

He'd been summoned by Jubal's housemaid when she found him – dressed in a suit - laying on top of his bed, with a note on the nightstand.

Not only did Amos publish the journal as a book, but for several years, he traveled around the country telling people of the man he called, Uncle Jubal.

Having no other relatives, Jubal left large sums of money to each of his employees, and donated his land to be turned into a state, wildlife park. And the rest of his money, which now amounted to several million dollars, was to be used to build a hospital and free medical clinic in the nearby town of Courtneyville.

As a footnote, once the dam was built and the tributaries were connected to the big river, it became a huge lake that is now called, Lake of the Ozarks…

ALSO BY JARED McVAY

__Other works by Jared McVay__

Jared McVay is an award-winning author who writes, Westerns: A western series: Historical Fiction: Action/Adventure: YA: Children's books: screenplays: teleplays: Short stories, and also does storytelling.

NOVELS:

Clay Brentwood western series:

Book 1 – Stranger on A Black Stallion

Book 2 – Unjust Punishment

Book 3 – Hammershield

Book 4 – Cinch Mountain

Book 5 – The Storm

Book 6 – The Chameleon

Historical Fiction: The Legend of Joe, Willy & Red – award winner

Historical Fiction: Silent Runner, Guardian Warrior

Western: Hacker's Raid – award winner

Action/Contemporary - Not on My Mountain – double award winner

CHILDREN'S BOOKS

Bears, Bicycles & Broomsticks – 11 short stories

Randal Gets A Hit

Santa's Magic Ring

SCREENPLAYS

The Hobos

Jared & the Warden

Talltree

TELEVISION PILOT SCRIPTS

McClusky [6 episodes] - Drama/Comedy

ACT Acute Care Transport - Drama/Comedy

Melinda: Award winning short story

THANK YOU FOR READING!

If you enjoyed this book, we would appreciate your customer review on your book seller's website or on Goodreads.

Also, we would like for you to know that you can find more great books like this one at www.CreativeTexts.com

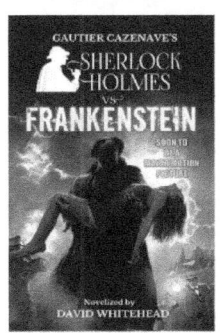

www.ingramcontent.com/pod-product-compliance
Lightning Source LLC
Chambersburg PA
CBHW072353020726
47506CB00004B/1099